HH

4 JUN 2023

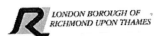

The Great Troll War

The Great Troll War

Jasper Fforde

Book Four of The Last Dragonslayer Series

HODDER

First published in Great Britain in 2021 by Hodder & Stoughton
An Hachette UK company

This paperback edition published in 2023

1

Copyright © Jasper Fforde 2021

The right of Jasper Fforde to be identified as the Author
of the Work has been asserted by him in accordance with the
Copyright, Designs and Patents Act 1988.

A CIP catalogue record for this title
is available from the British Library

Paperback ISBN 978 1 444 79996 5
eBook ISBN 978 1 444 79995 8

Typeset in Bembo by Palimpsest Book Production Limited,
Falkirk, Stirlingshire

Printed and bound in Great Britain by Clays Ltd, Elcograf S.p.A.

Hodde   ewable
and   able
for   to
conf   gin.

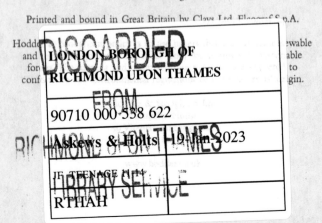

For my eldest great-grandchild.
Sorry about the state of the planet.
We knew what we had to do – we just didn't.
There was no excuse.

The Great Troll War

The Great Gatsby

Where We Are Now

Trolls. I was staring at one just then. He was about twenty feet tall, dressed in a loincloth, a pair of leather boots and on top of his unusually small head was a dead goat. I'm not a massive expert on Trolls, but apparently they wear rotting animals in the same way as humans wear perfume: to disguise their smell and make them more attractive. To each other, obviously. I like to think myself fairly broad-minded but even I would have to admit Trolls are pretty loathsome in manner, looks and eating habits.

So who am I? Jennifer Strange. S-T-R-A-N-G-E. Rhymes with 'Grange'. Y'know, the sixteen-year-old who was running Kazam, the House of Enchantment?

No?

Then how about this: I was the Last Dragonslayer. Right, *her*. The kid with the Dragons.

The Troll was holding a large club that was once the rear axle of a truck, and it looked as though he not only knew how to use it, but already had. His skin was rough, had the colour of mouldy bread and boasted an impressive display of intricate tattoos. Some were geometric and purely for decoration, but others were more practical: owing to a long mistrust of pen and paper, the left Troll leg is reserved for a part of their written history, and the right for recipes, to-do lists and bawdy limericks. But no fools when it comes to data integrity, Trolls back themselves up, just in case – they have often been observed with identical tattoos.

That the Trolls were here at all was due to Troll War V, which had been going for only two weeks but already had a clear winner: the Trolls. They had flooded out of Trollvania and rampaged rapidly southwards with little resistance from the various Republics, Duchies, Social Collectives, Fiefdoms, Principalties and privately run City States of the UnUnited Kingdoms. The rapid invasion was due to a favourable tactical advantage: *they were indifferent to us.* Hating humankind would have been easier to counter as at least there could be some sort of debating position between our species. What led you to hate us so much? How do we arrange some sort of peaceful coexistence? Will you please stop eating us? None of those questions meant much to the Trolls. They can't be swayed by reason or compassion or compromise for they regard humans as little more than vermin: an annoying pest that can outgrow the boundaries of their own environment in as little as nine centuries. Some humans think of rabbits in the same way: nuisances who damage the land, breed without conscience and are good only for the pot. The only difference between rabbits and humans as far as Trolls are concerned is that they can't wear us as a hat – although many have tried with varying degrees of success. In any event, there's little sense arguing with a Troll.

I had been in the Cambrian Empire when they invaded, searching for the Eye of Zoltar,[1] a fiery jewel with magical properties that the Mighty Shandar had tasked us to obtain in return for not killing the last two Dragons, something he had been contracted to do several centuries before. You'll hear more about Shandar later. All you need to know right now is that he's the most powerful sorcerer that has ever lived – and also turning out to be the least scrupulous.

I'd returned with the Eye and also Once-Magnificent Boo, who we had rescued from being ransomed. Addie, who had been our guide in the Cambrian Empire and in which capacity we owed her our lives, saw us safely to Cornwall, and made good on her promise to protect the Princess on the journey. She then returned to her village to fight the Troll. She had been reluctant to leave us, but the Princess had insisted.

'What's the Troll doing?' asked Princess Shazine of Snodd, who was standing next to me.

'Imagining us both inside a pie,' I replied.

'With white sauce, asparagus and badger's paws, I

---

[1] See *The Eye of Zoltar*, Jennifer's third adventure.

imagine,' said Tiger Prawns, who was also present. He was an orphan like me, only younger – ten, I think – and had a Moral Worth Index that was certainly in the top ten per cent. He had been due to take over from me the running of Kazam, the last house of enchantment, which is a sort of home for barely-sane sorcerers. But all those plans were upset by the Troll invasion: in what was likely a preemptive measure to stop us using magic against the Trolls, the head offices of Kazam at Zambini Towers were destroyed by a single and very powerful thermowizidrical blast, killing several dozen sorcerers, destroying countless volumes of spells and reducing the building to rubble. As soon as it was safe to do so, the dragons and surviving sorcerers headed to Troll-free Cornwall with Tiger Prawns among them. We'd joined him in Penzance a week later. That was five days ago and we'd spent the time trying to figure out a strategy of resistance and had so far not come up with much – I was due to convene a meeting later that morning.

Today's post-breakfast visit to the Button Trench was to ensure that it was holding firm – and to welcome any human stragglers who had crossed under cover of darkness.

'Badger's paws are hideously out of fashion,' said the Troll, whose ears, although only small holes in his head, made for surprisingly good hearing. 'We prefer a garnish of week-old goat entrails.'

'Two weeks,' said his wife, who was also on guard duty at the Button Trench. 'Goat entrails aren't *nearly* putrid enough in a week.'

They stared at each other angrily and both went the colour of a radish, the veins in their temples standing out like tree-roots. A Troll's temper is short and explosive and usually accompanied by extreme violence.

'It's warmer this far south,' said the Princess, who always spoke her mind, even to Trolls. 'You're probably both right regarding goat putrefaction rates when seen as combination factors of temperature against time.'

This was likely, as all Trolls lived until recently in the far North of the Kingdoms where the weather is disposed towards the inclement.[2]

'I can put it in a spreadsheet if you like,' she added.

'I like spreadsheets,' said the Troll Wife thoughtfully; like her husband, she was quick to temper yet quick to lose it. 'I have one that calculates the correct cooking rates for humans based on their Body Mass Index.'

'Undercooked humans present numerous health hazards,' explained the Troll Husband helpfully. 'It's a bit of a worry. Spending a day in bed after eating a dodgy human is rarely agreeable.'

'It's not a worry I share,' said the Princess, 'but if you're going to eat us, why haven't you done so?'

[2] Translation: very cold.

It was a pointlessly dangerous remark to make to a Troll, but the Princess was always forthright, even for a princess. She was the same age as me but we could not have been more different. While she grew up in a palace wanting for nothing and with forty rooms of her own, I was in an orphanage with nothing but my dignity and forty other girls in the *same* room. She had joined us on the quest[3] for the Eye of Zoltar because her parents, the King and Queen of Snodd, felt she was too horribly obnoxious to successfully lead the Kingdom if the need arose, and a slice of real-life experience would be good for her. Her mind was switched into the body of a lowly royal dog-mess clearer-upper to further her lesson in humility, and after several high-jeopardy adventures and a few interesting digressions into the knotty question of supply-side economics, the Princess had transformed from a hideously spoiled princess into a confident young woman of considerable courage. She was also, following the death of her parents at the hands of the invading Trolls, the rightful heir to the wealthy and influential Kingdom of Snodd on the Welsh Borders.

She was also now permanently residing within the royal dog-mess clearer-upper's body, her own lost

---

[3] Technically speaking it wasn't a quest at all but you'll have to read *The Eye of Zoltar* to find out why.

during the invasion — ringlets and dimples and royal birthmark and everything.

'Once we find a way to cross that trench,' said the Troll Husband, eyeing the glittering collection of buttons nervously, 'we will definitely eat you.'

'*Without* the badger's paws,' added the Troll Wife, who must have felt the issue had not yet been resolved.

'Right,' said the Troll Husband.

The trench ran for nearly four and a half miles along the route of the railway line from Penzance in the south of Cornwall to Lelant Saltings in the north, just to the east of St Ives. The ditch was barely ten feet wide and only a foot deep — humans could wade across it with ease. But the Troll, whose cunning, appetite and violent ruthlessness made the worst despot of the Kingdoms look like little more than an enraged infant,[4] had several unaccountable fears: swimming, a certain shade of cerulean blue, and buttons. And that's precisely what was protecting us now — millions and millions of buttons. They had been pulled from coats, shirts and blouses, or liberated from haberdasher's shops throughout the Kingdoms, then carried in bags, buckets or wheelbarrows by those fleeing the Trolls and dumped in the trench dug wizidrically by

---

[4] Coincidentally enough, the worst despot in the Kingdoms actually *was* an enraged infant.

Wizard Moobin, who had given everything to his last and greatest spell, the years piling on to his weary body as he sacrificed his remaining life-force to create a final line of defence against the invaders.

'Where would you place a human on the tasty scale?' the Troll Wife asked her Troll Husband.

'Somewhere between stoat and seal pup,' replied the husband thoughtfully, 'but they've never been my snack of choice, to be honest. Too stringy past the age of twenty-six. Some say their tendency to escape can offer up good sport, but I just think it's plain tiresome, myself.'

'A good sauce is key,' added the Troll Wife, 'and we'd best get used to them – it's about all we'll be eating for the next ten years.'

And they both laughed, a soft, galumphing, you're-so-trashed-as-a-species kind of laugh.

Magically digging the four-and-a-half-mile trench that now cut off Land's End, St Ives and Penzance from the invading Trolls had been the easy part. Spreading the 'bring every single button you can find to Cornwall' message on the low-alpha-suggestive telepathic bandwidth was actually what drained Wizard Moobin's power and ultimately took his life-force from him. The telepathic message was powerful enough to be heard by almost everyone in the Kingdoms, but only as a 'a vague idea that should be put into action', and only a small proportion responded. Luckily, the message was also picked up by magpies, who, as natural thieves, may have contributed at least a million buttons to the defences before falling, exhausted, from the skies.

It was a bold yet timely construction. The Button Trench kept the Trolls from crossing over into the last bastion of the UnUnited Kingdoms where lay encamped the free. The ones who had been the quickest to react to the threat, the ones who could run the fastest, the ones with a death-by-devouring promise on their heads, and those with specialist skills who had also been drawn here by a call on the same telepathic wavelength – specifically: expert fencers, keen-eyed marksmen and warriors.

'Tell you what,' said the Troll Husband, who had been staring at the Princess for some time and drooling in a truly unpleasant manner – great gobs of sticky saliva that fell from his upswept tusks like melted mozzarella, 'hand over the scrawny one and we'll guarantee that once we find a way across this trench, you' – he was pointing at me – 'will not be killed and eaten. You shall be *spared*. It is a promise.'

Oddly, the Troll would be as good as its word. Although murderous in nature and utterly dismissive of a human's right to life, they could still barter effectively with the ultimate bargaining chip: they would promise to spare your life. It was a gesture that was particularly effective for negotiating the surrender of the UnUnited Kingdoms as they swept through the island.

Offer resistance? Be killed and eaten.

Bow to your new overlords and follow their every demand? Be spared.

Guaranteed.

'How could they promise such a thing?' asked the Princess, whose schoolwork had centred more around deportment, strategic tantrums and estimating a prince's net worth and marriageability at a glance, rather than learning about the other inhabitants of our island.

'They have several active strands of Hive Memory,' said Tiger, knowing quite a bit about Trolls, as *not* learning which fork was which at a state banquet really freed up some time. 'It's thought that memories are shared by the same familial affiliation – and once shared, they effectively have the same memories. If you want all Trolls to have the same memory, you'd only have to share it with all the tribal affiliations, so it never takes long.'

'A Hive Memory could be useful,' said the Princess.

'Yes and no,' said Tiger. 'Within each memory-sharing tribe there are no secrets, double-dealing or lying. On the downside, card games within the Hive Memory affiliation are almost impossible, telling jokes pretty much pointless, and they have to binge-watch a TV series all at the same time to avoid spoilers.'

'That's true,' I added. 'When *Bergerac* came out on DVD, a Troll named Urgry watched it the night before they planned to do so and ended up being stoned to death by those in her affiliate for filling their heads full of spoilers.'

Trolls were particularly fond of crime TV shows from the seventies and eighties, with *Murder, She wrote*, *Columbo* and *Bergerac* being their favourites. They watched them again and again, as the aforementioned Hive Memory discouraged them from watching anything new because of the whole 'spoiler stoning to death' issue.

'I've not heard of *Bergerac*,' said the Princess, 'but that's easily explained: Mummy said TV was for the dull and uneducated – a princess's place is *on* the telly, not watching it.'

The Princess's upbringing had been horribly sheltered, but had lent her a very peculiar skillset. She could quote Tacitus, differentiate seventeen bottles of expensive mineral water by clarity alone, was able to guess the value of a tiara at forty paces and could skilfully project shallow indifference into a room long before she'd entered. All this, but she didn't know how to open a window, use a telephone kiosk or boil an egg.

'*Bergerac* was actually a really good TV series,' I mused, 'but well before my time. The series seven set were the only DVDs we had in the orphanage. We played them hundreds of times until they got scratched, then just re-enacted the stories from memory. I got to play Bergerac's ex-wife Debbie, which was kind of fun. We performed episode three at the Courtyard Theatre in Hereford.'

'That's the one where the diamonds got stolen,' said Tiger, something of an expert.

'And,' I added, 'John Nettles sent us a nice note when he found out and donated a new minibus to the orphanage.'

'Who's John Nettles?' asked the Princess.

Tiger and I looked at one another. As far as anyone in Mother Zenobia's orphanage was concerned – nuns, children, everyone – there was no greater star than John Nettles.[5]

'He's the—' I began, then: 'Never mind.'

'So how about it?' asked the Troll Husband, who was still waiting for an answer. 'The skinny handmaiden or your life?'

'Looks a bit bony for a snack,' said the Troll Wife, sizing up the Princess expertly, 'unless you like your humans crunchy and lacking in nourishment.'

'Not for a snack, silly,' said her husband, 'as a *pet*. They can be quite adorable – although sometimes

---

[5] As you might have guessed, John Nettles played Bergerac in *Bergerac*. He later found success in *Midsomer Murders*. But just so we're clear on this, he wasn't in *Murder, She wrote* or *Columbo*.

you have to pull their tongues out to stop them squeaking.'

'Okay,' said his wife, 'but remember to feed it this time – oh, and you *must* keep the males and females in separate cages or they'll breed. And – yes, agreed – the babies can be very cute but before you know it some fool will give them names and we'll be stuck with them, like, *for ever.*'

Trolls were, dismayingly, quite happy to keep humans as pets and, equally dismayingly, weren't very diligent when it came to looking after them.

'Hang on, what about me?' said Tiger indignantly. 'Why is Jennifer's life threatened and not mine?'

'You're too small to be troubled with,' said the Troll Wife in a dismissive manner. 'It would be like you threatening a Dorito. How about it?' she added, turning back to me. 'For we will cross this trench eventually, make no mistake about *that.*'

'No deal,' I said without hesitation.

'Then you shall be devoured,' said the Troll simply, 'and while alive. Probably raw as a snack,' he added thoughtfully, 'dipped in humus – no, wait, dipped in toejam. Jam, made of toes,' he added, in case I mistook his meaning. 'Nummy nummy.'

'You do what you have to do,' I said.

'What she said,' said the Princess, pointing at me.

'And I'm not a Dorito,' said Tiger.

'Sorry,' said the Troll Wife, whose mind had

wandered, 'did you say something? I was just wondering: do you have to use people called Frank to make frankfurters – or can it be anyone?'

I decided not to answer and we turned and walked away from the Trolls and the Button Trench.

'Thank you for not handing me over,' said the Princess once we were out of earshot. 'I'm really not cut out to be a bony snack.'

'We don't do deals with Trolls,' I said.

'If I'd been the old me, the Princess me, the obnoxious me – would you have traded my freedom for your life?'

'If you'd been in your princess body rather than the body of a malnourished servant with lank hair and skin complaints that don't seem to go away no matter how diligent the cleaning,' I said, 'they would have asked you for me – and I'm sort of thinking you would have given me up.'

'Without hesitation,' said the Princess in a sombre mood, 'and probably asked for a receipt to claim on my Princess Insurance. Goodness, I was so utterly obnoxious back then. Is royalty always this bad?'

'I don't think it's being a royal that does it,' I said. 'Just the ridiculous abundance of wealth, opulence and levels of undeserved privilege that go with it.'

The Princess nodded her head in agreement. She had matured quickly during the search for the Eye of Zoltar as it had been an adventure that would have taught even the most narrow-minded and utterly indulged child a few things about teamwork and sacrifice. Perhaps the Princess's ex-sorceress mother, who instigated the bodyswap and placed her in my care, sensed the Trolls were coming, and engineered the trip to not only keep her safe, but actually do her some good. Nothing like a bit of jeopardy and loss of prestige to make the overprivileged understand the important things in life.

We walked back to where I'd parked my Volkswagen Beetle, the only link with my parents. I had been left on the front seat when barely two months old late one December night, wrapped in a blanket, the engine running, the heaters on. Often, foundlings are left with talismans to identify them if their parents return to claim them. The Volkswagen was that talisman. If they had wanted me, they would have returned and presented the spare ignition key as proof.

They never did.

I opened the car door and took the sword Exhorbitus[6] from where I wore it on a scabbard on my back and stowed it using the clips on the roof

---

[6] The sword that Jennifer wielded when a dragonslayer. It was called 'Exhorbitus' owing to the unreasonably high cost of manufacture. Tell a swordsmith they're making something for Dragon or magical intent and they'll always add three noughts to the bill.

lining, then tried the glovebox for about the thousandth time. It was locked, and always had been.

'You'll eventually want to break into that.'

It was the Princess, who knew the strong bond I had with the car.

'I know,' I said, 'but what if it were empty, or just full of junk?'

'What if it's not?'

The Sisterhood at the Orphanage had tried to trace the owners of the car through the registration but that had only led as far as the owner before last, who had sold it on: 'to a middle-aged guy' who paid in cash, two months before I was found in it. The new owner had not reregistered the car in his name, so there was little to go on. Although the glovebox was locked it had never been forced as the Sisterhood saw this as damaging someone's property, and, interestingly, the car had only clocked up seventy-two miles from when it was sold to when I was found in it. Wherever I was from, I was local.

We drove the mile into Penzance, the Quarkbeast sitting in the back, staring at his paws mournfully. He didn't like Trolls any more than the rest of us, but stayed well hidden as Trolls didn't look at a Quarkbeast and see the most terrifying creature on earth: a three-way split between a labrador, a velociraptor and a liquidiser with all the safety features removed; a creature with razor-sharp fangs, a coat of carbide-tipped steel scales that could explosively detonate off his back and embed themselves in concrete. No, the Trolls saw a Quarkbeast as a sporting opportunity: put them in a ring with three bears, two rhinos, a hyena and six dozen enraged, adrenaline-fuelled badgers – then take bets on how long the Quarkbeast took to despatch them all.[7] Despite their fearsome looks, Quarkbeasts only ever attacked when they, or a loved one, were threatened. They usually felt guilty about it for years afterwards, with lots of sighing, mournful looks and overwhelming feelings of self-loathing. There were never any winners when it came to Quarkbaiting.

On the way back into Penzance we chatted about recent events, and Tiger related his escape to the Princess, who hadn't heard the story yet. She had warmed to him since they first met, when her initial instinct was to have him beheaded for impudence.

'Myself, Moobin, the Quarkbeast, the Mysterious X and Monty Vanguard were giving X his annual gaussing[8] in the basement,' said Tiger, 'as the weak

---

[7] According to most betting offices this would be somewhere between fifteen and twenty-six seconds.

[8] 'Gaussing' is the manner by which you might place a magnetic field onto something. It's really not that vital to know, although to the Mysterious X, whose particles do not have any bonds to keep them in place, it's vital. Maybe.

electromagnetic force holding its particles together needed a bit of a boost to keep them all in one vaguely coherent location. The human equivalent would be like watching your right foot drift off your leg and sail quietly out of the window. Although,' he added, 'that was only what we *thought* it wanted as no one is sure whether the Mysterious X exists or not. He communicates mainly by giving you vague ideas that sort of pop into your head unannounced.'

'Ah-ha,' said the Princess, who was still trying to get her head around the somewhat strange residents of Kazam.

'We were trying to coax him back into his Kilner jar when the air started to tingle and a thermowizidrical detonation wiped out Zambini Towers. The explosion left the building as nothing but a pile of rubble half turned to glass and killed thirty-seven residents instantly. It might have been worse if it had gone critical.'

'What's not critical about thirty-seven dead?' asked the Princess.

'"Criticality" is the term we use to describe the effect of a runaway thermowizidrical detonation,' I said, 'where every spell turns in on itself and annihilates itself and the next in a devastating chain reaction.'

'Even the simplest Worm Charm contains enough energy to take out a medium-sized house if you can tap right into the core of the spell,' added Tiger. 'Sorcerers always build in safeguards, but anyone who sets off a thermowizidrical detonation is dicing with destruction the likes of which you will never want to witness. If the attack on Zambini Towers had achieved criticality then most of Hereford would be a smoking hole in the ground – palace included.'

'That would not be good,' said the Princess. 'Go on.'

'We were trapped in the cellar but decided to lay low, as this was clearly a magic attack by a sorcerer of considerable power. We could hear someone looking for survivors – Trolls, we learned later – but even that stopped after an hour. We waited until after dark when the Dragons came to dig us out, then we were ferried on the carpets all the way down here while Moobin dug the Button Trench and put out the request for buttons on the low-alpha as Full Price put out a similar call for marksmen and women, warriors and expert fencers to make their way here.'

'Full Price is a sorcerer?' asked the Princess.

'"Full" is a nickname,' I said. 'His brother was known as "Half Price" and they were easy to tell apart – the nicknames weren't subtle.'

'Half died in the attack,' said Tiger in a quiet voice, 'but we did finally hook up again with Kevin Zip – if he hadn't been kidnapped at the time, we might have been prewarned and saved more sorcerers.'

'The Remarkable Kevin Zip is our finest precognitive,' I explained, changing down a gear as we drove across the swing bridge on the harbour front at Penzance. 'He can shuffle through the millions of possible futures and latch on to the one most likely to occur. He's rated the third-best there has ever been.'

'Does he tell how this all turns out?' asked the Princess.

'Precognition is more of a craft than a science,' I said, which was basically a shorthand admission that: 'no, he almost certainly doesn't'.

After driving past the Penzance Lido in bright sunshine and along the promenade in low cloud and drizzle – weather is very changeable in Cornwall – we parked behind the Queens Hotel, the base of our operations.

About six thousand people had taken refuge in the far tip of Cornwall, about a quarter of whom belonged on the Hive Memory 'Eat List', me included as of twenty minutes ago. The survivors were a mixed bag, and despite having many courageous individuals who favoured fighting over ending up as *sapien en cocotte,* we had no armoured vehicles, no artillery and only the weapons that the displaced had managed to carry with them. Annoyingly, bullets just tend to bounce off a Troll's thick hide and make them more violent and hungry – neither of which generally ends well for humans.

I'd consulted my go-to person for all matters on everything, a friend named William of Anorak, and he was desperately frustrated when it came to answering, as, unusually for him, he had few fascinating Troll facts at his fingertips. He told me he'd call me back if he found anything, then reeled off all the citrus fruits, first by size, then in alphabetical order.

Without any anti-Troll strategy so far, the only two weapons we had that could possibly make a difference were Colin and Feldspar, the Dragons – but even with sound logistical support, it would be only those two youngsters against several million Trolls. Annoyingly, little more than an hour after the Button Trench was dug, a Spellsucking incantation started up which effectively hoovered all the wizidrical energy out of the air, rendering us magically powerless. Technically speaking a Hex Energy Neutralising Reversal Yieldiser, it was more often known by the acronym HENRY.[9] This and the attack on Zambini Towers pointed a finger at the culprit: the Mighty Shandar. It takes a very powerful sorcerer indeed to spell up a Spellsucker or a thermowizidrical detonation. If there were a solution to the Troll invasion, it wouldn't be magically based until we could take out the HENRY.

Anyway, the Troll invasion reeked of the Mighty Shandar's assistance.

[9] The name of a popular brand of vacuum cleaners are called 'Henry' for precisely this reason.

'What's the plan?' asked Tiger as we climbed out of the VW Beetle.

'Yes,' said the Princess, 'what *is* the plan?'

'I don't yet have one,' I admitted. 'Tiger, weren't you running some numbers on the possibility of success when the Trolls inevitably cross the Button Trench?'

Tiger had indeed run the numbers – he was good with numbers.

'93.7 per cent chance of success,' he said.

'That's not so bad,' said the Princess.

'For the Trolls,' he added.

'Okay, that's actually very bad.'

'Yes,' said Tiger, 'the sort of odds that would give even the sunniest of optimists a lump in their throat.'

'We can't out-magic or out-fight them,' I continued as we entered by the back entrance of the hotel and climbed the steep steps to the lobby, 'so we'll need to outsmart them. But how *exactly* we might do that is a matter for discussion. The Troll is more powerful, more violent than us, and has accepted unconditional surrender terms from every single one of the Kingdoms aside from Cornwall. What used to belong to humans now belongs to the Troll.'

'They could in theory call on their human subjects to fight *us*,' said Tiger. 'Trolls regard human-on-human battles as rollicking good entertainment, and often take large side bets.'

'True,' I said, 'which is why we need to build a strong coalition. First, we need a figurehead to be our nominal leader, someone we can all rally behind, and whom the members of the ex-Kingdoms might hesitate to attack.'

'Oh yes?' said the Princess innocently. 'Anyone in mind?'

Tiger and myself exchanged glances. We'd been discussing this earlier.

'You,' I said.

'Me?'

'Yes. An uncrowned queen of a large Kingdom will fit the bill perfectly.'

'I don't have a Kingdom any more. It's all now Greater Trollvania.'

'The land is still there,' said Tiger, 'it's only the ownership that's in contention.'

The Princess looked at us both in turn.

'I don't know the first thing about ruling,' she said. 'I bossed an archduke around a bit once, but he was only six at the time. That's as far as it goes.'

We stepped into the hotel lobby, a large atrium that rose three storeys to a glazed roof above. The wind had got up and I could have sworn I saw a jellyfish, two catfish and three terrified-looking Sea Scouts in a dinghy blown clean over the hotel.

'If it's not you it will be one of the others,' said Tiger, nodding in the direction of what was clearly a group of princesses, all big dresses and the always fashionable wimpole hat, 'and you're *way* better than anyone in this motley bunch of royalty.'

In an improbable coincidence, there were twenty-six princesses in Penzance at this moment in time, all of whom had been attending a conference entitled 'Is too much ever enough? Modern princessing and the defence of opulence' at the Queens Hotel when the Trolls invaded. And while only four of them were now actually uncrowned queens, all of them thought they were uniquely capable of leading a vanquished nation to freedom. Or being the one in charge, at any rate. Indeed, the fact that we were based in the Queens Hotel at all was something of an annoyance to the princesses, who wanted to keep the hotel and everyone in it for their personal use while demanding to know why they should have to slum it 'just because of an invasion by human-eating homicidal lunatics'. No one had thought it wise to tell them that anything connected to royalty was, as far as the Trolls were concerned, 'good eating'. When they baked 'Queen of Puddings' they took it literally.[10]

The princesses and I had been dodging each other all week as our priorities were at polar opposites, but

[10] The recipe reminded Troll chefs to 'take extra care to remove any tiaras, rings and corsets as if they are swallowed this may be regretted later'.

it seemed that this was the morning they were going to try to flex their royal muscles.

'You there, servant and Dragon-person,' said the most spoiled-looking of the princesses, pointing at me, 'curtsy in the presence of your betters, commoner, or the royal executioner will have a new head for their collection.'

Princesses

The one who had spoken was pencil thin, sumptuously dressed, and seemed to glide when she walked, as if she had spent the first ten years of her life balancing a book on her head to aid elegant deportment.

'That's Princess Jocamanica,' whispered the Princess, who had also been avoiding the princesses. 'She spent the first ten years of her life balancing a book on her head to aid elegant deportment.'

'I never would have guessed. They're not *actually* going to execute us, are they?'

'Of course not. It's all princessy trash talk. We always boast we can have you beheaded or bricked up in a cellar and starved or fed to crocodiles in the moat, but we never actually do. It's seen as a little unseemly these days – and the price of crocodiles is *astronomical*.'

'I'm sorry?' I said to Jocaminca, in no mood to be threatened with execution. 'Are you addressing me?'

Princess Jocaminca visibly rankled.

'I shall be addressed as "Her Royal Highness the Princess of Shropshire, uncrowned queen, Jocaminca

Dabforth Pipplesqunge IV"',' she announced in a haughty manner, 'and I would expect all others of low birth to address the royalty present in this hotel in the correct fashion. Isn't that right, girls?'

The others all nodded their heads vigorously, except the ones who thought it below them, who had their servants do it instead.

'I made some notes as to the correct way we should be addressed and treated,' said Princess Tabathini, who seemed more pleasant than the rest, probably because she was a second-tier princess, meaning she only had a single castle and fewer than a dozen servants. I think she had only been at the Princess Convention because someone pulled out and they wanted to make up the numbers.

'It runs to almost ninety pages,' she continued, 'so you may have to hand it round once memorised.'

'On another matter, Miss Strange,' said Princess Jocaminca, 'I am hereby informing you that I, as the ranking uncrowned queen of the largest Kingdom here, place myself in charge of negotiating the manner by which we shall surrender to the Troll. I understand there is a Sorcerer's Conclave planned. I shall preside over it and take control in all matters relating to how we shall proceed.'

'Oh yes?' said the Princess, who had obviously been thinking about the whole 'nominal leader' deal and decided that now was the moment to reveal herself.

'Three things: first, we are not going to surrender. Not now, not ever. Second, as uncrowned queen of the Kingdom of Snodd – a bigger and *way* more prestigious Kingdom than yours – I believe the honour of presiding over the method of resistance should fall to me. Third, I have the support of Jennifer Strange, who is Dragon Ambassador to the world, the nation's Head Mystician and manages the only House of Enchantment in the Kingdoms. If we are to vanquish the Troll, we need magic on our side, Jennifer as our trusted adviser, and to work together as a team.'

Princess Jocaminca gaped like a fish at what she saw as a servant's gross impertinence.

'I beg your pardon. You are emphatically *not* Princess Shazine. That princess is tall and graceful and lovely, while you are short and ugly and utterly lacking in grace. If I had a servant right now I would command them to horsewhip you for your insolence.'

It was a fair point as the Princess had indeed been bodyswapped, so she related as proof things only a princess could know, such as the optimal temperature when bathing in rabbit's milk, and the ascending order of eligible princes in the Kingdoms, with all their titles and star ratings for good looks, personality and cash.

'Anyone who reads *What Prince Monthly* would know that,' said Princess Jocaminca in a sniffy tone, 'it means nothing.'

'Okay,' said the Princess, who knew full well that there was no *physical* proof she was anyone but Laura Scrubb, a lowly servant, 'let's ramp this up a notch. You and I and Cheryl and Candice and Tabathini over there were together in *I'm a Princess Get Me Out of Here* two years ago. You were voted out of the palace in the first round because you refused Task One: shaking hands with a poor person without grimacing.'

'That was never broadcast.'

'No,' said the Princess, 'and neither was the round where Princess Stellerini threw a massive 3.2 Richter Scale tantrum when she was told to reduce her entourage to only six servants and wear the same dress twice. None of you even got to the round where you had to do ironing or sew a button on a shirt.'

'Who won?' I asked out of curiosity. The show had been a big ratings winner, more popular than *'No Money but an Impressive Title*, in which five princes of impecunious means but an impressive bloodline had to battle it out to win the hand of a Grade VII princess, the sort whose Kingdom is barely larger than a couple of football fields.[11]

---

[11] Not the smallest Kingdom recorded. The Duchy of Bryn Mawr was only the size of a double garage with seventeen inches of coastline. It gave them the legal right to a navy, though not a very big one.

'Princess Organza of Midlandia,' said the Princess, and they then set about talking about how awful she was, how she would soon lose her looks, how she had 'certainly let herself go since the wedding' and was also – shock horror – far too nice to her servants, something that 'would only lead to ruin'.

'I was there when Princess Shazine was body-swapped by her mother the Queen and entrusted to me,' I said, before the princessy trash-talk got them all too distracted, 'and as Royal Mystician to the Court of the Kingdom of Snodd, I can vouch for her.'

'Not conclusive,' said Princess Jocaminca. 'Besides, your "princess" currently has her finger up her nose.'

I looked at the Princess, who did indeed have her finger up her nose.

'I think I've found an impressively large booga,' said the Princess. 'It's been bothering me all morning.'

'It was the bodyswapping,' I explained hastily. 'Some of Laura Scrubb's personal habits came across with it. If she ever asks you to pull her finger, please don't.'

'Eugh,' said Jocaminça.

It was time to play my trump card. I had wanted to keep it for the coronation, but the time was now. I reached into my pocket and pulled out a small leather pouch that contained a gold signet ring with the seal of Snodd cut into turquoise, surrounded by oak leaves, a Dragon and a very small advert for Fizzi-Pop.[12]

'Queen Mimosa gave me this in secret,' I said, 'for a moment such at this.'

I took the Princess's hand and slid the heavy gold ring on her third finger. She stared at it for a moment, and tears welled up in her eyes. She looked at me and I nodded. Her mother had been an ex-sorceress herself, and likely had a premonition something bad was going to happen, and that bodyswapping her with a lowly maidservant was the only way by which the spirit of the royal bloodline could be preserved. I think Princess Jocaminca realised it too.

'Your Royal Highness Crown Princess Shazine Blossom Hadridd Snodd,' she said politely. 'I humble myself in your presence and await your bidding.'

And she curtsied. As it turned out, the princesses who had signed up for the conference were all Grade II princesses of middling-sized Kingdoms, and none of them had the clout the Princess had – and they knew it. Say what you like about princesses, they know their place within the nation's royalty.

'I may have the body of a handmaiden,' said the Princess, 'with bandy legs, lank hair and several unsightly skin infections which will be dealt with as

---

[12] It isn't unusual for royalty to have sponsorship deals. Running castles can be expensive.

soon as the tests come back from the labs, but I have the mind and heart of an uncrowned queen, and I will not rest until the scourge of the Troll is vanquished from this land.'

And without waiting for a reply, she turned and set off for where the Sorcerer's Conclave was being held: the ballroom of the hotel. I turned and followed her.

'Did that sound queenly?' she asked as we walked along the corridor to the ballroom.

'Very,' I replied. 'I'd better start calling you "ma'am".'

'Only in public. When we're alone I want you to call me "Shazza", and look, for what you've done so far and will do in the future, I hereby make you a Knight of the Realm of Snodd.'

'I'm honoured, of course, I think,' I said, 'but can girls actually *be* knights?'

'They can if I say they can,' she replied with a smile. 'No point being the queen if you can't make your own rules. Save me a place at the Conclave, would you? I'm bursting for a wee.'

And she hurried off towards the toilets.

'Well,' said Tiger once she had gone, 'Sir Jennifer Strange, eh?'

'I'm not sure it's official without the sword stuff,' I said, 'but on reflection, I think I'd wear the label "orphan" with greater pride.'

'Yeah,' said Tiger, 'me too.'

'Quark,' said the Quarkbeast.

We paused in the elevator lobby outside the ball-room, where Prince Omar Ben Nasil was working on his flying carpet,[13] a threadbare specimen that smelled of unwashed spaniels and would have been rejected outright by almost any charity shop you could mention. The carpet was hovering about two feet off the ground, and Nasil was dressed in overalls and lying on a wheeled skate, the way a mechanic might do working under a car. He seemed to be delicately patching the centuries-old carpet, and the inspection light underneath shone through to reveal quite plainly its age and woefully threadbare condition.

'How's it going?' I asked.

'Not good, Jenny,' he said, wheeling himself out from under the carpet to talk to us, 'the Angel's Feathers entwined in the warp gives it the ability to float, but it's magic that controls it, so with the HENRY still operative, we're not going anywhere.'

'Well, do your best,' I said, and he nodded, grinned, then wheeled himself back under the carpet and carried on whistling to himself. We were about to walk into the ballroom when I heard someone call my name.

'Oh, Miss Strange?'

It was Tabathini, the really tall princess, who was

---

[13] Technically it's actually a rug, but that and other details were covered in *The Song of the Quarkbeast*.

so ridiculously thin that if she were painted pink and taught to walk backwards, she would be indistinguishable from a flamingo.

'Yes?'

'It's about Her Royal Highness the Crown Princess Shazine Blossom Hadridd Snodd.'

'Yes?'

'She's *not* the Crown Princess.'

'I thought we'd established that's exactly who she was.'

'No – no, I mean she's not *just* the Crown Princess. She's technically . . . the queen of all the UnUnited Kingdoms. Or, as we should say now: the *United* Kingdoms.'

'What?' I said, as the whole point of the Kingdoms was that they had never been united, not once, not ever, not even the tiniest bit.

'It's Rule 35b,' she said, showing me an underlined section in her pocket edition of *The Rulebook of Rules about Ruling for Rulers.* The awkwardly titled tome was the technical manual that covered all aspects of ruling in the UnUnited Kingdoms, whether they be an insane tyrannical despot or a touchy-feely communal-led socialist collective. I peered closer.

'Chapter 9, Paragraph 7, Subsection D, Rule 35b,' said Princess Tabathini, running her finger along the line of fine text. 'If the Albion Archipelago is invaded by a hostile force, the most senior monarch/ruler still at liberty is to assume command of all the Kingdoms until such time as that ruler relinquishes leadership and/or invading forces are defeated.'

Tiger and I looked at one another.

'Wow,' said Tiger, 'she's now the supreme leader of all the Kingdoms. That's a lot of people to be responsible for.'

'Do we tell her?' asked Princess Tabathini. 'I mean, power like that can go to a person's head, and the next thing we know she'll be wanting a toilet of pure gold and have an honour guard dressed in peacock feathers and bacon.'

'Does that happen?' asked Tiger.

'More than you think,' said Tabathini, rolling her eyes.

'I'll speak to her,' I said, 'but keep this under your hat, eh?'

Princess Tabathini walked off and Tiger and I looked at one another again. The Princess didn't seem like the sort of person who would suddenly want a gold toilet, but you never knew with princesses.

As soon as we'd entered the ballroom for the meeting and been given our name badges, Monty Vanguard walked over. After escaping Zambini Towers, he'd been in the first wave of displaced citizens to get to Cornwall. As ranking sorcerer he'd directed the filling of the Button Trench, then set up a command post in the Queens Hotel, ostensibly because he had stayed there for a couple of nights in the eighties and really liked it.

'Hello, Monty,' I said, 'how's the Button Trench holding up?'

'Secure for the moment,' he said, 'although quite what's stopping them having a human contingent under threat of eat-death remove the buttons to allow them to cross is a little confusing.'

'Or simply a large tree felled to bridge the gap,' said Tiger, 'or a coach.'

'I agree,' said Monty. 'They're waiting for something.'

'Shandar was behind all this,' I replied, 'and I think it's something bigger than reluctance over giving refunds.[14] How are the observers doing?'

'Up and running,' he said. The first task after the Button Trench was completed had been to create a chain of observers who could report in with news of Troll movements to the Human Defence Control room situated in the hotel's Reading Room.

'We've got at least twelve observers in each Kingdom. They're also part of an attempt to set up splinter resistance groups who will be ready to move when we have a centralised plan to retake the islands. Since the HENRY has wiped out all wizidrical forms

---

[14] He had been paid a lot of gold to get rid of the Dragons – which he didn't.

of communication – shoe, conch or hubcap[15] – we're having to rely on antiquated telephone networks with two-way homing snails as a back-up.'

Snails, as anyone will tell you, are only slow through lack of motivation. Suitably enthused, the average snail could match a human at a fast trot, with several larger varieties able to outrun a horse, so long as their moisture content holds out.

'Okay, then,' I said, 'and how are *you* doing?'

Monty Vanguard was less of a spell maker and more of a spell *writer*. He wrote spells mainly using the modern ARAMAIC spell language, but could also edit with the ancient RUNIX, which was very useful when trying to figure out how old spells worked, and whether they could be adapted for a more modern use. His most recent triumph was finding a way to utilise the ancient spell that kept bicycles from falling over and rewriting it to offer an auto-stabilisation system for octogenarians who were now a little unsteady on their legs.

'I'm holding up okay,' said Monty in the sort of

---

[15] Suitably paired, any two identical receptacles can be used for two-way communication. Shoes only work over a short distance but are convenient to carry. A pedal bin will certainly work up to a hundred miles and a well-paired tuba can reach Australia, although the voice at the other end sounds like Vaughn Williams's Bass Tuba Concerto in F Minor.

way that meant he wasn't, 'but I do miss Wizard Moobin.'

'So do we all. Any late arrivals for the Conclave?'

He passed me a list of the attendees.

'No one significant has arrived for over twenty-four hours,' he replied. 'I've invited non-wizidrical interested parties, too, as you requested.'

I thanked him and walked inside the large and well-decorated ballroom, all chandeliers and decorative plasterwork, with large picture windows lining the side facing the sea. The hotel staff had arranged the tables in a rough circle, and I sat to gather my thoughts. A lot had happened in the past fortnight, and I was still trying to keep up with the rapidly changing sequence of events.

I sighed. The Great Zambini would have known what to do.

Zambini had been my mentor, employer and, after the Mighty Shandar, the most powerful mage on the planet.[16] He'd pulled Kazam together when magic was a dying art and had been working tirelessly to preserve the power and majesty of magic until he vanished while performing at a children's party. He only reappeared from time to time, and never for

---

[16] Even more powerful than either of them, if she hadn't had her index fingers removed, was Once Magnificent Boo – hence the honorific.

very long. In his brief appearances I learned he'd become suspicious that he had been taken out of the picture deliberately, and I was convinced he was right. Since only he could realistically challenge the Mighty Shandar, it would make sense for Shandar to remove anyone who could stop him. When sorcerers go to the bad side, things can get very bad indeed.

'Have I missed anything?' asked the Princess as she sat next to me. 'I've not been to a Sorcerer's Conclave before, it's rather exciting.'

'We haven't started yet. Look, I need to speak to you about something.'

'Is it about Rule 35b?' she asked in a quiet voice.

'You know about that?'

'My mother insisted I read the *The Rulebook of Rules about Ruling for Rulers* several times. I didn't mention it earlier as being the supreme leader tends to make one a target for assassination and kidnappings by agents of a foreign power – and people start to grovel a lot and avert their eyes, which is just plain tiresome. It could be useful, though, leading the Kingdoms – and you know what?'

'What?'

'According to Rule 35b, I don't actually have to give the Kingdoms back once the Trolls are vanquished. With absolute power comes the absolute right to do what I want even when the threat is removed. I could leave everything as it was, or radically alter the island – even towards a unification: one land, one people.'

'You mean we could be a *United* UnUnited Kingdoms?' asked Colin the Dragon, who had been listening intently. 'Now that could be a thing. Standardised currency and education, a broad and attainable public health system for all, targeted financial assistance for those most in need and a centralised government that would promote trade by removing border controls. There could also be freedom of movement,' he added, suddenly getting quite carried away, 'equal opportunity employment rights, a banning of discriminatory practices and a responsible and workable constitution so citizens could enjoy broad and defendable rights and equality of opportunity. Best of all,' he added, 'domestic electrical plugs can all be the same. That one they use in Financia is just, well, *weird*.'

'Five prongs,' said Tiger, 'and two of them made of liquorice.'

'I like the sound of all that,' said the Princess, 'especially the plugs. I make you Minister for Good Ideas and Kingdom Integration – starting from now.'

'Oh,' said Colin, blinking twice, 'thank you.'

'No problem – but we've got to get rid of the Trolls first – *then* we can unite the country.'

'Which d'you think will be harder?' asked Tiger.

'I think they're probably about the same.'

The Princess removed the Helping Hand™ from

her wrist and placed it into sleep mode. A Helping Hand™ was a useful magical gadget that was in effect a disembodied hand that could be utilised to help drive a car with heavy steering, reaching up to paint places you couldn't reach and even playing accompaniment on a double bass. Since the Princess had lost her hand in hand-to-hand combat, she had come to rely on it, even though it was several sizes too big, was male, hairy, and had 'no more pies' tattooed on the back.

The doors to the ballroom opened at 2.20 and at 2.30 almost everyone was in place. At 2.34 Feldspar, the second Dragon, arrived, and although seemingly quite frightening, with scales and fangs and the occasional breath of fire – especially when excited – both the Dragons were so utterly non-Dragon and friendly that no one had much fear of them.

'Sorry,' he said apologetically, 'I was conducting an aerial survey of the neighbouring Kingdoms. Have I missed anything?'

'We were waiting for you,' I said.

'Oh,' he muttered, then tried to get to his seat, but not without some difficulty. Both Dragons were about the size of a largish Shetland pony by now, barely one twentieth of their adult size, and very clumsy – they were happier in the air, to be honest, or curled up on a sofa binge-watching TV series. I had told them about *Bergerac* in an unguarded moment, and they now loved the series so much they watched it again and again.

'Ow!'

'Sorry.'

Feldspar had trodden on the chief marksman's foot, and someone was sent to find a bag of frozen peas and some paracetamol. And so, after much apologising, everyone was seated. And at exactly 2.52 p.m., the Sorcerer's Conclave began.

The Sorcerer's Conclave

I took the sword Exhorbitus from my back-scabbard and laid it on the table in front of me, I guess to demonstrate the gravity of the meeting. Most enchanted swords had tastelessly overdecorated hilts and highly engraved blades, but Exhorbitus was more simple: perfectly proportioned and with a burnished dull finish and a ruby in the pommel, it was the weapon of a true warrior, to whom flashy presentation means nothing.

'My name is Jennifer Strange,' I said, 'and as Court Mystician to the Kingdom of Snodd and director of the House of Enchantment of Kazam, I think I am best placed to chair this Conclave, although I will hear arguments on why this should not be the case.'

'Shouldn't the Ruler of Cornwall be in charge?' asked Princess Jocaminca, who was clearly still a little chippy over losing her authority. 'Agreed, it's one twentieth the size it was, but while it remains unconquered land, the rightful ruler must still have authority.'

'It's a good point,' I said. 'Tiger, weren't you looking into this?'

Tiger stood up.

'All of Cornwall was bought by the Queen of Midlandia as a "second Kingdom" for her to enjoy ruling at the weekends. The Cornish Grand Vizier, charged to look after the Kingdom during the week, was also treating it more like a weekend thing, as was her deputy, the Attorney General, the Chief Judge and even the Minister for Pasties. They just governed as a kind of hobby. In fact, I can't find a single government job that wasn't done by someone who lives elsewhere.'

This was, sadly, all too true. After several centuries of weekend rule the indigenous Cornish now worked in a menial capacity beneath their weekending overlords. House prices were so high that the Cornish had to live in abandoned cars in fields until they were priced out of them, too, when 'living in an abandoned car in a field for the weekend' became the must-have holiday for Londoners with more money than sense.

'Is this true?' asked the Princess.

'Yes, ma'am,' said Tiger.

'My first decree as Ruler of all the Kingdoms,' she said, 'will be to seize all land and property in Cornwall owned by anyone who doesn't live here, and have it redistributed to the Cornish. Make a note, Tiger.'

'Yes, ma'am.'

'Okay,' I said, 'that's Cornwall sorted. Now: any other objections to me leading this Conclave?'

There were none, so I carried on:

'Before our discussions begin I would like to observe a minute's silence for those who did not survive the invasion and gave their lives in the struggle for freedom.'

We bowed our heads in the silence, and once the minute was up, I continued:

'As you all know the Trolls invaded two weeks ago led by Emperor Urdgg the Needlessly Violent. The invasion was well planned in that their strategy was very, very simple: advance through the UnUnited Kingdoms, killing and eating[17] anyone who tried to resist.'

It was a good strategy. The news spread quickly and the advancing Trolls found that their propensity for extreme violence and an imaginative flair for human-based recipes was enough to have humans falling over themselves to surrender, and the kings and queens, emperors, dictators, viziers and politburos all eagerly traded their and their family's lives for the keys to their nation. There was a murmuring at this and I looked around the room. This was meant to be a Sorcerer's Conclave but there were precious few wizards present. There had been talk of assistance from mainland Europe – they were quite enthusiastic to begin with, but then suddenly remembered they had

---

[17] Chillingly, not always in this order.

'a long-standing engagement of a pressing nature' and might have to 'sit this one out'.

'Okay,' I said, 'before we even begin to discuss tactics, we need to know how we stand as a potential army of resistance. Monty? Tell us what you've discovered.'

Monty Vanguard stood up. His once jet-black hair was now snowy white, yet combed in a manner that conveyed the appearance of a bank manager, a look reinforced by the circular horn-rimmed glasses, sensible suit, tidily knotted tie and ever-ready briefcase.

'As you might have heard,' he said, 'a powerful HENRY is currently active, nullifying all spells and rendering sorcerers powerless.'

'The more we try and damage it, the more powerful it becomes,' said Once Magnificent Boo, who was sitting on the other side of the Princess. 'We'll need to take it out by physical force.'

'Where is it based?' I asked.

'On Dartmoor,' said Monty. 'Colin took some aerial pictures. The HENRY is on the site of the TV mast, just near the prison, and surrounded by a forested enchantment – cut a bramble and two instantly grow in its place. If we want to destroy it we'll need to figure out some sort of countermeasure.'

'Okay,' I said, 'what else?'

Monty consulted his clipboard.

'Wizard Moobin was busy with the Trench and

button telepathy call, so he had Lady Mawgon and Full Price send out the requests for "Terrible Warriors" on the Low Telepathic Waveband to head to Cornwall along with marksmen and women, and anyone expert in fencing. All told, we have an army of just under two thousand.'

'That's good,' I said, taking a deep breath. When we failed to negotiate a deal with the Trolls then force would be inevitable.

Fight – or be eaten.

'Why didn't Full Price and Mawgon put out a call for artillery and heavy armoured vehicles?' asked Once Magnificent Boo.

'Cannons and tanks require heavy transportation and we didn't have the time,' said Lady Mawgon. 'Rifles are of questionable use as bullets simply make Trolls annoyed – but swords and rapiers are much feared, mostly because the scars can upset their intricate tattoos, of which they are hugely proud.'

'Warriors are resourceful fighters,' said Monty. 'They'll have a plan up their sleeves.'

'I agree,' I said. Since the UnUnited Kingdoms were so often at war, warrior was often a second profession on a part-time basis – when dentistry or carpet-fitting wasn't bringing in enough cash. 'Where are their representatives?'

Monty pointed towards where a woman and two men were seated between Tiger and the Mysterious

X, who was cosily sealed inside his Kilner jar, his particles sparkling like glow-worms. The representatives gave me a cheery wave while I consulted the register of Conclave attendees, which also listed the number of people they represented.

'So,' I said, addressing the Master Fencer, 'five hundred fencers and swordsmen and women, eh? That's impressive and, let me tell you, most welcome – at least that gives us *something* to attack them with.'

'Ah,' said the Master Fencer uneasily, 'I think there might have been a mix-up somewhere. We don't fence with rapiers and swords, we fence with *fenceposts and wire*. Lots of us will do hedge-laying as well. There are a few bricklayers too, if you'd prefer a wall. We're more into keeping cattle and sheep *in*,' she added, 'than keeping Trolls *out*.'

'Those five hundred fencers,' I said, trying to find a positive angle on this, 'are any of them handy with a sword?'

'They *might* be,' said the Master Fencer, 'but I know for sure they're handy with a billhook when it comes to pleaching.[18] I could always ask around, if you want.'

I looked at Full Price, who, along with the Lady Mawgon, had sent out the telepathic message. That

---

[18] The technique by which young tree saplings are bent and woven to make a living hedge. The 'billhook' is a large and very sharp sort of chopper.

was the trouble with magic. It often worked literally, and mistakes – or a misspelling – were common. If you were casting an enchantment, there was rarely any wiggle room for mistakes, and secondary spellings were quite common; even the simple incantation that runs temporary traffic lights could accidentally result in a shower of frogs.

'I've never done a low-alpha telepathic hailing,' said Full Price apologetically. 'We're lucky to have got anyone at all.'

'No blame is attributed,' I told him, 'but it's a good job we still have the marksmen. I know bullets just tend to bounce off the Troll's leathery hide, but they might be useful for delaying or distracting them.'

The keen-eyed marksman stood up.

'I represent the three hundred marksmen and women,' he said, 'and we too think there might have been an error in communication. We're actually people who paint white lines on turf for sporting events, although we'll also put yellow lines on roads to discourage irresponsible parking.'

'I'm not sure a double yellow line is going to keep any Trolls out,' I said. 'Why do you have "keen-eyed" in your title?'

'Most people use a string to help them keep the white lines straight,' he said. 'But we do it by eye alone.'

'Very useful.'

'It certainly saves a lot of time. I'm sorry we're not what you thought we'd be, but on the plus side we have given the local football and rugby grounds a bit of a freshen-up, and the parking regulations on the streets of Penzance have never been more unambiguous.'

'This is beginning to reek not of error but of sabotage,' grumbled Once Magnificent Boo. 'Somebody not so much jammed the magic, as subverted it.'

This was indeed possible – especially with telepathically transmitted ideas. Full Price, who had up until that moment looked downhearted given that he and Mawgon were mostly to blame for the misspelling, suddenly perked up.

'Okay,' I said, 'but at least we have a thousand terrible warriors. They'll be taking a bigger share of the fight, and if they are as terrible as their name suggests, they'll be more than useful. They'll be *indispensable.*'

'Oh dear oh dear oh dear,' came the voice of the third representative, who was wringing his hands in a desperate manner, 'this is all looking very frightening – we're all dead for sure. And what's more, I think I left the gas cooker on when I came out this morning, I have a rash on my foot that might turn out to be fatal and the gearbox in my car is making a funny noise.'

I looked at Monty Vanguard, who looked back with a resigned half-grimace. I turned back to the so-called warrior.

'You warriors are *worriers*, aren't you?'

'I'm afraid so,' said the terrible worrier, 'I don't think there is a single one of us who is expecting anything other than complete defeat under the Trolls – and is not fretting horribly about it. Will we be expected to pay for our rooms? I've not much money and I may have to go and live in an abandoned car somewhere. Am I being boring? I've had twenty years of therapy to make me less tedious. It was thirty pounds an hour. Do you think that was too much? I do. Unless you don't agree – and then I'll be conflicted.'

And he put his head in his hands and issued a long and melancholic sigh.

'It's fine,' I said, 'you're not boring and hotel management and staff are working for free while we figure out a way to beat the Trolls.'

'Oh,' said the terrible worrier, 'that's good – except for the Trolls. Do I look good enough to eat? You can be honest with me.'

'It's really looking like mischief now,' said Once Magnificent Boo.

'I'm thinking you're right,' I said. 'Do we have *anyone* here who is militarily trained?'

Monty consulted his clipboard.

'The Cornish army is absent as they only did it for fun at the weekends,' he said, 'but we do have about forty people who have some military training.

Haberdashers mostly – and after having a rummage we found eighteen swords, four firearms, three spears, six dozen pointy sticks, nine daggers and a trebuchet.'

'A trebuchet?' I said, as this was at least a viable weapon – a medieval siege engine designed to hurl rocks at castles. Although superseded by artillery and landships they were very 'in' at the moment owing to a recent fad for 'retro warfare'.

'Not a very large one,' said Monty, looking at his clipboard again. 'In fact, only a model.'

'We could bring it very close to the Trolls and hope that they don't fully understand the laws of perspective and mistake it for a full-sized one,' suggested the Guild of Fencer's representative.

'That's kind of a long shot,' I said.

'Or rather,' put in Colin with a snigger, 'it *won't* be much of a long shot.'

There was silence.

'Long shot?' he said. 'Trebuchet?'

No one laughed, and Colin looked crestfallen.

'Anyway,' I said, 'I think I only want to hear what we *do* have from now on. Assets we can exploit to bring our battle to the Trolls.'

Before anyone could say anything, the Remarkable Kevin Zip suddenly stood up.

'Something's going to happen,' he said in a quiet voice.

'What?' I said.

'I said: "Something's going to happen".'

'Yes, I know what you *said*,' I replied, used to Kevin's ways by now. 'I was just wondering what important thing will happen?'

Kevin Zip looked at us all, and we all stared back. When a pre-cog with a proven track record says something important is about to happen, you take note, although uncertainties over the precise time, nature and location of the event often make the prediction either useless or irrelevant – or it comes too late to do any good at all.

'The tea lady will arrive,' he said slowly, 'and she'll be short on Hobnobs and will instead offer us digestives.'

'*That's* the important thing that's going to happen?' said Colin. 'Like . . . big wow.'

'Two weeks ago I could see a month into the future,' said Kevin Zip, 'but when the HENRY fired up my Predict Event Horizon reduced to a maximum of eighteen minutes. This morning it had diminished to only twelve. If it carries on reducing at this rate I'll only be able to predict things *after* they happen. I think there's a word for it.'

'Memory?' said Tiger.

'That's the one. It's all a little annoying. But,' he added, scribbling on a piece of paper, '*immediate* things I can often see with great accuracy.'

'Is that useful?' asked Colin, and Kevin showed him

the piece of paper with 'it could be, not sure' written on it.

I took a deep breath and looked at Tiger, who shrugged. Usually a conclave is a well-ordered meeting offering a clear idea of where we are going with many sober, well-thought out and considered suggestions about the right course of action. With the Trolls quite literally an hour from this very spot — more if they chose to dawdle and admire the view — we needed to dispense with protocol and start dealing with practicalities.

'I'm going to throw the meeting open,' I said. 'If anyone has any good ideas on how to vanquish the Trolls, I want to hear all about it right now.'

'How about if we throw stones at them?' said a young man at the far end of the table. 'Just pelt them endlessly.'

'And you are?'

'Grover Ruckstell,' he said, 'representing the Guild of Haberdashers.'

'And what would throwing rocks achieve?' I asked, 'Since it would probably take a stone too big to lift and thrown at a speed impossible to accomplish to have any sort of effect.'

'It would make us feel better,' said Grover with a shrug.

'I think some sort of a stunt would be a good idea,' said Jimmy Nuttjob, noted daredevil and stunt performer. He had been wowing the audiences up and down the UnUnited Kingdoms for decades, and by royal decree had a bed reserved in every hospital, as most of his outlandish stunts went spectacularly wrong – such as the time he tried to fire himself from an air cannon through a brick wall, and set the cannon pressure a little too high and went through *two* walls, a parked car and embedded himself in a telephone box. Rumours persist that he has the image of a telephone dial permanently embossed on his left buttock.

'Okay,' I said, well used to Nuttjob's unique brand of showmanship/death wish, 'so what's your plan?'

'A skydive from thirty thousand feet trailing a huge banner reading *Ugg dugh lurgh hurg,*[19]' he said excitedly. 'That should make them see we're not a species to be trifled with.'

'A parachute drop doesn't sound *that* risky,' said Full Price, who was a huge fan of Jimmy Nuttjob but had also, in leaner times, enjoyed a bit of parachuting himself.

'Whoever said anything about a parachute?' asked Nuttjob with an excited gleam in his eye.

---

[19] A very vulgar taunt known to enrage Trolls everywhere. It suggests they 'would far prefer a sofa, potted plants and pale blue wallpaper' to the usual draughty cave littered with bones and as-yet uneaten entrails. The human equivalent would be calling someone 'a massive softie'.

'Teatime!' announced the tea lady as she walked in. 'I know you could all do with a cuppa but the Trolls have disrupted the biscuit supply chain, so it will be digestives only today.'

Zip's skill as a pre-cog was impressive but in this particular instance of little use – unless you were looking forward to Hobnobs, in which case it might have softened the disappointment.

'Actually,' said Kevin Zip, 'the Hobnob issue *wasn't* the important thing that was about to happen.'

'Glad to hear it,' said Colin.

'I think it's fairly clear,' said Once Magnificent Boo, 'that the Troll didn't do all this on its own, and we must—'

She had stopped talking because the doors had been flung open in a dramatic fashion and a tall and impossibly handsome man walked in. He was dressed in expensive embroidered silk clothes, had a long flowing mane of blond hair, an impressive lantern jaw and large blue eyes. It was Sir Matt Grifflon, and while I and most people who knew him groaned audibly, Princess Jocaminca strategically swooned at his striking, manly presence while Princess Tabathini fanned herself with a copy of *What Prince?* magazine.

Sir Matt Grifflon

He wasn't alone, as any knight worth their spurs always had a retinue of hangers-on which generally included a couple of lute-playing minstrels who would sing songs about the knight's achievements, several squires, an accountant, a make-up and hair stylist combined, a gun bearer, his agent, two valets, a dozen or so armed guards and, at the front, an ornamental hermit whose function was to spout meaningless aphorisms on demand. The latter bowed and took a deep breath.

'A man's word is the bond of past friendships in Kent,' he intoned gravely, 'and fish do not walk when there is water in which to swim.'

I looked at Tiger, who shrugged. He thought it was nonsense too.

'Consider the tadpole,' said the hermit as an afterthought, then bowed again and stepped aside with a flourish as Sir Matt took a dramatic pace forward.

'Please don't get up,' he said, although as far as I could see no one was going to, 'everything is now okay since *I am here*.'

Princess Jocaminca, recently recovered, swooned again, but more showily, hoping to gain his attention.

'United under my ruggedly masculine leadership,' he continued, 'we will vanquish the Troll and lead the Kingdoms into new and broad sunlit uplands. Furthermore . . .'

He carried on in this vein for several minutes. While he was talking about honour and loyalty and personal self-sacrifice – although not necessarily his own – everyone looked a little bored. Some people doodled on their pads, the Dragons started playing Scrabble with their neighbours and Tiger got out his yo-yo. The Princess leaned across to me and whispered:

'Have you come across this buttfish[20] before?'

'Several times,' I replied. 'He tried to kill me on the orders of your father. Weirdly, I was a huge fan when I was much younger, and even had a poster of him in my room.'

This wasn't unusual, as Sir Matt Grifflon, in addition to his role as the King of Snodd's favourite knight and enforcer, was also a successful recording artist. His last single, 'A horse, a song and me', had been a huge hit, and when not searching for a princess with a suitably large Kingdom to marry, he also did concert tours and was a dab hand at jousting.

---

[20] I never did find out what this meant.

'Don't trust him an inch,' said the Princess. 'He was always a pain in the bum back in the palace, strutting around the place and cosying up to Mummy and Daddy. My father wanted to sell him a marriage option but Mummy wouldn't allow it.'

'He'll want to marry you now.'

'What, me, in my scrawny handmaiden's body?'

'Knowing Grifflon,' I said, 'he'll have *definitely* figured out Rule 35b and will warmly embrace you with flattery.'

'. . . and leave no stone unturned as we expel this vile evil from our land,' concluded Sir Matt, and then, noticing Colin for the first time, yelled: 'Dragon!' and approached Colin menacingly, his large and very ornate sword now out of its scabbard. The Dragon, however, merely raised an eyebrow in a bored kind of way.

'Loathsome beast!' yelled Sir Matt. 'Destroyer of all that is good and wholesome, prepare to meet thy maker!'

He raised his sword to strike but Colin, with an almost effortless twitch of his tail, severed Sir Matt's sword neatly at the hilt – the blade of which clattered harmlessly to the floor.

Sir Matt stared stupidly at the broken sword for a few moments.

'That was *very* expensive,' he said reproachfully. 'You should be more respectful of other people's property.'

'And you should be more respectful of others' right to life,' replied Colin.

'The Dragons are with us,' said the Princess. 'You are to leave them both alone.'

'There are two?'

'Helloooo,' said Feldspar, giving him a cheery wave from the other side of the room.

'A *double* slaying,' said Grifflon excitedly, 'an honour I shall inscribe upon my coat of arms.'

'No one's going to be killing any Dragons,' said the Princess. 'It is my order.'

'I'm a knight,' he said simply, 'killing Dragons is what I do.'

'And burning idiots like you to powdered charcoal,' said Colin, 'is what *we* do.'

'Hmm,' said Sir Matt, and tried to put his broken sword back in the scabbard. It wouldn't go, not having a blade, so he passed the hilt to one of his squires, walked up to where we were sitting and made a deep bow and a flourish of high chivalry towards Princess Shazine, who stared back at him suspiciously.

'My queen,' he said. 'By an act of my selfless generosity your Dragons are now spared. I pledge my loyalty to my ruler, and offer myself as personal bodyguard, willing to die to protect the most inestimable jewel in these islands. Beautiful as you were when a princess, you are twice as lovely now, your external plainness, lank hair, mildly gawky appearance and unfortunate dentition confirmation that the soul of a ruler resides within. And,' he added, really pushing the boat out when it came to flattery, 'I think that beauty, good bone structure and a willowy physique are merely embellishments that have no bearing on inner character, and that far greater treasures lie beneath the surface. You and I were made for one another, and I think, given the dire circumstances, that we should be married straight away.'

'Oh,' said the Princess, 'isn't that a bit quick? I mean, you haven't even taken me out to dinner yet.'

'Or a movie,' said Colin.

'Yes indeed, a movie, thank you, good point,' said the Princess.

'They're re-running all the *Back to the Future* movies at the Savoy Cinema,' said Feldspar, who was looking at a copy of *What's on in Penzance*. 'That should be fun.'

'I've just had a thought,' said Colin. 'Was there a DeLorean Time Machine down the mineshaft throughout the first *Back to the Future*?'

'Nope,' said Tiger, 'it only came into being when Doc got struck by lightning at the end of Part Two.'[21]

'Are you sure?'

'Yes. Look.'

---

[21] You'll have to watch the movie.

And he started to draw the timelines on a sheet of paper to explain.

Sir Matt Grifflon stared daggers at them briefly, then dramatically knelt before the Princess, took her hands in his, and stared at her earnestly.

'In most circumstances, yes,' he said, 'I would be taking you to dinner and the movies and then we'd be running towards one another in slow motion on a beach, but by utilising Subsection 12, Paragraph 9, Rule 11F, "Males to become king if they marry female heirs to the throne", I can bring, as King of the United Kingdoms, my considerable expertise and rugged manly leadership qualities to the issue of the Trolls – and you can fall back into the role of supportive wife, and think about shopping and crochet and kittens and which private school the nation's royal heirs should attend. Say yes, and we can perform the nuptials now – I've even brought a bishop with me.'

He pointed towards where a bishop was indeed part of his entourage, although he looked a little more like a shabby curate as his clothes were cheap and poorly laundered, and his hat was too big and nearly covered his eyes.

'I think I've seen it all now,' I muttered.

Sir Matt flashed me an angry look, but, to his credit, at least he recognised me.

'Oh, look,' he said dismissively. 'Dragon girl. Well,

I'll give you a free pass this time, kiddo, but here's a spot of advice: ordinary people are *never* to address knights without first being addressed. It's in the *Manual of Chivalry* foreword and not hard to miss—'

'I'm a knight too,' I said, suddenly realising this could be useful, 'so can say what I like to you when I wish to do so.'

'Nonsense,' he scoffed, 'girls can't be knights. I mean, *really* – we'll be making spotty orphans into earls next.'

And he laughed for a bit until he stopped because the Princess wasn't.

'They can be knights if I say they can,' said the Princess in a stony voice. 'Isn't that right, Tiger, Earl of Prawns?'

'Me?' said Tiger, looking up from his convoluted diagram of *Back to the Future* timelines and seemingly taken aback by his new-found status. 'I mean, yes, your Majesty.'

'Did I say they couldn't?' said Sir Matt, changing his mind instantly. 'I meant to say they could and s*hould* be made into dukes if that's what the reigning monarch decides.' He turned to me. 'Sir Jennifer, I am truly sorry about all that silly attempted murder business. I think I was having a bad day, and it was only *attempted*, after all – not like the real thing, eh?'

'That you did not succeed is no credit to you,' I said.

'Well, look,' he said, trying to sound all conciliatory, 'we could play the blame game over the whole "tried to kill you issue" but I've moved on. Anyway, there are more important things right now, such as me and the Princess getting married — now if—'

'This isn't it either,' said Kevin Zip, who also didn't worry about interrupting knights. 'Grifflon isn't the Something that's Going to Happen. It's way bigger than him.'

'Exactly,' said Sir Matt, '*way* bigger: the wedding.' He patted his pockets, eager to hurry this all along so he could become Supreme Ruler of all the Kingdoms. 'I've got a ring somewhere.'

'I don't think a wedding is the Something that's Going to Happen,' said Kevin.

'What would you know?' said Sir Matt. 'Now, shall we perform the ceremony here or in the local cathedral?'

'Not so fast,' said the Princess, finally getting her say. 'What sort of a queen would I be if I did not show due diligence over my choice of consort? Would my subjects respect a queen who said *yes* to the first knight who asked, irrespective of lantern jaw, flowing blond mane and impressively successful recording career? No, my people would expect more of me. You are to prove yourself worthy of my hand in marriage, so I will set you a task.'

Sir Matt Grifflon bowed low. Tasks for hands-in-marriage were fairly routine in the Kingdoms – it was even a long-running reality TV show.

'I have already pledged not to kill those horribly disrespectful Dragons over there so it can't be that,' he said, 'but yes, I accept the challenge, whatever it is.'

It sounded as though he were suspecting something quite easy, which it usually was. Tasks were generally of a difficulty tailored to the average prince's IQ: find your own head with your eyes shut, identify a zebra in a line-up of elephants, spell your name, state your favourite fruit, that sort of thing.

'You are to find the tallest building in Penzance,' said the Princess.

'No problem, can do,' said Sir Matt, getting up from where he had been on bended knee. 'I shall do that in a jiffy and be back to claim your hand.'

'There's more. Once you've found it, you shall leap off singing "God save the Queen!" at the top of your voice.'

'Could I jump off a lower part of the tallest building?' he asked. 'I'm thinking a ground-floor window.'

'No,' said the Princess, 'because otherwise you'd not have enough time to sing: "God save the Queen!" on the way down.'

'I could sing it very fast,' said Sir Matt.

'No, I want it clear and unhurried,' said the Princess. 'How far would Sir Matt need to fall to achieve that? Anyone?'

'Sixty-four feet,' said Tiger. 'You'll be travelling at about forty-three miles per hour when you hit the ground.'

'That will sting a bit,' said the Princess. 'Well, toddle off, then. Let us know when you'll be jumping so we can come and watch.'

Sir Matt Grifflon muttered something, then left the room. There was a pause and then Tiger started giggling, followed closely by Colin.

'Do you think he'll actually do it?' said the Princess to me.

'He'll find any excuse not to. Besides—'

I didn't get to finish as a pillar of fire opened up in the middle of room, accompanied by a clap of thunder. It was not hot, just dramatic, and in an instant the fire was replaced by two people.

I'd met them both before. One was Miss D'Argento, a woman only a few years older than myself. She was Shandar's agent, had short bobbed dark hair, was dressed elegantly and carried a clipboard. The other person was tall, good looking and wore a dark suit with mauve pinstripes – which went, oddly, horizontally instead of vertically. He had a youthful bounce to his stride, carried a long cane and had bright green eyes.

It was the Mighty Shandar.

'*This is it!*' said Kevin Zip, suddenly becoming all animated and excited. 'This is the Something that was about to Happen!'

The Mighty Shandar

'All those present,' said Miss D'Argento, 'take heed and listen: you are now in the presence of Super Ultra Grand Master Sorcerer, mover of mountains, he-who-the-storms-obey, commander of oceans, speaker of tongues, keeper of the sacred spells, creator of beasts, wiser than the ancient ones and purveyor of fine enchantments, no reasonable terms refused, his most powerful, bountiful worshipfulness: the Mighty Shandar.'

She gave a dramatic flourish and a low bow, but if she had thought we would all follow suit, she was to be disappointed. The honorific was long winded, but correct. Technically speaking, *all* practitioners should be introduced this way, but it just soaked up useful time that might be otherwise spent drinking tea, or chatting. The only one of our bunch who liked this sort of nonsense was Lady Mawgon.

Nonetheless, at least one of us needed to offer the official reply, and since I was Court Mystician, it fell to me.

'This house welcomes you, O Mighty Shandar,

Super Ultra Grand Master Sorcerer, mover of mountains, he-who-the-storms-obey, commander of oceans and keeper of the sacred spells, creator of beasts and wiser than the ancient ones.'

To a sorcerer of Shandar's power, the correct honorific was all-important. You didn't get to this level with just skill and hard study. No, you needed ambition, a massive personal ego, a keen sense of entitlement and a streak of vanity a mile wide.

And he had all of them.

In spades.

'We return your salutations, noble Court Mystician,' said Miss D'Argento, going into the second line of the official salutation. I think there were four calls and returns in total. 'Our pledge is peace, our reason here a parler,[22] our fingers are bent, there shall be no subterfuge.'

She waited me to return the salutation.

'I'm sorry,' I said, 'I don't know the rest. I've never got this far before.'

'I think you just repeat it back,' said Colin.

'You do *not*,' said D'Argento indignantly, 'but if you so require, this person can write it down if you wish.'

Miss D'Argento usually referred to herself in the

---

[22] 'Parler' meaning a talk, from the French 'parler', meaning to speak.

third person. Out of all her affectations – jet-black suit, constant reference to her clipboard, fashionable indifference – it was the one I liked least. Shandar, however, merely glanced at D'Argento and waved away any objections, so she fell silent while he looked around carefully. His gaze paused briefly on Colin and Feldspar, then on Once Magnificent Boo, Monty Vanguard, the Princess, and finally me. He proffered me a faint glimmer of respect and stepped forward, his footprints remaining aflame for some seconds after he had moved on. That he was the most powerful sorcerer alive today was beyond doubt.

Shane James Alexandar was a child magical prodigy. By the time he was six he could levitate pianos and charm badgers from their burrows in broad daylight. He'd conjured up his first house by the time he was ten, and by his fifteenth birthday had demonstrated an eighty-foot free teleport, then a world record. By the time he was eighteen he had mastered arboreal transformation, weather manipulation and the transmutation of matter. He passed out First in Class from Sorcerer College and was awarded the 'Mighty' honorific eight years later when he spelled up the Quarkbeast, winner of the coveted 'Most Terrifying Beast' prize at the 1592 'Wizard of the Year' awards.

His dazzling career encompassed almost every aspect of the mystical arts, finally culminating in dealing with the Dragon Question,[23] for which he was paid enough[24] to retire twenty times over. He was so key to the industry that the unit of wizidrical energy had been named after him, and there were few who considered him anything but the finest exponent of the wizidrical arts. After the Dragons were dealt with his reputation began to tarnish as he became known as a sorcerer who would do pretty much anything if the price was right, ethical or not. By the time he was middle aged he was more of a loner, and rarely sought the companionship or counsel of his peers.

'Miss Strange,' he said cordially, 'you are looking well.'

'And yourself, sire,' I returned, 'you look barely a day over ninety.'

'You will treat His Mightiness with the proper respect,' growled Miss D'Argento.

'It's okay,' said Shandar, 'I think Miss Strange intended it as compliment.'

He was right. It was. Shandar was actually somewhere in his mid-four-hundreds and this was highly unusual. The magical holy grail of Eternal Life had remained stubbornly beyond the reach of sorcerers.

---

[23] See *The Last Dragonslayer* for a full explanation.
[24] Twenty-eight dray-weights of gold, a dray being a very large horse. It was about a third of all the gold in the world at that point. Today it would be worth about 1.2 trillion moolah.

The oldest wizard to ever live in a continuously human form had finally clocked out at an impressive 173 years and nine days. Others had achieved greater longevity by spending their weekends as tortoises or lobsters but Shandar had achieved his old age by simply turning himself to stone, a spell that had been invented to avoid income tax by outliving the current tax regime or waiting for the paperwork to be lost, as it inevitably was.

'So,' I said, 'how may we serve you?'

'Straight to the point?' he replied. 'I admire that. So here it is: no doubt you have seen that the Trolls are currently in complete possession of these islands. You may already have surmised that I had something to do with it.'

We all knew it was him, but the confirmation made my temper rise, and I could feel I was not alone – the tension in the room rose markedly.

'You murdered my friends,' I said in a quiet voice, 'innocents, sorcerers, your own. Everything that the Sorcerer's Charter holds to be true and just – you rejected.'

'The Charter does not recognise forward thinking; it is rooted in the old ways. And they were not friends of mine, Miss Strange – but I will meditate upon their loss, in time. To business: you will have seen that I have shortened Zip's predictive powers, set up a HENRY Spellsucker and interfered with

Price and Mawgon's telepathic shout-out. As things currently stand you have only two sorcerers, no wizidrical power for them to use, and less than forty people militarily trained, eighteen swords and four firearms.'

'Nineteen swords,' I said, 'if you count Exhorbitus, but let's not quibble.'

'I . . . exactly. The point is, you are poorly placed to resist the Troll, and the next step is up to you. They can rule for thousands of years with humans as little more than edible staff, or they can be gone by Monday teatime. I can make that happen, or I can leave them to their impressive levels of culinary invention.'

'We understand the threat,' I said slowly. 'What do you want?'

Horse-trading was a little below him, so he signalled for Miss D'Argento to step in.

'It's very simple,' she said. 'His Mightiness wants the Eye of Zoltar he asked you to secure and . . . your Quarkbeast.'

This was worrying. If you were foolish enough to let two identical yet opposing Quarkbeasts conjoin, they would generate huge amounts of wizidrical energy – always to the 'Criticality' level discussed earlier, usually with enough power to take out a good-sized city block. But as I sat there staring at them both, I realised that if you could *focus* that energy – such as

73

through the Eye of Zoltar – then you could use it to enrich yourself with some very powerful magic. With a sense of growing unease I thought I understood what he was up to. Not what he actually wanted to *do*, but a methodology to his demands: he was after power – and lots of it. This was a tricky situation, and in moments like this you needed time to figure out how to find yourself another, bigger chunk of time – and maybe, just maybe, you could find a solution in that.

Or just more time.

'Agreed,' I said almost immediately, as hesitation suggests indecision. If you're going to lie, don't dither for a second – and make it a whopper. The bigger the fib, the greater the chance that people will believe it.

'I will supply both to you,' I continued, 'just as soon as the last Troll hoof is off the nation's soil. We also want the Great Zambini returned to us, intact, now, as a sign of goodwill.'

The Mighty Shandar stared at me for a moment, impressed. Few, if any, would have dared to speak to him like this, but growing up in an orphanage under Mother Zenobia's often tyrannical method of child-rearing toughened you up.

'That any of you are alive at all is the mark of my supreme benevolence,' he said slowly. 'The magpies that helped fill the Button Trench – that was me. I have spared you once, but you will not always find me so magnanimous.'

'Zambini stays vanished,' added Miss D'Argento. 'You will give His Mightiness the Eye and the Quarkbeast right now, and the Trolls will be gone in a month.'

'The Mighty Shandar said he could get rid of them by Monday teatime,' said Tiger, who had been brought up in the same orphanage as me, and it showed. The Mighty Shandar turned to glare at Tiger, who didn't seem fussed at all.

'His Mightiness merely meant,' said D'Argento in a testy manner, 'that he can *start* to get rid of them by Monday morning.'

'He should have been clearer.'

'Put the little twit on the Troll Eat List,' said Shandar, 'and have him fast-tracked to the head of the banquet for his impertinence – on a large platter, covered in glaze and with an apple in his mouth. That'll shut him up.'

D'Argento made a hurried note and I smiled inwardly. Tiger was trying to distract him. Zambini had told me that when negotiating, keep negotiating, keep engaging, and even if you're making little headway, find some small concession. Come away from the first stage of a negotiation empty handed, and you'll *always* come away empty handed.

'We will consider your offer and let you know on

Monday,' I said, trying to buy some time over the weekend, 'so long as we can see a reduction in Troll numbers at the Button Trench.'

'His Mightiness is the one dictating terms,' D'Argento said. 'I thought that was obvious.'

Shandar looked at her and raised an eyebrow.

'But,' she added, taking it down a notch, 'since His Mightiness has more pressing matters to occupy his time, you may give us the Eye of Zoltar now, and as soon as we take possession of the Quarkbeast on Monday morning the Trolls will be instantly transported to beyond the Troll Wall, which will then be sealed. We do not know where Zambini is.'

'Take the deal,' added Shandar, 'or the next thing you will be wearing is garnish.'

There was a long pause.

'Jennifer,' said Boo, 'we should give His Mightiness the Eye of Zoltar.'

I wasn't sure about this, but trusted Boo implicitly, so nodded my assent.

'I'll get it,' said Monty Vanguard. As he hurried off, the Mighty Shandar looked around.

'So that's what Maltcassion[25] became, is it?' he said. 'Not much to look at, are you?'

---

[25] The Last Dragon, as killed by the Last Dragonslayer. Wise beyond measure, as old Dragons generally are. He became a good friend.

This was kind of true. Both Feldspar and Colin were only young, and looked like baby birds just coming into feather – sort of untidy, with feathers and scales pointing out in all directions.

'The name's Colin,' said Colin, 'and I will have my vengeance upon you for destroying so many of my kind.'

'I'm quaking in my boots already,' said Shandar. 'I'll deal with you and your silly brother in due course, have no fear of *that.*'

'Here it is,' said Monty, walking back in with a galvanised pail. We kept the Eye in a bucket of water, which is a good moderator[26] of wizidrical energy. But even so we had to change the water every week as the magic the Eye attracted turned the water first to Ribena, then to rose petals, then butterflies. It pays to be cautious. To expel energy in a focused beam, the Eye had also to be able to absorb it. Shandar delicately took the large and fiery jewel from the bucket, stared at it and smiled. We'd thought he'd sent us to find the Eye as something of a wild goose chase, but from the look on his face, it was an integral part of his plans.

---

[26] In this context, quenching the power of the magic. You would have to be very powerful indeed to do any useful spells under-water. It also explains why getting rainstorms to start is easy, but getting them to stop is almost impossible.

'You have until dawn on Monday to deliver the Quarkbeast,' said Miss D'Argento. 'If you fail to do so, His Mightiness will undertake some instant bridge-building across the trench, and then set out deckchairs for us both to watch the invasion of your pitiful little safe haven in comfort, and the devouring of all those within.'

'Well,' said Shandar, clapping his hands and giving us all a smile, 'this has been a lot of fun and I think we understand each other. Good day.'

And he vanished in another overly dramatic pillar of fire.

Oddly, Miss D'Argento *didn't*; she was left standing in the middle of the ballroom very much on her own. She looked at her watch, then the clipboard, then found an invisible piece of fluff on her lapel.

'He's forgotten you, hasn't he?' said Tiger after an awkward few seconds.

'His Mightiness has much on his mind,' she said, 'but I am central to his needs. He will return.'

'Leave Shandar and side with us,' I said. 'With your help we can beat him.'

'My destiny is inextricably linked to that of my master's,' she said, staring at me with a glimmer of sadness. 'As, I believe, is yours.'

'We have something in common, then. Is this how you see yourself?' I added. 'The lackey of a despot?'

'Your taunts will not sway me from my course,' said

D'Argento. 'There is a bigger picture that you cannot see, a story that is not yet revealed.'

'Riddles, D'Argento?'

She cocked her head on one side and regarded me without emotion – and was suddenly gone in another pillar of fire. Shandar must have wanted his socks washed or something.

There was a moment's pause as we took all this in.

'Quark?' said the Quarkbeast.

'No,' I said, staring into his expressive mauve eyes, 'we'll not give you up. Not now, not ever.'

'What was all that "bigger picture" stuff about?' asked the Princess.

'I'm really not sure,' I replied. 'Messing with our heads, most likely.'

'Is he going to make good on that promise to instantly remove the Trolls?' asked the Princess.

'An assurance from Shandar assures precisely *nothing*,' I said, 'so assume not. If we have until Monday morning, that's two days.'

'A lot can happen in two days,' said Tiger.

'True. Why were you keen to give him the Eye of Zoltar, Boo?'

She nodded towards Monty.

'While handing it to him I may have *accidentally* slipped a Lump of East in his pocket,' said Monty, taking an east-pointing compass from his own pocket. 'It's such an old spell he may not notice he's got it on him.'

Monty put the compass on the table and we stared at it. The needle swung around lazily.

'What are we looking at?' asked the Princess.

'The spell that makes any iron point to magnetic north is the only remaining part of an ingenious Global Magic Navigation System spelled by the Phoenicians around two millennia BCE,' explained Monty. 'There were going to be four fixed compass points around the globe, each with a separate metal-based compass that would point to them. Simple trigonometry would then be used to give your location anywhere in the known world with an accuracy down to about five hundred yards.'

'What happened?' asked Colin.

'Budget overruns, mostly – and sabotage by other seafaring nations. The one they planted in the far north is the only one still functioning today.'

We continued to stare at the compass, and the needle swung freely for a while, then turned and pointed fixedly in one direction.

'Okay,' said Boo. 'He's out of teleportation and somewhere on that line.'

'He could be as close as Padstow or . . . in Siberia,' said Tiger.

'Exactly,' said Boo. 'Feldspar? I need you to take this compass to the end of the harbour, get a reading, then fly to the north coast and get another reading. Repeat several times, and when you think you have a reasonable accuracy, come back and we'll figure out the trigonometry.[27]'

'Right,' said Feldspar, happy to be doing some work. He flew out of the open window with a raucous beating of wings and an enthusiastic 'Tally ho!' then returned a minute later to take the compass that he'd forgotten, and flew off again, only without the 'Tally ho'.

'Okay,' I said to everyone present, 'just so we're clear on this: Shandar will not keep his word. The negotiation you saw buys us one thing: time. We've got until dawn on Monday morning to figure out a winning strategy. After that, Cornwall will look less like a picturesque peninsula with a rugged coastline and reasonably priced teashops, and more like a Troll's all-you-can-eat buffet. The Princess's closest advisers are going to try and formulate a plan of action, and I may call on any one of you to help, so stand close by to await orders. Any questions?'

No one said a word, and I called an end to the Conclave. The attendees all filed out in something of a daze, leaving only myself, Boo, Colin, Tiger, the Princess, Full Price, Kevin Zip, the Mysterious X and Monty Vanguard. Once everyone else had

---

[27] With this method, Feldspar would ascertain two angles and one side of a triangle. Enough to figure out the other angle and sides – and a fix on where Shandar was based.

departed, I asked Tiger to go and fetch Lady Mawgon.

'Okay,' I said, 'we need to discover Shandar's overall plan, and once we know exactly what it is, the chances of thwarting him might move, with a lot of luck, from "utterly impossible" to a more workable "highly improbable".'

'My kind of odds,' said the Princess.

We discussed Shandar's possible plans, making little headway until Tiger came back accompanied by a severe-looking woman who glided into the room dressed in a large black crinoline dress.

It was Lady Mawgon.

Troll Defence

Lady Mawgon was in charge of the Operations Room, which was just down the hall and opposite the main reception. The converted reading room was now full of desks, telephones and hastily employed clerks who were taking calls from the network of observers dotted around the country. All the information came through Mawgon, who decided what was relevant and necessary as opposed to what was hearsay and exaggeration. At the same time, she coordinated the regional resistance groups.

'Good evening, Lady Mawgon,' I said. 'How are things looking in the Troll defence network?'

She was ex-Zambini Towers, one of the few who had escaped the Troll/Shandar attack. She and I had not really got along until this moment of National Jeopardy, following which she had transformed herself – I hope permanently – from 'openly hostile' to 'mostly disapproving', a huge step forward.

'The situation is not looking favourable, Miss Strange.'

She'd get round to calling me 'Jennifer' eventually,

and perhaps even 'Jenny', if either of us lived that long. Lady Mawgon curtsied to the Princess, whose new role as Queen had got about, and made a short speech of loyalty, then nodded respectfully to Once Magnificent Boo, who she saw not just as a mentor in the mystical arts, but the finest exponent of the often tricky art of looking perpetually moody without really trying.

Lady Mawgon moved to where there was a large map of the UnUnited Kingdoms on the wall. She didn't so much walk as *drift* across the room. I knew for a fact she wore roller skates under her large black crinoline dresses, an odd affectation that softened her a little in my and Tiger's eyes.

'We've just heard that Wales has finally fallen,' she said, pointing at the map with her stick, 'and the last two hold-outs of the Duchy of Portland Bill and the economic City State of Financia surrendered last week rather than be eaten. The only part of the UnUK at liberty aside from this tip of Cornwall is the Seagoing Nation of the Isle of Wight, but they will not be of any help: in their eagerness to get away they ran themselves aground on Iceland in the fog.' She paused for a moment. 'So aside from a few pockets of resistance where they had either hidden up trees or are marooned on islands, the UnUnited Kingdoms are now Greater Trollvania.'

'To *them*,' said Tiger. 'The United European Nations

will never accept the Troll as legal owner of islands that were invaded against their will.'

'Actually,' said Lady Mawgon, 'that's exactly what the UEN did. It *really* is now known as Greater Trollvania. I think it was part of a deal whereby the Trolls didn't further their territorial ambitions into Europe.'

We stared at the map of the UnUnited Kingdoms for a moment. We really were on our own.

'If it only took two weeks to conquer the entire UnUnited Kingdoms,' I said slowly, 'the biggest question is why they haven't done it since the Romans last expelled them beyond the Great Troll Wall in AD 130.'

'The Wall was designed to keep them out,' said Monty, 'and as far as anyone knows, they never once tried to invade us – all the Troll Wars since then were instigated by humans.'

'As a precautionary measure against the Trolls attacking?' asked Tiger.

'It was more likely so Daddy and others could sell shedloads of military hardware,' said the Princess sadly. 'Nothing like exaggerating a non-existent threat to sell rocket launchers, field artillery and a few hundred landships.[28]'

It had long been suspected this was the case. The

[28] Vast tracked vehicles four storeys high and with a crew of eighteen; there is one described in *Song of the Quarkbeast*.

King of Snodd's Useless Brother had once tried to declare war on the ocean so he could sell thousands of his 'anti-sea' artillery shells – all guaranteed to hit the target with one hundred per cent accuracy. But Monty was right. The Trolls hadn't once tried to invade in nearly two thousand years.

'They are a distraction to aid Shandar's plans,' said Full Price. 'With the Kingdoms under the heel of the Troll, no one could oppose him.'

'That sounds logical,' I said. 'Carry on with your report, please, Lady Mawgon.'

'Our observers have been reporting in hourly,' said Mawgon. 'Estimates vary but it looks as though there are currently two million Trolls in the Kingdoms and their numbers are still rising.'

She pointed at Trollvania on the map – everything north of the Troll Walls. There were two walls, the second about ten miles north of the first, reputedly the result of a mix-up during the wall-building contract-tendering stage. They ran roughly from the River Clyde in the west to Stirling in the East. Mawgon explained that although the area north of the walls was large in size,[29] the number of Trolls ever seen from the air on photo reconnaissance missions was nil.

'Where are they coming from?' asked Monty.

---

[29] You would know it as Scotland, more or less.

'We don't know,' said Lady Mawgon, 'but it explains why the last five Troll Wars have resulted in utter defeat and failure: the visible number of Trolls was always low, yet their numbers were massive when attacked.'

We mused on this for a moment.

'What about Shandar's interest in Quarkbeasts?' I asked.

'While I was being held for ransom in the Cambrian Empire,' said Once Magnificent Boo, 'Quarkbeasts from all over the planet were being traded, cajoled, trapped and tricked into returning to the UnUnited Kingdoms in Shandar's private aircraft. There are thirty-six of them in total and I think we should assume he's almost got the full set.'

'Quark,' said the Quarkbeast, who was under the table, licking the chrome off an aircraft's undercarriage he had found.

We all fell into silence after this, thinking about just how bad this might be.

'Oh, I get it,' said the Princess, who was lagging behind. 'Shandar wants to harness not just the power of a pair of Quarkbeasts conjoining – *but all thirty-six together.*'

'And focus all that power into himself with the Eye of Zoltar,' I added.

Monty gave a low whistle and even the Mysterious X seemed to glow more brightly in his Kilner jar for a moment. It would be an awesome amount of wizidrical power. And given that Shandar was already powerful, it would put him on another level entirely.

'How much crackle are we talking about?' asked Tiger.

'With all thirty-six conjoining simultaneously,' said Lady Mawgon, 'there would be about 2.1 TeraShandars.[30] Enough to do some pretty strong magic – but he must need every possible ounce of power if he wants your Quarkbeast as well.'

'Wait a minute,' I said, recalling an earlier conversation with Once Magnificent Boo, back when I first met her at her home – a sort of refuge for abused Quarkbeasts, 'didn't you say that as soon as the combinations are fulfilled, they will come together and merge into a single Quota of fully Quorumed Quarkbeasts, and all the great unanswered questions of the world will be answered?'

'I did indeed,' said Boo, 'but I wasn't expecting this.'

'2.1 TeraShandars is a lot of power,' mused Full Price, 'enough to achieve world domination.'

'Is that what he's after?' asked the Princess.

'Megalomaniacs generally are, ma'am,' said Lady

---

[30] A thousand Shandars is a KiloShandar, a thousand KiloShandars is a GigaShandar, and a thousand GigaShandars is a TeraShandar. It's a lot.

Mawgon. 'It's very tiresome. We'll assume it's what he wants until we know otherwise.'

'It might explain,' I said, 'why he was willing to sit out most of the last three centuries as stone: so he could wait until there were thirty-six pairs of Quarkbeasts, then harvest the awesome power of a mass conjoinment to feed his plans for planetary conquest.'

'So the Quarkbeast was simply a Wizidrical Energy generating device?'

'Looks like it.'

'There's a problem here,' said Full Price, '2.1 TeraShandars is big, sure, but could only maintain world domination for about a year – maybe two if you economise on palaces, go for a less extensive wardrobe and cut out crowd-pleasing yet pointless demonstrations of power.'

'Even a year of being World Emperor is still four months and three days longer than anyone else has managed.'

'Maybe he's going for the record,' said Tiger.

'It's possible,' said Boo, 'but there are easier ways of getting into the *Guinness Book of Records*.'

'He'll be in for a sticky end once his power fades,' said Full Price. 'There's a very good reason why there isn't a murderous ex-megalomaniacs club.'

'I have a question,' said the Princess.

'Go on.'

'Shandar already has tons of power. Teleportation, setting up that HENRY, helping the Trolls, turning in and out of stone, destroying Zambini Towers, that sort of thing, right?'

'Right.'

'So why does he need to negotiate with us at all? If he's so powerful, he could just kill us all and take the Quarkbeast. We have no magical powers to counter him, and even if he couldn't or doesn't want to kill us, he could just remove the Quarkbeast spookily, quietly, and without us even noticing. I can understand why he asked us to get the Eye of Zoltar as he wanted us out the way, but his recent demands? We're missing a trick here.'

This was a very good point.

'He must have a vulnerability,' I said, 'something that can stop, alter or ruin his plans. And if that's so, it's something we can exploit.'

I paused. 'Why are you all staring at me?'

'It's you,' said Lady Mawgon. 'The Quarkbeast chose you to be its keeper, and you single-handedly brought the power of magic back into the world when you did that whole Berserker thing with Exhorbitus. Shandar foretold you would be the Last Dragonslayer – it was etched on the sword's blade. *You* are part of this, *you* are the fly in his ointment, *you* have the power to oppose.'

'That's complete and utter nonsense,' I said,

knowing full well that's *exactly* what it looked like. 'There's nothing chosen about me. I can't do magic, I've never had that power.'

'Maybe your power is the power to channel.'

'That makes no sense. Sorcery is only ever about channelling.'

'Copper has no power of its own,' observed Colin, 'but can transmit vast quantities of electricity.'

'You're all wrong,' I said. 'I'm just an orphan with accidental relevance. I'm going for a walk. Let me know when Feldspar gets back with a fix on Shandar's location.'

And I walked out of the door feeling hot and annoyed.

The Troll

I walked out the back of the hotel and to the car park. I wasn't annoyed because of what they said, I was annoyed because it was very likely true. I had felt the power channel through me when I held up Exhorbitus back in the Dragonlands the day I slayed the last Dragon, and it had felt as though every cell in my body was being pulled apart. Pain I would never want to feel again. But there had been something else, too – I felt that my purpose, my destiny, was not yet fulfilled.

There was more for me to do. D'Argento had been right: my destiny, like hers, was inextricably linked with Shandar's.

I opened the bootlid of my Beetle, pulled out the dipstick, cleaned it, put it back in, then looked at it again. The oil was clean and perfect and filled *exactly* to the line. It had been the same since I'd started work at Zambini Towers, soon after leaving the orphanage. The tyres had always remained the same pressures, too, and never wore out. Tiger said it was because I was still running cross-plys over radial tyres,[31] but I had a better idea: secretly, the sorcerers at Zambini Towers had been helping me out with a few simple car maintenance spells as they knew I earned almost nothing. Although I did still have to put fuel in the car, it never returned less than a hundred miles to the gallon – an impossible feat.

I busied myself thus, attempting to hide from the serious by undertaking the banal. I kept a dustpan in the boot and swept up the small bits of twisted metal left by the Quarkbeast in the footwells. He would insist on chewing metal when riding in the car, no matter how many times I asked him not to. I think he was a nervous passenger.

Tiger walked up.

'Any news from Feldspar?' I asked.

'Not yet. The Princess wanted me to come and check on you.'

'I'm fine,' I said, which is what people who aren't fine always say. 'I'm going to wander up into town. If you need me, come up and find me.'

He left and I wandered out of the car park and up towards the main part of the town, absently staring into store windows as I went. There was a shop selling spares for the many steam engines that still pumped

---

[31] It's not important. This is just Jenny distracting herself with the minutiae of driving fifty-year-old cars.

water out of the mine workings in the area, and another which sold tourist trinkets made out of tin and fossilised scones. There was even a museum dedicated to Richard Trevithick,[32] and a pasty shop that boasted proudly that it held the record for the largest pasty in the world, a monster that tipped the scales at almost six tons, and looked like a beached whale that had overindulged in a tanning booth.

I reached Chapel Street, then spotted a familiar figure making a call from a telephone box outside the Co-Op. It was Sir Matt Grifflon, and close by were his small group of hangers-on, which included the shabby curate in the oversized bishop's hat. The minstrels were singing what sounded like the Catalina Magdalena Hoopensteiner Song, but had changed the words to something about how Sir Matt 'married the frumpy Princess and made the Kingdoms a better place by his wise and not-at-all corrupt leadership', but they soon stopped when they saw me.

'Everything okay?' I asked them.

They all looked shifty, then pushed the ornamental hermit out in front to quote some more of his meaningless aphorisms, presumably to confuse/ impress me.

---

[32] An early pioneer of steam engineering, both of pit pumps and locomotives.

'Complexity,' he said in a grand tone, 'is the second cousin of needfulness.'

'I have absolutely no idea what that means,' I told him, 'and I strongly suspect that you don't either.'

'Oh,' he said, then, in an equally grand and expansive manner: 'Why dig a hole in the garden, when potatoes grow wild in Finland?'

'Nope,' I said, 'that's actually even *more* pointless and unintelligible.'

'Damn,' said the ornamental hermit, 'how about: "Every journey starts with the first step"?'

'Better,' I said, 'but still so hopelessly open ended as to be utterly meaningless.'

'Hello, Jessica,' said Sir Matt, suddenly noticing me and stepping out of the phone box, while indicating for one of his valets to take the receiver. 'Come to apologise, have you?'

'Not even close,' I said, 'and it's *Jennifer*.'

'Same thing. Look, you and I should come to an agreement of some sort. I will be King of the Greater Kingdoms soon, and it makes sense for you to back me up on this, what with having the ear of the Dragons and Head Mystician and stuff. Just advise the little princess that I'm the one for her, get her to cancel the whole silly jumping off a building lark, and there could be a little something in it for you.'

'That's very generous,' I said sarcastically. 'What were you thinking of? A lounge suite? A set of steak knives?'

'No,' he said, blinking twice, 'I was thinking more along the lines of giving you . . . Wales.'

'Wales?'

Yes, it's a small country to the west of here about the size of . . . Wales. How about it?'

'Wales is *about* the size of Wales?' I asked. 'Isn't it *exactly* the size of Wales?'

Sir Matt Grifflon looked at his retinue for guidance; they all nodded their heads vigorously.

'As you said,' he agreed. 'Do we have a deal?'

'No.'

'Think carefully, Juliet, these are uncertain and volatile times, when pointlessly stubborn servants of the Crown might be found severed in two lengthwise. That sort of thing happens in Penzance all the time – no one would ever ask any questions.'

'I'm not so sure that it does. And it's Jennifer.'

I grasped the hilt of Exhorbitus as I saw Sir Matt's hand move towards his own sword. I felt the power of the sword feed into me. I only had to *think* the sword in front of me, and there it was. Exhorbitus had the power to change thought instantaneously to action.

'That was really . . . quite fast,' said Sir Matt, who had only been able to grasp the hilt of his own sword in the time I had drawn my own, 'but I am fifteen people and you are one.'

'Fourteen,' said a voice at the back. 'Jerry's gone shopping.'

'Yes, okay, fourteen. But still enough to defeat you, given that you are small and girly and weak looking to boot.'

His bodyguards, I noticed, as they took a step towards me, were not just shiftless hangers-on, but armed with swords and daggers and eager to back their leader up. There was a wiry one at the front with wide-spaced eyes who looked *specifically* like trouble – he didn't seem to blink much and had a dangerously indifferent look about him.

'I am not a violent person,' I said in a quiet voice, 'but I will kill anyone who tries to kill me, or harms anyone I am sworn to protect.'

'Quark,' said the Quarkbeast in agreement; he was sitting just behind me and licking his own bottom nonchalantly – it was clearly intentional: he wanted to demonstrate his contempt for them all. He knew I had this, and would only intervene if he thought I was in danger.

And I wasn't. Not even the slightest bit.

'So who's first?' I asked.

The indifferent-looking one with the wide-spaced eyes didn't move, but one of the minstrels did. Exhorbitus and I moved again in a harmonious flash of light and steel. The minstrel stopped, shocked at my speed. He then nervously checked his own body to see whether there was a part of himself no longer attached. I could have sliced off his belt buckle and seen his trousers fall to the floor, but I wanted a more arresting demonstration of my power. After a two-second pause, the top of the iron post box next to me gently slid off and fell to the ground with an angry clang. Exhorbitus could cut through cast iron as though it were tissue paper. If I had chosen, I could have done the same to them, and they knew it. Their swords were cautiously replaced, and Sir Matt took his hand off the hilt of his. The one with wide-spaced eyes was the last to relax his grip, and I made a mental note: this one would fight not caring if he won or lost – the most dangerous of them all.

Behind me, the Quarkbeast yawned and scratched his ear with a hind leg. His effortless nonchalance in the face of their threat spoke volumes. He could have killed them all without even breaking a sweat, but sometimes wielding awesome levels of power is all about not wielding it at all.

'So,' I said, deftly returning Exhorbitus to the scabbard on my back. 'How are you doing with the task the Princess set you?'

Sir Matt looked at me coldly.

'You will beg my forgiveness before the weekend is out, Dragon-Girl. Mark my words: I will marry the Princess, and I will be king.'

'The Princess will never marry you,' I said, 'no matter how many buildings you jump off.'

'We'll see.'

And he took the telephone back off the valet, and carried on talking.

'I'm now *very* interested,' I heard him say as I walked away. 'How soon can you find your way down here?'

I carried on up the road, unworried about Grifflon's threats or intimidation. I'd weathered them before.

I took a right into Market Street with its imposing domed-roof bank building and the bronze statue of John Nettles, Cornwall's most famous son. I knew the statue was here, but I'd not wanted to view it merely with a disrespectful glance so had avoided the main street while driving around town over the past week. No, I wanted to gaze upon it at my leisure, as I could now. The thing is, it wasn't just his performance as Jim Bergerac in *Bergerac* that so impressed us at the orphanage, but that he had been adopted at birth, and that sort of made him one of us. Elsie Hopkins at the orphanage once claimed to have seen Mr Nettles in the Aldi in Hereford, but she often told tall stories, so we didn't think it was true. Tiger thought it might actually have been Christopher Timothy,[33] which was more likely as he had been performing his one-man show in the Courtyard Theatre; it was based on the life of Jeb Malick, the adventurer who not only

---

[33] Another TV star that you might not have heard of.

successfully navigated the River Wye in a barrel, but also invented the trampoline.

I sat on a handy bench in front of the Nettles statue and pulled from my pocket the photograph of my parents I always kept with me. Mum and Dad were smiling brightly in front of a shiny new land-ship. They were wearing overalls with the shoulder chevrons of engine room technicians first and second class of the third division of the Fourth Armoured Brigade. They fought in the third Troll War – that's two before the current one – and had been in the first wave of the attack.

Actually, it wasn't their picture at all – just a random one pulled from the pages of *Picture Post*. Aside from the note left for me in the Volkswagen which said I *was* a Troll War war orphan, there was no concrete evidence that I was anything of the sort.

I dug a Pollyanna Stone out of my pocket, a simple device which caused the holder to see what they wanted to see. It was lick-to-activate, spelled by Bartelby the Mildly Creepy in the fifteenth century. I licked the stone and the saliva bubbled and fizzed as the enzymes from my mouth reacted with the five-hundred-year-old spell. In an instant Mum and Dad were standing there in front of me.

'Hello, sweetie,' said the person I imagined might be my father. He was dressed exactly the same as he was in the photograph, but because of the HENRY in black and white and a little flickery. My similarly imagined mother was standing behind him, holding a spanner. Both had streaks of oil on their faces, and I could sense a faint odour of hot oil and diesel exhaust.

'Look at you!' beamed my mother, sitting down next to me. 'All sort of warrior-like. Did you find the Eye of Zoltar?'

'Yes,' I said, 'but the Trolls invaded in our absence and now I'm not only responsible for a ramshackle army of resistance, but am chief adviser to the Queen, a position that might unite the Kingdoms once and for all – supposing we live that long.'

'You've always delivered before,' said my father kindly. He was always kind, but this was how I wanted him to be, so it was how the magic made him appear. I looked down at the Pollyanna Stone, where my saliva was bubbling on the surface. They'd only be here for another ten seconds or so.

'I often wonder,' I said, 'how different my life would have turned out had I been indentured to a hotel or fast-food outlet instead of a House of Enchantment.'

My mother put her translucent hand on mine.

'Where you are now is where you were always going to be,' she said. 'You were always going to be the Last Dragonslayer and nothing would have altered it. This is your destiny, Jenny, and for better or worse, you will fulfil it.'

'The Mighty Shandar is the most powerful wizard yet known,' I said, 'and planned much of this in advance. It seems likely he removed the Dragons for precisely the same reason he removed Zambini – so nothing could ever stand in his way.'

'*You* stand in his way,' said Dad, 'so he's not that powerful. He can't kill you, vanish you, turn you to stone or even teleport you to the Antarctic. You control your own destiny, but you also control his. Where you go, so must he.'

'What do you mean?'

'Jenny,' said my mother, 'all that you have ever done is leading to a single decision point where everything hangs in the balance and nothing will ever be the same again. A moment where only you can make things right, where only you can make the difference that matters.'

'Really?'

'Yes. You're different and you've always known that.'

She was right. I'd always felt it. At the orphanage I'd been respected rather than popular. Bullies never troubled me. Strange by name, strange by nature, I'd heard them say.

'Tell me what will happen,' I said, 'tell me what I should do.'

They smiled at me.

'We're not real,' said my mother, 'we're only saying

102

what you want to hear. Our knowledge outside of this is limited.'

I looked again at the Pollyanna Stone as the last of my saliva boiled away, and by the time I looked up, they had gone and I was left staring at the empty space.

'Quark,' said the Quarkbeast, who was sitting on my foot, something he often did, I think because he found it comforting.

'What do you think, boy?' I asked, folding up the photo of my parents and returning it to my pocket with the Pollyanna Stone.

'Quark,' he said again.

'I know,' I replied, tickling him behind the ear, 'uncertain times.'

'Miss Strange?'

I turned. It was the representatives of the fencers, marksmen and worriers. They had elected to come out and have some fish and chips instead of eating in the hotel.

'Fancy a chip?' asked the worrier. 'I hope I haven't overdone it on the salt.'

'Thank you. Perfect,' I said, not telling him that, yes, they did indeed have too much salt on them. I budged up on the bench so they could sit down.

'What's Christopher Timothy doing as a statue all the way down here?' asked the Chief Fencer.

I decided not to correct her.

'How many people do you have under your control?' I asked instead. 'All of you, like, in total?'

The number, it turned out, was eighteen hundred, more if the haberdashers wanted to help out.

'That's good,' I said, as at least there was a command structure of sorts in place. 'Were any of you in the military?'

'I was,' said the worrier, 'but I've a bad feeling you're going to give me something important to do and I would then fail utterly and bring dishonour on my family to the end of recorded history.'

'That's a worst-case scenario, right?' I asked.

'Is there any other?'

'From personal experience,' I said, 'things can and do come out all right. What rank were you?'

'A second lieutenant in the Queendom of Mercia's land army.'

'Have you seen combat?'

'I was in the catering corps, but it was still traumatic. Have you ever thought just how stressful it is making spaghetti and meatballs for six thousand soldiers? I forgot the cheese one evening and had to demote myself. Look, don't you think Sir Matt Grifflon would be better suited to lead us all? I think I saw him just now in the Co-Op.'

'No, we need someone we can trust,' I said, 'and I speak for the Queen when I say this: I promote you to General Worrier, commander of the resistance army. These two will be your second- and third-in-command: Major Worrier, and Private Worrier.'

'I'm not sure I can do this,' said the general.

'Nonsense,' I said. 'Besides, I appointed you in full recognition of the facts – so any failure of yours is a greater failure of mine. I promoted you; the responsibility is all mine.'

'Oh,' said General Worrier, pondering this for a moment.

'Right,' I said, 'so I want you to all put your heads together and figure out who conceivably might be useful in a scrap. Shandar gave us two days and since we're not doing a deal, we need everyone we can muster with whatever weapons we can find along the Button Trench at sunrise on Monday morning. Questions?'

'What if we fail?'

I shrugged.

'Shandar triumphs and we all get eaten, I guess. But that's not going to happen. Let me know when you have set up some sort of command structure. Discipline and focus will be everything.'

They looked at one another, saluted smartly, gave me the remainder of their chips and hurried off.

I dawdled back down the hill soon after, and took a short cut through the rather lovely Morrab Gardens, full of rare shrubs, trees and perfectly manicured grass. As I was walking out of the garden's exit near the Queens Hotel, the Quarkbeast said: 'Quark.'

'What is it?'

He was pointing at a small car: an Austin Mini. I think it was a Mark I estate version from the sixties as Kazam's cook, Unstable Mabel, had one just like it. The car seemed to be moving slightly and snoring, but as I looked closer I could see that inside the car was a young female Troll, curled up on the rear seats, mouth open, fast asleep. The car was sagging on its suspension, and I think the roof actually bulged outwards when she turned over in her sleep.

I stared at her intently, feeling quite safe as, firstly, I had Exhorbitus and the Quarkbeast with me, and secondly, the Trolls were notoriously slow and jam-headed for at least half an hour after waking. In fact, Jimmy Nuttjob's father, Timmy Nuttjob, toured with one of the captured Trolls in the 1950s, performing his ever-popular 'putting my head in a Troll's mouth' act, a feat he could only perform within twenty minutes of the Troll waking. Sadly, one day at a Royal Command Performance, the pantomime horse act preceding him overran while performing their trade-mark 'Dobbin Quickstep', which brought Timmy Nuttjob's career to a very swift end – and with no chance of an encore.

Intrigued, I examined the Troll minutely. She was not as big as most, and because of the small size of the car, had somehow managed to fold herself up in a manner that looked staggeringly uncomfortable. One arm was behind her head, the other was under her body, and she'd draped her legs over the front seats so her feet were pressed against the inside of the windscreen.

I felt conflicted. Conventional wisdom should have had me dragging the creature from the car and striking her head clean off her shoulders before she woke. True, Trolls would show us no mercy and had already murdered over two hundred thousand people, with many of those not eaten currently bottled in aspic,[34] but it seemed wrong to kill them as a routine, no matter how indifferently barbarous they were. Trolls had been captured only twice before, and neither of them divulged a single piece of intelligence, and without fail took every opportunity to savage their captors.

I was just wondering whether there wasn't some other way of handling this when I noticed that the Troll had something written with a Sharpie on the back of her hand. Even viewed upside down it made me stop and take notice, for I recognised the unmistakable cadence of Zambini's handwriting in the elegantly lettered script. I wiped some dirt off the Mini's window to read it.

---

[34] It's sort of a gelatine made from boiled-down bones that can be used to preserve previously cooked meat.

Contact Jennifer Strange in Penzance and tell her everything. She will not harm you.

I could feel my heart beat faster. The Great Zambini popped out of non-existence every now and again, and never more than for a few minutes. I had to assume that he had met with this Troll, found a friend, had a few words, and then sent her off to find me.

I had to know more.

Still keeping a wary hand on Exhorbitus I slid the window open, and poked the Troll to wake it up. She groaned, farted and rolled over, and I poked her again.

'Jenny?' came Tiger's voice from just behind me. 'What are you doing?'

'There's a Troll in this Mini.'

'Crumbs,' said Tiger when he saw what I'd found. 'How did she get across the Button Trench? No, wait, scrub that – how did she even get herself inside that Mini?'

I told him I had no idea, showed him what was written on the back of her hand, then asked Tiger why he had come to find me.

'Just that lunch is ready,' he said, 'and it's macaroni cheese.'

'My favourite,' muttered the Troll, lifting its eyelids a fraction to stare at us both with a sleepy expression.

'Fetch an armed guard,' I said. 'Actually, make that

several. Tell them to blindfold her, lead her to one of the hotel basements, then say that I, Jennifer Strange, will be along to see her just as soon as I can.'

'I need to stay in the car,' said the Troll in a sleepy voice.

'Why?'

'Wide open spaces don't agree with me. Or with you, come to think of it.'

'I don't understand.'

She opened an eye fully and regarded me minutely.

'It's a Troll thing.'

I took a deep breath.

'Okay,' I said to Tiger, 'have a guard drive our guest to the hotel garage and tell them to watch her like a hawk until I come and see her.'

'Shall I tell them to use lethal force if she doesn't comply?'

'You know what?' I said, staring thoughtfully at the massive creature. 'If her favourite meal is macaroni cheese and she likes Mini Travellers, I have a feeling she'll be no trouble at all.'

Dinner

The restaurant in the Queens Hotel was offering a reduced-service buffet owing to circumstances, but had to keep their waiting staff on hand to assist the princesses, who didn't know what a buffet was and, even when it was explained to them very, very slowly and in great detail, could not really get their royal heads around the concept of 'waiting in a line and serving yourself'. After half an hour of fruitless explanations, the staff went and got their food for them, and everyone was happy.

The weather had worsened while I had been walking in town, and a small water spout had descended from the storm clouds a few hundred yards offshore. It moved in rapidly, picked up some salty old sea dogs who had been mending nets on the beach, and then blew them in tight orbits around the promenade outside the hotel. The gnarled men of the sea seemed entirely unfazed and presented us with a medley of sea shanties as they were blown past the dining-room windows. After five minutes of this, the clouds lifted, the water spout collapsed, the fishermen went back to their nets and it was a bright summer's day again.

I selected some food and sat down at the table that had been reserved for the UnUnited Kingdoms government-in-exile. One of the other princesses tried to join us but was beaten to the last place by Once Magnificent Boo, who could move quite fast when she wanted to.

'I found a female Troll hiding in a Mini,' I said, and when I'd answered 'no' to the 'did you put her to death without hesitation?' question and 'I don't know' to the 'why was she in a Mini?' question, I explained about the message from the Great Zambini on the back of her hand and added that I thought it needed further investigation.

'If Trolls have a Hive Memory,' cautioned the Princess, 'anything she witnesses here could be useful intelligence to every other Troll.'

I told them I would take precautions.

'It might be a trick,' said Lady Mawgon.

'I'm not sure Trolls do tricks,' said Monty. 'They're more of a "go on a rampage and kill everything in sight" sort of creature.'

Everyone nodded in agreement. The Troll had little need or use for sneaky subterfuge; in fact, they positively hated it. When you met a Troll, there were few, if any, surprises. A meeting invariably went like this: capture, death, snack. The only real variation was the time interval between the three.

'This Troll seems different,' I said, 'but I'll be careful.'

'Sorry I'm late,' said Colin, padding up to the table on his hind legs and laying some photographs on the table. 'Feldspar got a fix on where the Mighty Shandar was holed up, so I went on a photographic reconnaissance trip to have a look.'

He placed the pictures on the table and we pored over them.

'Isn't that . . . the Chrysler Building?' I asked, staring at where the Art Deco New York skyscraper was now sprouting out of a cow field in Devon.

'A full-size replica,' he said. 'I called the New York Tourist Information bureau and they said they weren't missing one, although I did get them to go and check, just to be sure.'

'The building is just north of Exeter,' said Feldspar, 'presumably for convenient access to the M5 inter-Kingdoms motorway.'

I stared at the pictures. Although incongruous, the seventy-seven storey Art Deco skyscraper was peculiarly lovely, with tasteful decoration in stone, glass and steel. If I had vast amounts of power and money and was an overly flamboyant character with a penchant for con-spicuousness, I might have created something similar.

'I flew lower for some oblique views too,' added Colin, 'but they're a bit blurred as I was travelling quite fast.'

The skyscraper had steel shutters on the lower windows and main entrance, and what looked like a heavily guarded service entrance that gave handy access direct from the motorway.

'How do we attack it?' asked Tiger.

'Right now I'm not sure we can,' I said. 'Shandar would detect a thermowizidrical device – even a small one – long before it got close enough to do any damage.'

'And,' said Lady Mawgon, 'we don't have enough crackle to levitate a chair, let alone build a TWD.'

'What are the defences like?' I asked.

'Anti-aircraft fire opened up as soon as I was within a thousand yards,' said Colin, taking a large handful of food and tipping it down his throat. 'And look, you see these white dots scattered around outside the building?'

We looked at the picture closely. Although the image was blurred, I knew what they were.

'Hollow Men,' said the Princess, who had lost her right hand to one. 'I *hate* Hollow Men.'

We'd battled Hollow Men before in the Cambrian Empire. They were basically dark suits and white shirts, a hat and a pair of gloves given life by the Mighty Shandar. When not in use they were simply a folded parcel of clothes with a hat on top, but would spring into life in a moment ready to do Shandar's bidding.

'Can we defeat them the same way we did last time?' asked the Princess.

'Without any magic we're not doing much of anything,' said Full Price. 'The HENRY is sucking up the wizidrical energy as a sponge absorbs water. I tried mining my own life-force to see if I could utilise that in the same manner as Moobin,' he said, 'but I have nothing left on tap.'

Since magic was essentially based on emotional spirit, using one's own remaining life-force was always a ready solution if you needed a lot of crackle in a short amount of time. It would, unfortunately, take years off your life – literally. My good friend Perkins had sacrificed himself in this manner during our adventure to find the Eye of Zoltar only a few weeks before. Wizard Moobin had done the same to construct the Button Trench. But I also knew what Full Price meant when he said he had 'nothing left on tap'. His life would probably end soon – he was like a battery that was almost flat.

'Firstly,' I said, 'no one is using up their own life to do magic. I've seen too much of that. Secondly, I'm sorry to hear you have nothing left on tap, Mr Price – how long do you have left?'

'Not sure but not much,' he said. 'For any sorcery

you're going to have to rely on Lady Mawgon or the Mysterious X — that is, if he exists at all.'

We all looked at the Mysterious X, who wasn't eating, obviously, but was just sitting on the table in his Kilner jar, the charged electrons glowing like glow-worms and moving languidly in orbit around one another. X's existence was as nebulous now as it had ever been, but even with twenty sorcerers a lot more solid than X, they'd all be useless without any wizidrical energy.

'I managed to salvage a couple of Dibble Jars[35] from Zambini Towers after it was destroyed,' said Tiger. 'Any use?'

'You are close to redeeming your worthlessness,' said Lady Mawgon, which was about the closest thing to a compliment Tiger was ever likely to get. 'They'll hold about 720 KiloShandars of wizidrical energy each and are self-filling — all we need do is take them to the source of the HENRY.'

'Good idea,' I said. 'We'll leave at first light tomorrow for Dartmoor, and we'll go by Dragon.'

Colin snorted two jets of milk out of his nostrils when I said this.

'Wait, what?' he said.

---

[35] The Dibble Jar, despite its horribly uncool name, is a method of storing wizidrical energy, like a battery. There's more about them in *The Song of the Quarkbeast.*

'You and Feldspar can take us. You fly us in, we fill the jars and then you fly us back.'

'Oh, so we're just the same as carpets now, are we?' said Colin.

'Or little better than a horse?' added Feldspar. 'What do you want to put on us? Saddles? You might as well feed us with a nosebag.'

I looked at Tiger, who shrugged. Stupidly, we'd assumed that we could ride on them. Colin picked up on this immediately.

'Oh, I get it,' he said. 'You think we're being unreasonable? Well, it's just that Dragons fit into so many humancentric stereotypes. When we're not guarding princesses or turning knights to charcoal, we're wise and thoughtful and ponderous – and then all meek and compliant, allowing ourselves to be flown. Is that how you see us?'

'You do actually do all those things,' said Tiger.

'Maybe we do,' said Colin, 'but it's not *necessarily* because we're Dragons.'

'Go and ask at Penzance International Airport,' said Colin. 'They've been flying refugees in all day. I heard there were so many light aircraft they're pushing them into the sea to make room for new arrivals.'

'Planes are too noisy,' I said, 'and we need to be able to land on a ha'penny.'

But the Dragons weren't really listening.

'Besides,' said Feldspar, 'how do you know you won't fall off? All that "diving down to rescue you" stuff is only in the movies. If I try to pull steeply out of a dive the G-force would snap my wings like Twiglets, and all I'd be is a very large hole in the ground.'

'What's a Twiglet?' said the Princess.

'Honestly,' said Once Magnificent Boo, 'you two are such a bunch of fusspots.'

'You try being the last of your kind,' said Colin. 'I didn't ask to be a Dragon. I'd rather be a house painter, making people's homes bright and cheery.'

'And I want to run a restaurant,' said Feldspar, 'and say things like: "Good evening, madam, dinner or the bar?"'

And they then stared at the tablecloth in a sulky mood.

'If we leave now in your car,' said Tiger, 'we could be in Dartmoor by—'

'Oh, so now you *don't* want us?' said Colin. 'Well, that's really, really nice. A hazardous mission that could have far-reaching consequences and we get to sit on the sidelines?'

'I thought you didn't want to do it?'

'We *do* want to do it,' said Feldspar. 'It's just we don't want to be *expected* to do it.'

And they both got up and went off, grumbling as they went.

'What was that massive hissy fit all about?' said the Princess.

'They're still young,' I said. 'Dragons can live over eight hundred years, so they're toddlers for at least three decades. They'll fly us to the HENRY, and risk themselves to do so.'

'Good,' said the Princess. 'Let's go and talk to that Troll of yours.'

Moll the Troll

The Troll was being held in the hotel garage, which was situated a couple of streets away. The main door was guarded by one of the worriers, who apologised profusely about something trivial, then chewed his knuckles anxiously. We opened the door carefully and walked in, the Princess, myself and Tiger. The interior was large enough to hold about twenty cars, but these days was used as a storeroom for hundreds of extra chairs, hotel furniture and obsolete catering machines. The Mini was in the centre of the concrete floor, and table and chairs had been set up next to it.

We were all wearing neckerchiefs over our mouths and dark glasses so she wouldn't be able to send our likenesses into the Hive Memory, and I laid Exhorbitus on the table lest she try anything – although since she was still stuffed inside the Mini, it was difficult to see what she *could* do in a hurry. I then sat down, while Tiger and the Princess stood near the door, arms folded, leaning on some stacked furniture.

The Troll stared at me for a moment, then at the garage that surrounded us. She looked at the walls, the ceiling, then the large double doors.

'Will they open without warning?' she asked.

'Locked and guarded.'

She nodded, then carefully unlatched the car door and climbed out in a single unhurried movement that was peculiarly elegant. The car's suspension rose as she did so, and once out of the car she could stand up to her full height, which although not substantial for a Troll was still at least ten feet. Despite this, she wasn't as frightening as any of the other Trolls I'd come across: she was not armed with the usual assortment of clubs or knives hanging from her waist, just a potato peeler and a runner bean slicer. Her leathery skin was liberally covered with tattoos, and aside from the geometric patterns and the customary Troll history on her right leg – the events surrounding Troll War II, I think – the tattoos were mostly of vegetables. On top of her head was the customary small leather cap, but in this instance it was not decorated with a dead goat, but a rope bag containing rotten cabbage heads and blighted carrots that were slimy with age.

She stretched out on to her tiptoes, twisted left and right, then smiled broadly.

'Hello!' she said brightly. 'The name's Molly. Easy to remember. "Moll the Troll", that's me.'

'You can call me Truman,' I said. 'Truman . . . the human. And that's Roy,' I added, pointing at Tiger. 'Roy . . . the boy.'

'What about the scrawny one?' asked Molly, pointing towards the Princess.

'Pearl,' said the Princess. 'Pearl the Girl.'

The Troll narrowed her eyes suspiciously.

'I think these are all made-up names.'

I decided not to answer.

'Roy?' I said instead. 'The dinner.'

Tiger placed the large bowl he'd been carrying on the table and took off the tea towel to reveal a quintuple portion of macaroni cheese.

'For me?' asked Molly, and I nodded.

Most Trolls eat with their hands – they pride themselves on their lack of manners, in fact – but this one used a large wooden spoon, which looked out of place, like a poodle wearing a monocle.

'How did you get to be vegetarian?' asked the Princess.

'Does it show?' asked the Troll guiltily.

We all nodded and the Troll sighed deeply.

'Troll parents see vegetarianism as a sociopathic eating disorder,' she said quietly. 'It's deeply shaming, and cave prices plummet if a veggie is thought to be in the area. My parents were actually pretty good, for Trolls,' she said. 'Barely beat me at all and only left me outside in the winter for a week, not a month, as is normal to toughen us up. They were seen as overindulgent parents, but I still loved them. Dad conducted the Trollvanian Petraphonic orchestra. The sound of twenty per cent of the Troll population tapping rocks together is something to experience. My mother used to solo on river pebbles. She could tap like an angel and often reduced audiences to tears.'

She picked up the bowl and licked out the remains of the macaroni cheese.

'The thing is, *all* Trolls were once vegetarian. We were a peaceful race, harming no one. But a Troll named Qurrgg suddenly took a liking to meat, and the usually placid community fell to his power. The veggie trolls were maligned and pushed to the edges of society. We remain hidden these days, frightened to even *think* about cooking up a creamy mushroom tagliatelle, much less make it. Have you ever had moussaka?'

'Yes.'

'We used to clandestinely meet in forest clearings to secretly conjure up a moussaka and other non-meat specialities. We had to smuggle ingredients in. Then, one evening, on ravioli night, we were denounced. I was charged with making pasta "with intent to consume", and possession of an aubergine, a charge which was dismissed as they couldn't prove I was going to eat it. I, and by extension all the other vegetarians, were sentenced to a life of unpaid domestic work with no possibility of moussaka.'

She gave a doleful sigh.

'How did you escape?' I asked.

'We were called to the front line to man the mobile food kitchens – a thankless and disgusting job, as you can imagine – and that was when Mr Zambini appeared. He said you would help us out, so I abandoned my post, found somewhere restrictively small to hide and made my way over just before the Button Trench was filled. I guess no one was expecting to see a Troll driving a Mini. Is there any more of that macaroni cheese?'

I nodded to Tiger, who went and fetched another helping.

'So,' I said, 'tell me more about that.'

I pointed at her hand, and the message written in black Sharpie:

Contact Jennifer Strange in Penzance and tell her everything. She will not harm you.

She looked at her hand, then at me.

'You're Jennifer Strange, aren't you?'

'I am.'

'Ha!' she said. 'I *knew* you were using made-up names.'

I pulled down the handkerchief that was covering my face. There was no point to the subterfuge now.

'Your kind has a Hive Memory, so you can under-stand how it might pay to be cautious.'

'The shared memory only runs through individual strands of Troll society,' she explained. 'My memory only feeds into the other veggie trolls. Before I got in the Mini I could feel them, y'know, in my head, doing stuff all round the country. Back in Trollvania we used to share memories to hone survival strategies – and swap recipes. But once I was in the Mini, I couldn't feel them any longer. Do you think that's weird?'

'I can't think of much that *isn't* weird about all this.'

She paused for a moment.

'If I tell you all about your Zambini friend, can you offer a safe haven for all the veggie trolls? We're only 6.66 per cent of the Troll population.'

'How many is that?' I asked, thinking I could find out how many Trolls there were in total. But she cocked her head on one side and looked at me as though she didn't really know what I was talking about.

'Trolls prefer to work in percentages, fractions and ratios, as it allows a clearer overview of stuff, rather than getting bogged down in specifics.'

'Can you give us an example?' asked the Princess, who was aways interested in figures.

'Well,' said Molly, 'if the Troll agree to spare ten per

cent of humans from the pot, then we can say that without needing to count you all first, which would be time-consuming and tricky, since you spend a lot of time scurrying around and screaming idiotically. Here's another one. I represent twenty-five per cent of the creatures in this room, right?'

We nodded. There were four of us: Me, Tiger, the Princess and the Troll.

'Okay. Now, if the seventy-five per cent of creatures in this room that belong to the subset "non-Trolls" agree to share a cake of unit one, what would be the numerical value of each share?'

'.333,' said the Princess, before adding: 'Actually, the 3s would go on for ever.'

'And if you recombined the cake without eating any, would the sum return to unit one?'

'No,' conceded the Princess, 'by my reckoning it would come to 9.9999 recurring.'

'Then you see what I mean. Fractions are better for sharing cake, percentages for understanding sets within a large body without quantification. Numbers, well, they're quite good for precisely defining owner-ship, but not much else.'

'I disagree,' said the Princess. 'Numbers are not simply about raw quantity – they can be manipulated with others to calculate a future event with accuracy. If I know how far away something is, and have an idea how fast I will move, then knowing the time it will take to reach it is a useful asset. Similarly, if I have limited time and a destination to reach, I know how fast I will have to travel. And if I have both limited time and speed, I will know how short I will fall of my destination.'

Molly chortled.

'Your complex mathematics don't fool me, Human. Your calculations only have relevance if you place value on what time you get anywhere. We prefer a "we'll get there when we do" approach.'

'Some of our trains work on the same principle,' I said.

'So I heard,' said Molly. 'If you dispensed with timetables and defined arrival time as when they got there, all trains would achieve one hundred per cent punctuality.'

'By the same token they would all depart exactly on time, too,' said Tiger.

'Now you're getting it,' said the Troll. 'Numerical values are *seriously* overrated. Here's another example: if I were to tell you the mass of the sun is roughly 2×10^{30} kilograms then it would just be a meaninglessly high number – two with thirty noughts[36] after it.'

---

[36] Exponential notation allows us to express a high number without running out of ink. For comparison the age of the universe in years is thought to be only a trifling 1.3×10^{10}.

'I agree with that,' said the Princess.

'Right,' said the Troll, 'but if I were to tell you the sun has 99.86 per cent of the combined mass of the entire solar system, what would that mean?'

'It would mean . . . wow,' said the Princess.

'Exactly,' said the Troll, grinning broadly. 'Wow.'

'So hang on,' said Tiger, 'all the rest of the planets and moons and comets and stuff make up only, what, less than .14 per cent of the total mass?'

'To be honest,' said the Troll, 'most of what isn't the sun is Jupiter. All the rest of it – us included – is the galactic equivalent of the dust you missed when cleaning.'

'I've come over all negligible,' said Tiger.

'I try and keep all my counting to a minimum,' said the Troll. 'It saves a lot of time. So: will you give a safe haven to vegetarian Trolls, even if I don't have a numerical value?'

'I can't make that promise,' I said, 'but I know someone who can.'

The Princess removed her handkerchief too. Sometimes a little trust goes a long way.

'I am Princess Shazine Blossom Hadridd Snodd,' she said, 'uncrowned Queen of the greater United Kingdoms.'

'You seem a little spotty for someone who's going to be a great queen,' said the Troll after staring at her for a moment.

'And you seem a little lacking in grace for

someone who will one day negotiate peace between our species.'

They stared at each other for a moment, then smiled. They would go on to form a great alliance, but that would be later, in a time and place I wouldn't share.

'Wow,' said Tiger, who felt it too, 'I think I've just witnessed history in the making.'

The Princess put out her hand.

'I will offer the V-Trolls a safe haven irrespective of numbers,' she said. 'If a group of people are being persecuted for their beliefs, then assistance can only ever be a binary issue: yes or no.'

'Now you're speaking my language,' said Molly with a grin. 'So here we go: Zambini had four messages for me to pass on to Jennifer. The first was that the Mighty Shandar's plans were 'bigger and bolder than anything you can imagine'. Secondly, that you, Miss Strange, are the only one who can stop Shandar, and help will come from an unexpected quarter. You need to be brave, to be bold, and go where others fear to tread. The third message was less of a message, and more of a gift.'

She pulled a waxy object from her ear, where, she explained, 'she had to keep it in case she was searched'. The key was greasy and, well, a little disgusting – there were even some hairs and a couple of beetles attached. I took the key, wiped it on my handkerchief and stared at it closely. I knew which lock it would fit.

'And the fourth message?'

'Oh, yes,' said the Troll, 'but you have to come a little closer.'

I moved closer to the Troll, who, while not as grimy, smelly or as dribbly as her carnivorous kin, was still far more unpleasant than anyone I knew. She put her arms around me in the most gentle and tender of embraces and held me for a moment, rocking gently. She had emulated Zambini's trademark hug so closely that for a brief moment it actually felt I was there, transported back to my first few days at Kazam, when everything was strange and frightening and new. The Troll put her mouth to my ear and whispered, in a fine impersonation of Zambini's voice: 'This is goodbye, Jen. Had you been my own daughter, I could not be more proud.'

I now returned the hug, hoping that it would eventually make its way back up the line to him. I knew then I wouldn't see Zambini again, and not because he had stopped randomly appearing. It was just that the next time he did, I would, as likely as not, no longer be here.

Eventually, Molly released me from the embrace, and I blinked away the tears.

'So,' I said, wanting to move on, 'why are Trolls so frightened of buttons?'

'They're just *horrible*,' she said with a shiver. 'The randomness of their size and colour – and the noise they make when they touch. Ugh. The same goes for swimming. I mean, what's the point? The water gets up your nose and it's really slow. And that shade of cerulean blue? It's just, well, *nasty*.'

'Would jackets covered with buttons be any sort of defence?' I asked.

'Not really,' she said. 'The button suit would have to cover you head to toe, and it wouldn't stop Trolls killing you and then pulling the clothes off your shattered body with a long pair of tongs.'

'I suppose not. Tiger,' I said, 'send someone around the hardware stores of Cornwall and get as many blue paint swatches as you can to show Molly, and see if we can isolate the specific shade of cerulean they despise.'

'It's a *very* precise shade,' said Molly. 'Most blues we're quite happy with.'

'Also,' I added, 'I want you to source a long duster coat and fedora hat. I don't want the sight of our valued friend and ally causing consternation or accidental attacks.'

'Right,' said Tiger, and hurried off.

'I don't want to go outside,' said Molly, suddenly apprehensive. 'I can transfer from a car to a building but only at a run.'

'We can facilitate that,' I said.

'Well,' said Molly, looking at us all in turn, 'you turned out to be quite pleasant after all, and hardly dangerous or ill tempered at all. But you know what could really cement this friendship?'

'Moussaka?' asked the Princess.

This HENRY totally sucks

There was only the merest glimmer of the pre-dawn when we gathered outside the hotel the following morning. Tiger was there with the two Dibble Storage Jars[37] in a rucksack, and I was there with the warmest clothes I could find.

Once Magnificent Boo and Full Price were also present, there to see us off. Ideally, either of them should have come with me as they could do a little magic 'on the fly' if required, but Colin and Feldspar were still teenagers, and couldn't carry their weight.

'Tiger will have to carry the jars,' said Feldspar, who was fussing as usual. He'd found a set of bathroom scales to ensure the weight was evenly distributed and said it would help if Tiger took Exhorbitus, but I wouldn't be parted from it, so had to divest myself of all other items in order for him to take me at all.

'We'll try and figure out Shandar's plans while you're away,' said Boo. 'Monty's trying to figure out what 2.1

---

[37] It's not relevant, but each looked like a glass half-size Roman amphora sealed with a large cork bung.

TeraShandars of wizidrical energy will actually do and perhaps work backwards from there.'

'I just thought of something,' said Tiger. 'If Zambini had been *literal* when he said "bigger and bolder than anything you can imagine" then it's not world domination because, well, we've just thought of that and it's not a big stretch – all power-hungry megalomaniacs want that – along with adoring masses, a lot of gold and some very big statues.'

It was a good point.

'In that case,' I said, swiftly thinking this through, 'we need someone who can think bigger and more boldly than us. Someone who has fanciful notions and weird screwball ideas that fly in the face of logic and reasoning.'

'What about – I don't know – a fantasy author?' suggested Tiger. 'They're pretty unhinged and come up with all kinds of weird and crazy stuff. Maybe they can help.'

Boo said she'd get Princess Jocaminca on to it as it would be good to 'see those wasters doing some work for a change'.

'Okay,' I said, tying a handkerchief around my neck against the chill morning air, 'we're out of here. Happy and ready to go?'

'Yup,' said Colin.

'Yup,' said Feldspar.

'I'm ready,' said Tiger.

'Now listen,' said Once Magnificent Boo, coming over all motherly, which felt very alien indeed, unless your own mother was moody and distant and forbidding and didn't blink and stared at you oddly all the time. 'To recharge the storage jars just put them near the source of the HENRY and let them fill on their own.'

'You'll know they're full when they start to glow bright green,' added Full Price. 'It shouldn't take more than twenty minutes. Yes?'

'Yes.'

'Good luck, then. Think you'll be okay?'

I paused for thought. We had to defeat the most powerful wizard the planet had ever seen along with an untold number of Trolls with dinner on their minds – and had little to help us: a princess with no nation, two fussy Dragons, fencers and marksmen who were neither of those things, a bunch of terrible worriers, two sorcerers with no magic, no plan, a vegetarian Troll and forty-eight hours in which to do it.

'Piece of cake,' I said.

Full Price and Boo stepped back as Colin lowered himself to the ground so I could climb on.

'Don't jab me with that sword,' he grumbled. 'Now hang on tight and for goodness' sake don't fall off – I don't want your death on my conscience.'

'If that happened,' said Feldspar with a silly giggle, 'you'd be the *last* Last Dragonslayer slayer.'

'Yes, ho ho, very funny,' said Colin. 'It's all right for you, you've got the light one.'

They fussed like this for several minutes until eventually, after a long galloping take-off run along the promenade, they inched slowly into the air with a frantic beating of wings. Colin then flew in a long arc around the bay, not very fast, and never above twenty feet. I clung onto the rope halter, which was passed around his neck and nose.

'Are we going to gain any height?' I asked.

'I'm sorry,' said Colin above the sound of his beating wings, 'you're going to have to speak up a little.'

I repeated myself louder.

'Totally out of the question,' he yelled back. 'I'm . . . *unhappy* with heights after I was shot out of the sky and nearly died in that fall back in the Cambrian Empire.[38] Besides,' he added, 'low and slow allows you a survival potential if you fall off. I'm going to fly above water and trees for that very reason.'

'I'm not going to fall off,' I said.

'Yes, but if you do.'

Tiger was having no such issues with Feldspar, and

---

[38] Crossing over into the Cambrian Empire. He was saved by Perkins, who turned him to rubber before he hit the ground – and he remained as rubber for the next few days. See *The Eye of Zoltar* for the full story.

they were now high above us, wheeling in and out of the clouds. I asked Colin to pass over the Button Trench, and as we did I noted a thousand or so Trolls congregating at the barrier, who waved at us as we went over, and made eating gestures with their hands. Shandar had not been kidding over his 'forty-eight-hour' threat.

We took the sea route along the South Coast, startling seabirds and the occasional porpoise as we passed round Lizard Point. Colin sped up a little as he grew more confident, but twice had to stop to get his breath back as it was an effort to keep us both aloft. The first time was near St Austell, the second at Looe Island. Feldspar and Tiger joined us on both occasions, and although Feldspar suggested they swap, Colin refused. I think it was a matter of pride.

We carried on up the coast and at Plymouth took a left and headed inland, the route taking us across the city, where we could see the full effect of the Troll invasion. Overturned cars, fire-gutted buildings and prisoners corralled into fenced-off areas and guarded by Trolls.

As soon as Plymouth was behind us the land rose as we flew into the large massif that is Dartmoor. We passed across the turquoise pools of quarry workings, then scooted at almost zero height over the boggy terrain, eventually alighting just behind Foggin Tor, about two miles west of where the HENRY was situated, so we could take stock and make plans. While the Dragons sat and ate sandwiches and drank tea from a Thermos, Tiger and I trod cautiously up to the highest point of the tor, and then, staying low and out of sight, we peered across the tussocky, boulder-strewn moorland between us and our target, a lattice-work steel radio mast wrapped tightly with thick arboreal growth. There was little sign of life other than a few ponies and sheep quietly grazing, but we could see neat bundles of clothes placed on the ground at about hundred-yard intervals all around, each with a pair of shoes on top and a budget steel sword stuck into the ground near by.

'Hollow Men?' whispered Tiger.

'Hollow Men,' I whispered back. 'These will be proximity actuated – get too close and they'll jump into life. Believe me, you don't want to fight one.'

I'd tackled them before, and while a sole example could be despatched with relative ease, if three or more attacked simultaneously, you would soon be overpowered. When it comes to violent killing machines without reason, pain or fear, Trolls might be a more preferable foe.

'Here,' said Tiger, and handed me the binoculars. I focused on the impenetrable forest that had grown around the mast. It seemed to quiver as I watched, the forest thickening and moving as it absorbed the background wizidrical energy.

'So if there's no spelling going on anywhere,' whispered Tiger, 'how can it have anything to absorb?'

'Magic is a product of raw human emotion,' I murmured, scanning the tightly knotted trees for any place where we could gain access, 'and the wizidrical energy generated by the fear and stress of the Trolls' invasion is generating huge amounts of crackle. Presumably the HENRY will then transfer everything it gathers to Shandar, thus making him even more powerful.'

'D'you think he planned it all this way?'

'He's a fool if he didn't,' I said, still staring through the binoculars, 'but wizidrical energy derived from pain and loss is always tainted with the burden of sorrows, which in turn taints any sorcerer using that power, and draws them farther into a downward spiral towards anarchy and chaos.'

'Evil makes evil,' said Tiger.

'Yes,' I replied, 'but similarly, good begets good.'

'How's it going?' asked Feldspar, who had wriggled up behind us.

'Nothing so far,' I said. 'We'll watch and wait for a bit before we rush to action.'

'Jolly good,' said the Dragon. 'Here's a cup of tea and a KitKat. You'll have to share, I'm afraid. Listen, is Colin all right? He seems to be in something of a mood.'

'He'll be okay,' I said.

'Okay, then,' said Feldspar, and crawled off back to where Colin was waiting.

'So what's the plan?' asked Tiger as we stared at the knot of forest. There were no Trolls and no sign of life. As we watched, a crow perched on a sword hilt of one of the Hollow Men. The pack of clothes suddenly popped into existence as an empty human-shaped entity and expertly cleaved the crow in half. Then, when it observed no continuing threat, it collapsed back into a folded parcel of clothes.

'I don't like Hollow Men very much,' said Tiger.

'Me neither,' I replied.

Then, quite suddenly, several of the trees bent apart and opened on one side of the thicket that was wrapped around the mast. The gap stayed open for about ten seconds, then closed again.

'It's venting hot air,' I said. 'Make a note of the time.'

Tiger jotted in his notebook and started a stopwatch as I stared at the same spot to see whether it would reopen, and we sat in silence for several minutes.

'Jenny?'

'Yes?'

'The key Zambini sent to you via Molly,' he said. 'It was for the glovebox of your VW, wasn't it?'

'Yes.'

He paused to see whether I would volunteer more, but when I didn't he said:

'And?'

'Portal's opening,' I said as the trees parted again. 'Time?'

'Exactly twelve minutes.'

'Good. Let's see if it does it again.'

'Okay. And the glovebox?' he asked again, as Tiger seldom forgot about a question once he'd asked it. I dug into my jacket pocket and passed him a photograph.

'There was a spare set of headlamp bulbs,' I said, 'a car manual and service history, a bar of Cadbury's Fruit and Nut that was so old I scarcely knew what it was, and this.'

Tiger stared at the faded black-and-white photograph. It had been taken outside the orphanage where we both grew up. Zambini was standing next to the VW Beetle, holding a baby wrapped in a blanket, the Quarkbeast sitting attentively at his feet. Also in the picture was Mother Zenobia. She had run the orphanage for over half a century, and was a craggy ex-sorceress, who had always been scrupulously fair in the treatment of her charges: we took it in turns to sleep under the hole in the roof. The picture might have an innocent explanation, but it looked for all the world as though Zambini was leaving me at the orphanage.

'He might have . . . chanced along at the precise moment you were abandoned,' said Tiger, who was trying to put a positive spin on this even though it sounded as though he thought the same as I – that both Zambini and Mother Zenobia had known all along who I was.

'And posed with me, Mother Zenobia, the VW Beetle and the Quarkbeast?'

'I do confess it seems a little odd,' said Tiger.

'It's more than odd, Tiger. The picture being left in the glovebox with a key delivered from Zambini? He *wanted* me to see this.'

'You think Mother Zenobia knew your identity and kept it from you?' he asked in a shocked tone. 'She would *never* do that.'

'I agree – so if she did it was for a very good reason. And it also suggests I was not assigned to Zambini Towers randomly – and that the Quarkbeast didn't just chance along.'

'All this was planned?'

'If so, it was sixteen years in the making,' I said, staring at the radio mast, to which the entwining trees clung tightly like some sort of massive beanstalk, 'but if I want answers I'll have to find Mother Zenobia and ask her. Perhaps that's why Zambini revealed it to me now.'

'Is she still alive?' he asked. 'I mean, is *anyone* from the Lobsterhood still alive?'

'No idea,' I replied, then: 'The portal's opened up again. Interval?'

'Twelve minutes.'

'Good. Let's talk to the Dragons.'

I replaced the photo in my pocket and we picked our way back across the boulders to where the Dragons were waiting. They had eaten their sandwiches, our sandwiches, most of the biscuits and were now playing mah-jong while sipping tea from large tin mugs.

'Pong,' said Colin, staring at his tiles. 'No, wait, Chow. I always get that confused. What news?'

'The HENRY is a thick knot of beech, mixed with bramble,' I said. 'It's impenetrable, but every twelve minutes the tree trunks part to vent out hot air. They stay open for ten seconds, then close.'

'Okay,' said Colin, 'so one of us flies in there, drops the jars off at the core and comes back out, then we check on them every twelve minutes until they are full, right?'

'It's a good plan,' said Feldspar, 'but doomed to failure. That HENRY has got "trap" stamped all over it in big letters. Shandar is expecting you to come, expecting you to enter. When that closes with you and me inside, we're not coming back out until Shandar's plans have come to fruition. This is playing right into his hands.'

'You have a better plan?' I asked.

'Do you trust me?'

He was asking all of us, and we all agreed that we did.

'Jenny and I need to go off-grid for twenty-four hours, do some digging and be back in time for Shandar's deadline. Agreed?'

We all nodded again.

'Shandar might be doing mind sweeps of those loose with their thoughts, so this is the cover story: we attempted to gain entry to the HENRY but there was an accident and we fell into the water-filled quarry just over there. We did not re-emerge, and Colin and Tiger, you waited for four hours before returning home. You can tell only the Princess and Once Magnificent Boo that we are safe. We will send word as soon as we can by way of a homing snail that all is well, but that might not be for twelve hours or more. If you do not receive any word in twenty-four hours, then we are truly gone, and the fight is now yours. Do you understand?'

Colin and Tiger both nodded their heads.

'Good.'

Feldspar stretched his wings, then clasped his brother in a hug, and handed him the thumb ring that had been Maltcassion's. They then conversed in Dragon for a few moments, and pressed their foreheads together hard.

'Take care, won't you?' said Tiger, handing me the

backpack with the jars and the snails and the few snacks the Dragons hadn't managed to eat. 'Should we hug in case it goes wrong?'

'It's not going to go wrong,' I told him.

'No,' he said, chewing his lip.

'Okay, then,' said Feldspar once he had finished conversing with his brother, 'how long can you hold your breath?'

I recalled swimming in the Wye when I was little, just near the orphanage.

'Maybe thirty seconds.'

'Good enough,' he said. 'Climb on.'

We took off and then circled around the source of the HENRY.

'So what was all that hugging stuff you did with Colin?' I asked. 'It's not the standard goodbye I've seen you guys do in the past – and you gave him Maltcassion's ring.'

'That's easily explained,' he said cheerfully. 'I'm going to die soon. I can foresee it. Not how, or when, or precisely where – but certainly within the next twenty-four hours.'

'Then we need to turn back,' I said.

'The future, once set, won't change, Jen. If I were to head back now then my death would be something banal and avoidable, like being hit by a car or food poisoning or something. I'll turn back if you command it, but my end will have no value, and I will have entered the world as I left it, without changing anything for the better.'

He looked around at me with his large green eyes as his wings beat through the air. He was less than a year old and the head jewel in his forehead had not even begun to grow through. He wouldn't be adult for another century and a half. I knew what he said was true, knew that the end of his life could be spent wisely or foolishly. He was my friend, and I was his. But we both understood what had to be done, and about selflessness, and sacrifice.

Endgame is serious stuff.

Feldspar went into a slow spiral dive to lose height to the west, then made a low approach towards the HENRY on a route that took us over the flooded workings. As we passed over, Feldspar feigned a wing cramp, told me to take a deep breath and then rolled over and impacted the water.

It was immensely cold, and I gripped harder on his rope halter as I could now feel Feldspar swimming below me. The light dimmed, and after a moment or two I felt us stop, some hands holding me, and with a hissing noise the water drained rapidly from the small round chamber in which we found ourselves.

'You okay?' said a diver who was operating the controls of the airlock. I nodded. Once the water was out, a hatch at the bottom of the chamber was opened and we climbed down a short ladder. The first thing I saw when I reached the bottom rung was a naval officer with a kindly face. She saluted smartly.

'Miss Strange?' she said. 'I am Captain Lutumba. Welcome aboard *DCSV Bellerophon*.'

Aboard the Bellerophon

I was handed a towel and while I dried my hair I looked around. I was inside what looked like a storeroom of circular cross-section about thirty feet long and no more than fifteen feet wide and high. The hull was constructed with multiple circular bulkheads of riveted iron construction, and fore and aft were watertight doors. The sub had been awaiting our arrival beneath the waters of the quarry, and we had dived down and entered by way of a series of hatches between the craft and the water-filled quarry above.

Feldspar was dry almost straight away, and thanked the captain for the speed at which she had managed the rendezvous. She replied that, with a common enemy, all national differences were set aside. I thanked her too, and as we we watched, crew members busied themselves sealing the hatch in the ceiling and then stowing the breathing apparatus they had used to dive out into the quarry to guide us back to the craft. The crudely engineered interior looked very like one of the vast tracked landships that had often been used to wage war in the Kingdoms, but I knew I wasn't in one of those. I was in a Subterrain, essentially, a submarine that travels not through water, but land.

'You'll need some clean clothes until yours dry off,' said Captain Lutumba. 'My number two will take you to my cabin where you can change. I will expect to see you ASAP in the control room.'

The second-in-command took me to the captain's cabin, where I changed out of my wet things and handed them over for drying. Although I'd never been in a Subterrain I knew of their existence, or at least *supposed* existence. The Duchy of Cotswoldia, denied a land army or airforce as part of the peace treaty with the neighbouring University City State of Oxfordia, embarked on their own version of a land-locked navy: not one that worked in rivers or lakes, but underground. The sleek burrowing craft often spent months at a time submerged, and aside from a trembling of teacups in the corner cupboard, there was little sign a Subterrain was close – until one of their burrowing torpedoes hit home. They were almost impossible to detect – crucially, not even by magic. We could creep up on Shandar and he'd not suspect a thing.

I found Feldspar in the control cabin chatting with Captain Lutumba. The sturdy riveted iron construction was evident here, too, and the hull sides where not covered by dials and gauges were lavishly decorated with polished brass and wood, with several fine oil paintings. There was a small kitchenette from where a rating was about to serve tea along with several custard tarts, which I can reveal were very fine indeed. The control cabin was far less complicated than the bridge of a submarine as these vessels moved a lot slower, and were rarely in danger of sinking. The crew were composed mostly of engineers and geologists, who navigated the ground beneath the UnUnited Kingdoms by avoiding hard rock and instead opting for alluvial flood plains, clay, coal or, even better, soil.

'The *DCSV Tamaraire* was down here half a century ago assisting the Kingdom of Devon's unrestricted clotted cream campaign during the Scone Wars with Cornwall,' explained the captain to Feldspar as I walked in, 'so we used the TransDartmoor Subterranean Expressway to meet you. We can traverse Dartmoor in about an hour, barring roof cave-ins.'

'How long have you two been in touch?' I asked.

'A week,' explained Feldspar, 'through Lady Mawgon.'

'We accept Princess Shazine Snodd as the one true ruler and you as her proxy,' said the captain with a respectful nod and a click of her heels. 'The *Bellerophon* is now at your service. What are your orders?'

It was a no-brainer. I asked for them to go beneath

where the HENRY was situated. The captain gave the order to get under way, and we set off, the craft trembling and shuddering as it moved. Navigation when in a pre-dug tunnel was fairly simple, but out in the open ground it was more about following areas of the softest rock. Because of this, the navigators had the most up-to-date geological maps complete with locations of gas mains, train tunnels and everything else, but caution was still a watchword: there could often be unmapped obstructions such as wells, concrete pilings and enthusiastically deep underground car parks.

'We don't even *try* to get across London these days,' explained the chief geo-navigator. 'One of our small, two-woman fast pursuit craft broke into the Piccadilly Line near Ealing Common and there was hell to pay.'

It took us only fifteen minutes to move the half-mile or so, the rubber-shod wheels that were set into the craft's flanks driving it along the smooth tunnel. Once we were beneath the HENRY the captain ordered all engines halted. I took the storage jars from the backpack and opened the stoppers. Dibble Storage Jars glow when accepting a charge, but right now they were doing nothing of the kind. Wizidrical energy travels easily in air, but water or soil blocks its power very quickly. The captain, however, was not short of ideas and suggested we attach the jars to the periscope in a special container usually reserved for retrieving stores of pâté, ciabatta, avocados and so forth from resupply trucks, generally disguised as roadside catering vans.

The Dibble Jars so placed, the captain gently raised the periscope up to ground level, which also allowed us a quick view of the inside of the HENRY. There were six Trolls sitting around looking bored, and next to them, a large cage on wheels. Feldspar had been right. It had definitely been a trap.

'The Mighty Shandar is clearly unable to catch you himself if he assigns the task to Trolls,' said the captain, also having a look. 'He fears you. Where do you want to go once the jars are filled?'

'Time spent on reconnaissance is never wasted,' I replied. 'Think we can get beneath Shandar's skyscraper? It's just north of Exeter.'

Feldspar and I marked on a map where the replica of the Chrysler Building was sited, and the navigators pulled out their charts and found that they could follow the trans-Dartmoor Expressway, then hook up with the Sticklepath fault-line before hanging a right into the Crediton trough – and all through ready-dug tunnels.

'If we clear all traffic from the tunnels ahead of us we can get to Dig-Zero in three hours,' said the captain. 'After that it will take us seven more hours to burrow the mile to Shandar's tower, although I think we might be able to shave half an hour off that if we hoof it and don't stop for lunch.'

I told her that would be admirable.

'By your command,' said the captain, again saluting smartly, and the crew readied the craft. And as soon as the jars were full, we were off.

Breaking the Spaniel Barrier

There is no standardisation of measurement in the UnUnited Kingdoms. In Wales, for example, distance is measured in Coracles. A KiloCoracle is a thousand Coracles, a MicroCoracle one thousandth of a Coracle, and so forth. Because of this, measurements across the Kingdoms are often arbitrarily chosen so everyone has a vague idea of magnitude – weight is in apples, distance in telephone boxes and speed by comparison to animals. Subterrains in pre-dug tunnels were measured in Spaniel Speed.

As soon as the jars were glowing green with a full load of wizidrical power, the captain ordered 'Full Ahead Both Engines' and we were away, the communications officer alerting by radio any Subterrains in the tunnels to pull into a siding as they were on a 'Code Red: Vital War Business'.

This part of the journey was the most exciting as at least you could feel that we were moving along. We had to stop once to reconsolidate a tunnel owing to a partial collapse, then again to move past another Subterrain taking Eat List refugees down to Free

Penzance. I chatted to a few off-duty ratings and learned the Subterrain was crewed entirely by women as men were considered bad luck.[39] There had been loud grumblings of doom from the older earth-lags when Feldspar arrived as they considered him an omen of bad fortune. I had explained to them that he was only male by virtue of his default to a gender pronoun, and they then wanted to know why he was defaulted to male and not female or even nothing at all, for which I had no good answer. The crew calmed down, however, when the captain told them of the unique nature of the mission, and promised extra grog rations.

Time passed quickly, and after several hours we had made the journey – or at least, as far as we could go without digging a fresh tunnel.

'We're a mile from the building,' said the chief navigator to the captain as we walked in, having been summoned to the bridge. 'Open country, possibly sheep pasture.'

'Good. Depth?'

'Thirty-two feet keel to greenside,' said a rating.

'Constanza?' said the captain, addressing the geo-navigator.

[39] Whether they meant in general or just Subterrain-specific, I never did quite find out.

'Twenty-one feet of soft Permian breccia, then soil,' she said, staring at an instrument bolted to a bulkhead.

'Okay, then,' said the captain. 'Periscope up.'

There was a mild shimmering sensation as the periscope bored its way up through the rock. To avoid giving the sub's position away, the viewing head of the periscope could be disguised in many ways, depending on the area in which it was surfacing: a stone on a beach, a discarded crisp packet in a lay-by, a single shoe on a motorway or a duck in a pond. On this occasion, the periscope would be camouflaged as a fly agaric toadstool – chosen specifically because the red and white head is well known to be poisonous and would not be touched. The subterfuge was necessary. Because of its slow getaway speed, a Subterrain was vulnerable to attack – the most effective countermeasure being an earth-harpoon attached to a small car with a steel hawser. You'd soon know where the Subterrain was headed as it dragged the car through hedges and houses as it moved.

'Okay,' said the captain as she stared into the periscope and clicked the magnification to full, 'see what you make of that.'

I looked into the twin viewing eyeholes of the periscope and could now see the large skyscraper that was incongruously sprouting out of farmland in

Devon. Although I'd not seen the original Chrysler Building I knew it well enough from pictures as I was a big fan of Art Deco and had several scrapbooks containing pictures of notable buildings. This facsimile was every bit as beautiful as the original, the decorative tiles and burnished steel shining in the sun, the geometric patterns and automobile motifs quite lovely to behold. The tower was also indicative of just how much magic Shandar had at his fingertips: if he could build something like this as a base of operations, then it would have been with magical power he had to spare; like the loose change you find down the back of the sofa.

I moved the periscope around. There were Hollow Men in abundance guarding the building but no Trolls as far as I could see. Having studied Colin's aerial photographs, we knew there was a small entrance on the side facing away from us that gave direct access to the M5 motorway and Exeter Airport, where Shandar's fleet of Skybus aircraft had been moving in and out, presumably with the Quarkbeasts he was so keen to harvest. When I had seen enough, I thanked the captain.

'Periscope down,' she called, and there was a soft whirring sound as it retracted.

The captain called for Full Ahead Both and the Subterrain started to shake as the main cutters bit into the rock. I asked Feldspar whether we should send a homing snail but it had been less than four hours since we left Colin and Tiger and they would not yet be heading home.

'We'll be under the building in eight hours,' said the captain. 'We can probably manage twice the speed of mole in this stratum, more if we hit a softer section. Go and relax.'

It was good advice. Nothing happened very fast in the Subterrain Service. A battle between opposing fleets of Subterrains had occurred only once, during a totally unnail-biting three weeks in the winter of 1953. The slow progress of the engagement ensured that it was, descriptively and literally, the most boring battle in the history of warfare.

I went for a wander around the large craft, partly out of curiosity, partly out of not wanting to play poker with Feldspar, as he had suggested. There were torpedo rooms fore, aft and amidships, as turning the craft was not an easy manoeuvre. All torpedoes were designed like corkscrews and travelled very slowly, but that wasn't much of an issue as other Subterrains would be similarly slow to take avoiding action, and buildings couldn't take any avoiding action at all.

Living quarters were by necessity quite cramped, but the galley was Michelin-starred, and the food astonishingly good. The chef gave me a butterscotch parfait which melted on my tongue. Farther aft was the engine room, where two large in-line diesels ran on recycled vegetable oil, which made the whole sub, and everyone in it, smell very much like a fish and chip shop.

I moved on past the storeroom and came to the room where we'd entered the *Bellerophon* and sat on some sacks of potatoes near the escape pod. I took the photograph I'd discovered in the Beetle's glovebox out of my pocket and stared at it for some time in silence. I turned the picture over and looked again at a pencilled note in Zambini's hand that read: 'The Assetts', with the date of my induction into the orphanage. It had to be me. I paused then turned the picture back over and wondered *who exactly* he had been referring to as assets: Zambini, Zenobia, the Quarkbeast, me – even the car? I was just about to put the photo away when something caught my eye. There was a small hand pressed against the rear window, as though a child were inside on the back seat. I could just see the top of their head too, and they had bunches. Most likely a girl. If this were the day of my induction, then the mystery child had not been inducted at the same time. I had been the only one that week.

I took a deep breath, placed the picture back in my pocket and returned to the captain's cabin, where Feldspar eventually persuaded me to play poker. As we played, we talked about the enduring mysteries of the Troll: why they had never invaded until now, what did they eat when not eating humans, and crucially, their numbers. All the Troll Wars had been started by humans, usually through fear, a need to try out weaponry or even, as the Princess suggested, to keep the orphan-based economy supplied with free labour. On the issue of size, the estimated number of the invading forces was around two million, but given Trollvania was mostly rock and heather and without visible structures of any sort, it was difficult to see where they came from.

'Caves?' suggested Feldspar.

'They'd all be pasty and squinty and looking like mole-rats if that were the case,' I said. 'As far as I can see they're all very tanned and healthy looking.'

'Molly might know.'

'I asked her,' I said. 'Numerical values don't mean much to them.'

'Counting is overrated,' said Feldspar. 'I know that you have an above-average number of legs, and I can know that without doing any counting at all.'

'I have two legs,' I said. 'That's the average number, surely?'

'Someone, somewhere, is missing a leg,' he said, 'perhaps both. Which changes the average. You have the *mode* of human legs – that occurring most often in a data-set. The average number of legs on a human is somewhere around 1.99999 recurring, but without counting everyone and their legs, which is both futile and time-wasting, we'll never know for sure.'

'That's true,' I said, 'but if I asked all the Dragons on the planet whether they liked rice pudding, and fifty per cent said they didn't, that wouldn't really be very helpful, would it?'

'It would be *correct*,' said Feldspar, who hated rice pudding, 'but yes, statistically it's a little meaningless – when you hear about percentages as the result of a survey, it's always a good idea to find out the size of the sample. Flush,' he added, laying down his cards, 'queen high.'

'Zambini always said that with surveys it's useful to find out who paid for it before accepting the findings,' I replied, also laying down my cards. 'Pair of nines.'

After several hours of pointless speculation over the Trolls, more chat about hard numbers versus ratios and me losing all the money in my pockets, we were summoned back to the control room.

'We're almost there,' said the captain. 'Chief geologist?'

The geologist looked up from her Ground Penetrating Sonar screen and told us that Shandar's building carried on beneath the soil for a good seventy or eighty feet – the normal depth of foundations for a building this size – so the captain ordered us to dive and we felt the sub pitch down as we bored deeper into the rock. Ninety minutes and a game of Scrabble and mug of cocoa later, the geo-navigator reported that the sub-basements were guarded by six feet of reinforced cement and two-inch-thick steel plate.

'Problems?' I asked.

The captain replied no, as they had something called a 'thermic lance' for just such an eventuality, and had just given the order to halt the main engines when I felt the craft lurch oddly. A warning klaxon went off somewhere and the geologists rapidly consulted their instruments.

'Speak to me, Number Two,' said the captain.

'Exterior temperature is rising,' she said, twiddling a few knobs and staring at some dials.

'What?'

'Twenty-five degrees under the hull and rising.'

'Impossible! Sensor error?'

'They're all reading the same, ma'am.'

'Explanation?'

'Working on it now, ma'am.'

I could sense by the urgency in the captain's voice that this was not something they had experienced before. I looked across at Feldspar, who stared back at me and shook his head resignedly. *This felt like magic.* The navigation officer pressed a few buttons and the Ground Penetrating Sonar, more usefully directed forward or upward, was now looking directly below, and it seemed as though there was something large beneath us – and quite hot. The craft lurched again and pitched downward. I grabbed hold of a bulkhead to steady myself as several pencils and a coffee mug slid off the navigation table to land with a clatter on the floor.

'We're descending,' said the helmswoman, 'deck to topside one twenty feet and increasing.'

'Permission to fire seismic charges, Captain,' said the chief geologist.

'Granted.'

The geologist opened a spring-loaded access panel marked 'Emergency Only' and pressed four red buttons. There was a pause and we heard two pairs of muffled concussions. To figure out the nature of the rock strata, small charges are detonated and the return echoes studied to give an idea of the under-lying geological structure. I figured the charges were used sparingly as they would give away the craft's position.

'Full astern both,' said the captain, and a shudder ran though the craft – but with apparently no effect at all. The craft lurched again and pitched down more markedly, while at the same time several control panels fused in a flurry of sparks and we were plunged into darkness.

'Captain,' said the geologist once the red emergency lights had flickered on, 'sensors indicate the heat below us is a . . . magma chamber, and we're heading straight into it.'

'Don't be ridiculous,' said the captain. 'There's not been any volcanic activity on this island for over fifty million years – the crust here is eighteen miles thick.'

The geologist switched the Ground Penetrating Sonar to the main screens so we could see what lay beneath. It seemed that Shandar had opened up a well that plunged down eighteen miles, and up this channel was rising a steady stream of molten rock, to pool in a large subterranean lake of magma beneath his skyscraper, into which we were now heading, out of control. It didn't take an expert to realise that when we hit the magma lake, the most sophisticated underground weapon of war would be nothing but molten steel.

'Deck to topside now two hundred and twenty feet,' said the helmswoman. 'Rate of descent now seventeen moles per second.'

'How long until hull rupture?' asked the captain.

'Twelve minutes,' said the second-in-command, looking at the dials and screens in front of her, 'but,' she added, 'we're only a minute inside the safe window for escape pod activation.'

'Very well,' said the captain, 'tell the crew to stand down from duties; you are to update the log and fetch Last Letters from my safe. Miss Strange, with me.'

I followed her down the boat, the crew stepping aside to let us past and tipping their caps respectfully. We arrived at the aft cabin where we'd come in and walked to the escape pod hangared in the far bulkhead. The captain pulled a lever and the door popped open. The pod was about the size of a pillar box: there was room only for one. The lack of urgency among the rest of the crew meant only one thing: there was only the one pod. One was all that was needed – smallest out, pinpoint the stricken craft, call in an excavator or a group of miners, depending on depth. If that failed, the crew could fire torpedoes and climb out through the voids made by those. But with the exterior rock now the consistency of toffee and the temperature rising by the second, none of those options was possible.

'But—'

'The Subterrain Service was always a hazardous assignment, Miss Strange, and we knew that when we signed up.' The captain smiled. 'Listen, any sorcerer powerful enough to create a magma chamber for defence is quite outside my realms of expertise – but conversely, he's well within yours.'

She stepped back as the second-in-command handed me the ship's log and an envelope that contained the crew's Last Letters. They both saluted and wished me the very best of luck. Already I could hear the crew singing a soft-ground shanty:

> *Proud subterraneans we be*
> *and Terra is our nation*
> *The subsoil is our dwelling place*
> *the worms our destination*

Feldspar had accompanied us. I said to him, 'You can fit in here too, can't you?'

'I don't think I'll be opening that restaurant after all,' he said. 'Tell Colin I'm glad he's the last Dragon and not me. He'll be much better at it.'

'I'm staying with you,' I said.

'If you do then our sacrifice has been for nothing,' said Feldspar. 'This is the only play, Jen.'

I opened my mouth to speak, but I had no good argument. He was right. It *was* the only play. I took a deep breath and turned to Captain Lutumba.

'Thank you, Captain.'

She smiled.

'It has a been a pleasure sailing with you, Miss Strange. Make us proud, make us *matter*.'

'I will.'

'And listen,' added Feldspar, 'kick Shandar's butt big-time, right?'

'You have my word.'

I took another deep breath and stepped into the escape pod.

'Goodbye, Jen,' said Feldspar. 'Love you.'

'Love you too,' I said. My eyes began to fill with

tears as the captain slammed the pod door shut. Almost instantly I felt the small craft shudder as it moved vertically out of the Subterrain, my feet growing hot from the small solid-fuel booster that was pushing me upwards, the revolving auger on the top of the craft cutting through the soft medium as it rose. A minute later and I felt the auger start to bite – but not to take me through the roots and turf into the fresh air of the Devon countryside as I had expected, but into something else: something hard. Sparks and hot metal drifted past the porthole as the carbide-tipped cutter bored deep into the barrier above me. In another minute or two the porthole cleared and I hastily unlatched the door and stepped out onto a smooth concrete floor. I grabbed my bag, sword, paperwork and storage jars as the escape pod sank slowly back into the ground. Within a minute it had disappeared from view and the concrete had self-repaired itself so perfectly there was no evidence the floor had even been breached.

I leaned against a packing case, sank to the floor and silently wept for the loss of not only a good friend, but the crew of the *Bellerophon*, who had so stoically accepted their fate – and now trusted me to make their sacrifice matter. I sighed and wiped the tears from my cheeks. If my resolve was not already cemented before this, it was now. I would defeat Shandar, no matter what it took.

I took a deep breath, calmed myself and looked around at the sub-basement in which I found myself. There was work to be done.

Inside Shandar's Tower

The basement was single-storey, and in the centre was a service elevator large enough to hold a truck. The floor space was about half the size of a soccer pitch but roughly trapezoid in shape with solid steel uprights spaced at regular intervals supporting the building above me and diagonally cross-braced to the walls and each other. The area was filled with floor-to-ceiling storage racks, all meticulously labelled and stocked with a bewildering variety of goods: clothes, tinned food, ping-pong balls, spare dishwasher parts, bottles of wine, packets of seeds. There was even an entire rack devoted to movies and TV series on DVD[40] – more than one could ever watch in a lifetime.

I walked towards the service elevator and stairway block, intending to continue my explorations on the next floor up, but when I turned a corner I stopped dead as a Hollow Woman was walking towards me, pushing a shopping trolley full of empty jam jars.

[40] *Bergerac* wasn't there. I checked.

Unlike the Hollow Men, who typically wore a dark suit, hat and white shirt, the female version of the Hollow Man was dressed in denim dungarees and a gingham shirt. She wore gloves, but instead of a hat she had a red-spotted headscarf wrapped around where her head would have been. Although devoid of life and essentially nothing but a set of clothes given movement and purpose by Shandar's power, these dungaree-clad drones seemed more to do with store-keeping than defence, because as I stood there, hardly daring to move, the Hollow Woman simply walked straight past me and carried on to place the items in the trolley on a shelf, then make a quick note on a pad detailing what was stored where.

I turned and climbed noiselessly up the stairs to the next level, which was more of the same: racks and racks of stores. Clothes, huge forty-gallon drums of peanut butter, a complete set of *National Geographic*, and a lot of really good art – much of which I knew rightly belonged to the regional galleries that were dotted around the UnUnited Kingdoms. It wasn't just paintings that had been stolen, either. There were sculptures, tapestries and priceless silver and tableware. The next level up from this was furniture – mostly ornate and upholstered with brocaded patterned work, all far more intricate and beautiful than could ever be conjured up by magic. There were eight sub-basements in total, each full of everything that might be needed for a lifetime of luxurious living. The last sub-basement before I reached the ground floor was the loading dock, which had a large opening to an exterior ramp.

Hollow Men were milling around while trucks offloaded more goods to be stored either in the sub-basements below or the office space above, as the large service elevator went both ways. There were too many Hollow Men here to avoid being spotted, so I hastily made my way up another flight of steps and came to a door marked 'Lobby'. I pushed it open a crack and peered out.

The entrance atrium was triangular. The sunlight had turned a deep orange in anticipation of setting, and was now throwing a warm glow upon the wood marquetry, stainless steel and marble interior. The high ceiling was covered with a large painting that depicted the Mighty Shandar's numerous achievements – magical exploits, created animals, finest spells, biggest castles. It all looked very much as though the painter was eager to massage Shandar's ego – the wizard was always portrayed in a heroic way, his foot on the head of a defeated Dragon, dopey things like that. To my right I could see the main entrance with what looked like airtight doors, currently secured open. There were eight Hollow Men in the lobby, all motionless. I took a homing snail from my bag and wrote on the shell in very small letters:

Alive, Feldspar and crew of Bellerophon *heroes of resistance, more later.*

I then took the tiny hood off the snail's head and they[41] yawned, waved both sets of antennae at me and looked around. I laid them on the floor and then, after a moment's pause to get their bearings, they were off like a rocket, zigzagging towards the entrance. If the Hollow Men on guard duty saw the snail, they did not consider them a threat and the last I saw of the heroic gastropod was as they slid out into the daylight and then hurtled off in the direction of the M5. Snails often navigated by motorway – fewer obstructions, well signposted and the white lines a low-friction surface conducive to sustained speed. They'd probably get the message in Penzance in about two hours, so long as the plucky mollusc could figure out the Button Trench.

I gently closed the lobby door and carried on up the tower, but this time more cautiously, one hand on the hilt of Exhorbitus. My caution was unnecessary: the first floor was empty. I went to the window and looked out onto a landscape bathed with the long shadows of the setting sun. It was the end of a very

---

[41] Homing snails are technically *Helix velocitas pomatia,* and are both male and female, hence the 'they' and 'them' pronouns. I could have written 'it' but that would be disrespectful.

long day by now, the dawn trip to the Spellsucker radio mast with the Dragons feeling like weeks before, the memory relegated to misty forgetfulness by the drama of the rest of the day's events.

The window, I noted, was sealed tight shut and made of thick glass, but with nothing else to see here I worked my way upwards, exploring the floors as I went, which wasn't so very hard as each floor was pretty much open plan, a square space around the central core that carried the elevators, stairs and service shafts. I noted that the building was strengthened by more steel girders that were criss-crossed by bracing bars, some of which were in awkward places and needed to be stepped across.

I carried on trudging up the steel stairs as outside it turned from day to dusk to night. Most floors were empty, but others were notably in use: four floors were allocated to Hollow Men and Women storage – rows upon rows of shelves upon which were placed parcels of folded clothes wrapped in cellophane, ready to leap into life at Shandar's command. Three more floors were made over to market gardening and another two seemed to have been converted into a double-height library, with a dizzying collection of books contained upon oak shelves, and a reading area of plush green leather armchairs in front of a crackling fire. By the time I reached the thirty-ninth floor, Quarking noises from above told me I was closer to something more relevant. I quietly opened the fortieth-storey door and, once I'd ensured no one was about, crept in and found myself in a floor entirely devoted to Quarkbeasts. The creatures were all held in their own sumptuous living quarters, fully equipped with all the things Quarkbeasts really like, which generally revolved around chewing on a zinc-plated anchor link while sprawled on a large sofa sipping rusty water and watching TV.

I looked around the individual rooms cautiously and could see that our theories regarding Shandar and the Quarkbeasts were correct – each Quarkbeast was housed in a room next to his or her identical yet opposite twin, and a shared door between their quarters could open when required and the Quarkbeast, naturally curious, would meet their twin – and being *entirely* opposite to one another, would cancel each other out with a staggeringly large release of raw wizidrical energy. But instead of leaving North Devon as simply a smoking hole in the ground, the energy of all those simultaneously conjoining Quarkbeasts would be channelled through large silicon-coated steel funnels in the ceiling that led up a long vertical shaft that disappeared into the gloom high above – presumably to where the Mighty Shandar would be waiting to receive all that extra power.

I had a scout around and found that all Quarkbeasts except one were present – mine. After finding the room destined for him, I felt a cold shudder of revulsion go through me. The recent loss of Feldspar and the *Bellerophon* and the damage that had been wrought by Shandar's assistance to the Trolls bubbled to the surface. I felt hot, and twitchy, and all of a sudden I didn't really care what happened to me or who knew I was here. I headed straight to the main passenger elevator and pressed the call button.

I didn't have to wait long for the car to arrive, and the doors opened to reveal . . . Miss D'Argento, surrounded by a half-dozen Hollow clerks who were so startled by my sudden appearance that they spontaneously collapsed into six neat piles of clothes, the papers they were carrying now scattered in the air like a ticker-tape parade. If Miss D'Argento was surprised to see me, she didn't show it. She merely raised a jet-black eyebrow.

'Miss Strange,' she said, inclining her head in greeting.

'Miss D'Argento,' I said.

There was a pause, until she asked:

'Which floor?'

'All the way up,' I told her.

She leaned across and pressed a button marked 'Control Deck'.

'What are you hoping to do?' she asked as the lift rose. 'Shandar's power will soon be without limit, and no one will be able to withstand his might.'

I looked at her for a moment.

'They all say that,' I said, 'every single despot who ever tried to take what was not theirs by force. And you know what? They always end up ignominiously defeated, vanquished by events they can't predict, from a quarter they don't expect.'

'I don't think you understand the Mighty Shandar well enough,' said D'Argento, who seemed no longer to refer to herself in the third person, to my great relief, 'nor of what he is capable, nor his plans.'

She was right. Zambini had sent a message to the effect that his plans were 'bigger and bolder' than anything we could dream up. But that didn't matter right now.

'I understand him perfectly,' I said, 'but you don't. If you did, you'd be helping and not hindering.'

'Our destinies are inextricably bound,' she said. 'I've known that for a long time, and learned it from someone wiser than you.'

I didn't really understand D'Argento and Shandar's relationship. She was too smart to simply be a minion, yet not outwardly evil enough to stand by his side. She was basically his agent – an employee. Insanely loyal or simply in it for the cash? I couldn't tell – but people who stood on the right-hand side of tyrants usually ended up on the wrong side of history.

'What's your play?' I asked her.

'What's yours?' she retorted as the bell sounded and the lift doors opened. I made no answer and she stepped out of the elevator and indicated the room with a flourish.

'Welcome,' she said, 'to the Tower of Knowledge.'

I stepped into the room. The doors slid shut behind me and I looked around.

Whatever the real Chrysler Building looked like inside, I was willing to bet good money it was nothing like this. The floor area was smaller than on the lower storeys as the building narrowed as it rose, but the room was still large and sumptuously furnished with leather armchairs and walnut tables and desks. To one side on a low dais a string quartet of Hollow musicians were neatly folded next to their instruments, and on the other side of the room a log fire blazed in a grate within an ornate fireplace. Centred on all the four walls were large semicircular windows, giving far-reaching views in all directions. Above our heads was the interior of the tower's spire: an empty void of at least six storeys in height, with the distinctive triangular windows allowing a clear view of the dark sky outside.

I noticed a large aperture in the centre of the room, across which was placed a stainless steel grate. I walked across and peered into a vertical shaft which plunged into darkness far below, from where I could hear faint Quarking noises.

'During the mass conjoining,' said Miss D'Argento, who had walked with me, 'the raw wizidrical energy will flow up this conduit, and will be absorbed and then focused by the Eye of Zoltar into every cell of his body. No one has ever been that powerful before. He will, quite literally, become—'

'A living god?' came a voice from behind us. I turned. It was the Mighty Shandar, and he looked younger and fitter than when he had appeared last in the Queens Hotel ballroom.

'Practising your humility, Shandar?'

I purposefully left off the 'mighty' honorific. His eyebrow twitched and I saw D'Argento flick a nervous look towards me. A lesser mortal would have been vaporised into dust where they stood, but I was not frightened of him, and it was best he knew that.

'There is a fine line between boldness and stupidity,' he said, commenting either on the absence of the honorific or my sarcasm, but I wasn't sure which. He snapped his fingers and the Hollow string quartet popped into life, picked up their instruments and began to play softly in the background.

'D'Argento,' said Shandar, 'bring us coffee. Jennifer and I need to talk.'

D'Argento nodded respectfully and departed. We stared at one another for a few moments.

'Are you going to kill me?' I asked.

'If it were that simple,' he said, 'I would have done it years ago, the first time I realised who you were, the moment I realised Zambini had put a plan in place, the moment I saw you for the threat you are.'

I thought about the photograph I found, the one of me at the orphanage, with 'The Assetts' written on the back. Me and the Quarkbeast. I had to know more.

'Enlighten me.'

'I shall not,' he said, wagging a finger at me. 'The supreme delight I will get from destroying you lies in the fact that you will *never* know what it is you could have done. But the people you failed, the people you left behind, I'll make sure they know how absolute was your blundering stupidity. The name of Jennifer Strange will be synonymous with complete and utter failure.'

And he laughed.

My temper spiked and in an instant Exhorbitus was out and had sliced him cleanly in half. Or rather, that's what I had intended – but Exhorbitus, who could change thought into immediate action, was still too slow. The instant before the blade struck him, Shandar had teleported to a position beside the fire, where he stared back at me laconically.

'What do you think?' he asked, indicating his creation, the tower.

'Vulgar and ostentatious,' I replied, taking two steps

towards him. He effortlessly teleported to one of the windows, then another, each time accompanied by a faint 'pop' as the air rushed in to fill the area left empty by his departing form. If I were to beat him, it would not be with a blade. I calmed, and placed Exhorbitus back in its scabbard.

'You're already all-powerful,' I said. 'Why annihilate all those Quarkbeasts in the mass conjoining? What could you want that you do not already have?'

'I have plans far bigger and bolder than you could possibly imagine,' he said. 'You will never find out what I am going to do until I have done it.'

'We're working on that,' I said, wondering whether the team back in Penzance had managed to find a fantasy author with a suitably aberrant imagination, 'but really,' I added, 'centuries of planning to give yourself, what, two TeraShandars of power? It's big enough to achieve world domination, but not enough to keep it.'

He smiled.

'Who did your maths? That Full Price nincompoop, or the perpetually moody Lady Mawgon? "She who no-one obeys".'

'It's more?'

'*Considerably* more. You don't total the power of each conjoinment, you *multiply* them. The power available to me is roughly two raised to the power of sixty-three.'

He placed the figures in the air as smoke so I could better understand them.

$$2^{63}$$

'Doesn't look like much, does it?' he said. 'But when you consider that the notable Carl Sagan[42] calculated that two raised to the power of eighty was likely the number of elementary particles in the universe, I think you will agree I will have more crackle on tap than I'd really know what to do with.'

'More skyscrapers in North Devon?' I asked.

'You're very sarcastic, aren't you?'

'I learned it from a friend,' I said, thinking of Tiger.

'It's not skyscrapers I want to build,' he said after a moment's thought, 'it's *enlightenment*.'

'I'm listening.'

'The acquisition of knowledge follows broadly established lines: research, collation, evaluation, testing, modification and conclusion. These can all be done by others and deposited in libraries. Terrific if you're a specialist, but if you are looking for a broader and fuller understanding of exactly what all this is here for and how and why it works, then you will need an all-encompassing overview, a full

---

[42] You need to look this guy up.

and complete understanding of an almost infinite host of subjects. A lifetime is not long enough to do that.'

'I don't disagree with that,' I said, 'so far.'

'In the pursuit of knowledge,' he continued, 'humans fight, regimes fall and knowledge is lost, forgotten or warped for political gain. With a clear objective and time enough in which to do it, I can achieve full enlightenment. If you stop to think for a moment, Jenny, I'm actually making the greatest possible contribution to human knowledge. I call it "The Everything Project".'

There was a pause in the conversation as D'Argento reappeared and handed Shandar a coffee, and me a banana milkshake, my favourite.

'All the great unanswered questions of the world will be answered,' I said, recalling Yolanda of Kilpeck's prediction of what would happen when the Quarkbeasts came together.

'Correct,' said Shandar. 'The Quota of fully Quorumed Quarkbeasts will allow me to become what will be known as "the Shandarian Oracle".'

He paused for a moment.

'But to ultimately know everything I need to transcend the boundaries imposed by human biology. When the Quarkbeasts conjoin I will have the power to achieve immortality. An eternal life to answer the Eternal Question. Better still, I will have enough spare power to bestow it on others. Like the loyal Miss D'Argento, for instance – and you.'

'You're offering me eternal life so I can help you figure out the riddles of the universe? That's quite an offer.'

'The best you'll ever get,' he said. 'Give me your Quarkbeast, and live a life eternal at my side, learning all there is to know about everything.'

'That's all I have to do?'

'Pretty much – oh, and you have to be my friend, stop all this hating and occasionally help me out in times of need.'

I thought for a moment. Not about his offer, which would have massive strings attached – but what he was *actually up to*. There was more to this, and it certainly reeked of world domination – but we'd already discounted that. There was something more.

'Tell me your plans and I'll give you an answer.'

'Give me your Quarkbeast and after the conjoining I'll tell you everything.'

'Why not just take it?'

He paused.

'It's . . . not as easy as that.'

'But all this Troll mass murder is?'

'I didn't kill anyone,' he said, 'I simply allowed the Trolls to express themselves in an openly geographical manner. It's not my place to instruct the Trolls as to their eating habits, any more than you can insist I be vegetarian.'

'So you're okay with all that "being eaten alive" stuff?'

'Of course,' he said, mildly puzzled that I should ask. 'Looking at it objectively, there is no difference between Trolls eating humans and humans eating sheep. Thinking otherwise strikes me as actually a little hypocritical, wouldn't you agree?'

I had been vegetarian for years, although not militant, but there was a point buried deep somewhere in his twisted logic.

'May I ask a question?' I asked.

'Shoot.'

'How does someone get to be as utterly immoral as you?'

'You've got me all wrong: I'm not immoral, for that would make me at worst deceitful or unprincipled, as I would understand the wickedness behind my actions. No, I am *amoral* – without any morals at all. I see, I want, I take – without guilt, pity, mercy or sorrow.'

'And how's that working out for you?'

'It's working out very well,' he said, indicating the surroundings, 'as you can plainly see.'

He stepped closer.

'Look into my eyes, Jennifer, and see if you can tell me what is missing.'

He was uncomfortably close, and I could smell the salt and vinegar crisps on his breath. But I did what he asked, and stared into his eyes. They were dark and empty like Once Magnificent Boo's, but while the ancient sorceress's eyes had a sense of bruised yet defiant humanity within them, Shandar's had none, and I shivered.

'Oh my goodness,' I said in a quiet voice, 'you have no soul.'

'Correct,' he said, 'and it's *so* much easier. A conscience is as much a barrier to knowledge as biology is to eternal life. Eventually, I will have both.'

'So long as you get the Quarkbeast.'

'You'll come round to it,' he said, 'and you will join me on this journey, as will Miss D'Argento – you will not be friends to begin with, but will learn to enjoy each other's company, like sisters.'

'Very cosy.'

'I'm offering eternal life and the ultimate answer to everything. What's not to like?'

'There'll be *something* not to like,' I said. 'I can smell a catch in all this. It permeates your words, like cheap cologne.'

He smiled again, but I could see now that it was utterly devoid of warmth, humour and humanity. I shivered. There is little defence against someone with no soul. Even a Troll can keep a promise.

I'm going home now,' I said, 'and once there, I will figure out a way to vanquish you.'

'Good luck with that,' he said. 'You've been an exciting adversary, but I think we're pretty near the endgame. I *will* have the Quarkbeasts, they *will* conjoin, I *will* have eternal life, you *will* join me on my journey. It is foreseen, it is inevitable.'

'The one thing I've learned about premonitions,' I said slowly, 'is that they come true in unexpected ways.'

'I think we've talked enough, Jenny. If you haven't surrendered the Quarkbeast to me before sunrise on Monday morning, then the Trolls will come into Penzance, and I will have the Quarkbeast anyway.'

He touched me on the shoulder and I felt the warm fizzy sensation of a user-defined enchantment.

'When you're ready to go,' he said, 'just click your heels twice and name your destination.'

And he vanished.

I looked across at D'Argento, who smiled back at me. Unlike Shandar's smile, hers appeared almost genuine.

'You agree with all that?' I asked her.

'Of course,' she replied. 'The Mighty Shandar is a true visionary. The Everything Project is a venture of extraordinary scope and ambition in which I am hugely honoured to play a part – as will you be.'

'Cosying up to a man with no soul isn't going to end well, D'Argento. It never does.'

'Undertaking a self-soulectomy[43] is just one of the many sacrifices Shandar has made on the altar of human enlightenment. Dispelling the Better Angels of his Nature was a difficult decision – but necessary.'

I stared at her for a moment in silence.

'C'mon,' I said, 'he's gone. Tell me what you really think – and what he's actually up to?'

I saw the briefest flicker of doubt cross her face, then it was gone. It was a loaded question, and her reaction was what I was looking for. She couldn't tell me anything even if she wanted to. Shandar would be watching and listening right now. She may even have been beguiled; possibly her will was not her own.

'The Everything Project was four centuries in the making,' she said. 'Once His Mightiness has the Quarkbeast he will reveal all – and you will clamour to be by his side.'

'Don't count on it, D'Argento – and look, thanks for the milkshake.'

I tapped my heels twice and murmured 'Queens

---

[43] As you might imagine, 'ectomy' is a medical term relating to the removal of something, in the case of 'Soulectomy', a soul. The word can also apply to tonsils (tonsilectomy) or bone (ostectomy).

Hotel, Penzance'. There was a sound like a thousand crisp packets being scrunched in unison, and there I was, outside the main entrance just across from the promenade. All the street lights were on and scattered groups of people were out for a walk in the warm night air. The Quarkbeast, who usually sat on the top step to soak up the sun when it was sunny and the water when it was rainy, sat up and wagged his weighted tail happily.

'Quark,' he said.

'Hello, boy,' I said, stepping forward to tickle him under the chin. 'What's been going on?'

'Qu-ark,' he replied, and his tail dropped. This didn't sound good at all, so I hurried up the steps into the hotel.

Wedding bells

I pushed opened the main door to the hotel, hoping to tell the Princess and everyone else what had happened as soon as I could, but there didn't seem to be anyone about. The ops room was locked although I could still hear people working inside, and while yesterday the reception area had been busy with clerks moving about with reports and paperwork and suchlike, there was little movement in the hotel at all. It seemed a little eerie – and worrying.

'Where is everyone?' I asked the man on the main desk.

'They're at the wedding,' he said, grinning with an annoying level of royalty-based rapture. 'I would have liked to go but I couldn't move my shift. How was your day?'

'It could have gone better. Room 266, please.'

He handed me a message from my pigeonhole. It was from William of Anorak, and he'd come to the conclusion that since he had no factoids about Trolls, someone must have stolen them from his head – and

188

maybe that's what Shandar had been up to: fogging any memories over how to stop them.

'Bad news?' asked the receptionist.

'Not unexpected,' I said. 'Isn't it a little late in the day for a wedding?'

'The city runs a twenty-four-hour Harry and Sally marriage service,' he replied, handing me my key, 'because when you realise you want to spend the rest of your life with somebody, you want the rest of that life to start with them as soon as possible. Also, I think the Princess said there was some constitutional urgency in it.'

'Which princess?' I asked, although only reluctantly, as royal weddings were, along with tapioca, boy bands and celebrity biographies, things in which I had zero interest. 'The tall gawky-looking one or Jocaminca?'

'No, no, the *Princess* – you know, the uncrowned Queen of all the Kingdoms – your friend – the one with the funny skin rashes.'

I suddenly had a very nasty feeling.

'Who . . . is she marrying?'

The receptionist grinned fit to burst.

'Why, Sir Matt Grifflon, of course. Such a lovely couple. I've managed to reserve a dozen commemorative plates; they're going to become collector's items one day – do you want to buy one? Actually, I think I've over-ordered so can let you have five at the extra-special price of anything you want to give me.'

I hurried across to Penzance's cathedral, a neo-industrial design built entirely of red brick, oak beams and riveted iron, the material of choice of Cornish architects, who were more used to designing mine workings and engine sheds than ecclesiastical architecture.

The crowds were about twenty deep outside the cathedral, but I pushed my way to the main doors with some difficulty, as it seemed that almost everyone had over-bought commemorative plates and now wanted to sell them on. I confronted a guard who tried to stop me getting in by saying something threatening, and I, in return, said something so frightening back that he shrank in horror and let me past.

The interior of the packed cathedral was filled with the sound of muted snivelling, but I trotted nosily up the nave as fast as I could, the Quarkbeast at my heels. Six more guards tried to confront me but I simply glared at them dangerously and clasped the hilt of Exhorbitus, and they instantly retreated. I may even have gone a little red in the face as my temper, once up, can be frightening to behold. When you've been in a berserker frenzy, it pays to put it about: you'd be surprised how many people treat you with caution.

The couple were at the altar. Matt Grifflon in his best armour, buffed to a high sheen, his long hair coiffured to look like a blond wave about to break on the seashore. The Princess, greatly smaller than he, was by his side, dressed in a wedding gown and veil, with the best tiara anyone could find atop her head as a makeshift crown. Worse, she had her hand in his.

'I have an objection!' I yelled, as the nuptials, it seemed, had not yet been completed. Both Sir Matt and the Princess turned.

'What utter nonsense is this?' I asked, striding up. 'A coerced marriage is unrecognisable in law.'

'Oh dear,' said Sir Matt, rolling his eyes, 'it's little grumpy-chops again. Are you jealous it's not you I'm marrying?'

'Me? *What?* No.'

'Jenny,' said the Princess, 'I know this is a shock to you, but Sir Matt explained *everything* and we are now very much in love. You and I are very competent, but we do not have the ruggedly male leadership qualities necessary to see this through. We need a strong man like Sir Matt to guide us in these difficult and subversive times.'

'You're kidding me, right?'

She stepped forward and hugged him tightly.

'My mind is made up. Sir Matt is the person best suited to lead the nation to a negotiated settlement with the Troll and Mighty Shandar. I also ask that you respect our views in this matter and not stand in the way of our happiness.'

And she smiled at me and biffed Sir Matt affectionately on the nose – which I have to say was so nauseating I actually felt the bile rising in my throat.

'But, but wait,' I managed to stammer, 'what about Subsection 12, Paragraph 9, Rule 9G of the *Rulebook of Rules about Ruling for Rulers*: "Males to become king if they marry heirs to the throne"?'

'What of it?' said the Princess. 'I think this is definitely man's work, and I will be a good, submissive wife and leave all decisions up to hubby – except choice of schools for the royal children, and those perilously difficult decisions over soft furnishings, curtains and banquet guest lists.'

I looked at Sir Matt, who was smiling at me.

'It's one of my faults,' he said. 'I just have far too many star qualities. Now, if you will excuse us?'

I didn't know quite what to do and suddenly felt very stupid. The curate in the oversized bishop's hat said: 'May I proceed?' to the couple, and they turned their backs on me. There was the sound of tutting from the twenty-six princesses who were all maids of honour in the front row, their faces an odd mix of jealousy and happiness, but mostly jealousy.

'Pssst!' came a voice from behind a column in the north aisle. It was Tiger, and I hurried across. He was standing with Once Magnificent Boo, and neither of them looked very happy.

'What the hell's going on?' I whispered when I

reached them. 'Has the Princess gone *completely* insane? I mean – marrying Grifflon? The man's a dangerous idiot.'

'Totally lost her mind, if you ask me,' said Tiger. 'None of us can understand it – and the Princess won't even see us to discuss it. More importantly, we got your snail. Is that true about Feldspar?'

'I'm afraid so, and Shandar is a Quarkbeast away from almost unlimited power. Can we talk somewhere else? If I have to listen to any more of this garbage I think I might actually throw up.'

Sir Matt Grifflon and the Princess were exchanging vows, and when I say 'exchanging' it sounded like it was all going Grifflon's way – lots of 'obeying husband' stuff and little or nothing in the other direction.

We made our exit from the cathedral, past the increasingly desperate commemorative plate sales-people, then went and sat in a small café opposite the John Nettles statue. We ordered three hot chocolates and a cinnamon bun each, and any 'bent or unwanted' cutlery for the Quarkbeast to chew on. I told them about Feldspar and the crew of the *Bellerophon*, and we held hands around the table and lowered our heads in respect of the loss. I then outlined briefly what had happened, about my meeting with Shandar, the Subterrain and the magma chamber.

'But aside from two full Dibble Jars,' I said, 'there's

not much else I gained – except that we got the Quorum power wrong: it's closer to 2^{63} TeraShandars – so long as all the Quarkbeasts are conjoined simultaneously.'

Boo gave a low whistle and raised her eyebrows.

'That's a seriously large amount of juice.'

There was a pause as our drinks arrived.

'Did Grifflon even do the task she set him?' I asked.

'Not at all,' said Tiger. 'Soon after you left Sir Matt requested an audience with her. Next thing we know, he's completely won her over.'

'A beguiling?' I asked, but Boo shook her head.

'There's not enough power around to change a mouse's mind from Cheddar to Brie, let alone the mind of someone as headstrong as the Princess. It all strikes me as completely out of character.'

I told them both I would speak to the Princess alone just in case there was a bigger plan to all this, and they told me that Sir Matt had taken over the running of the Human Resistance Movement, and would be acceding to all Shandar's demands – including the surrender of the Quarkbeast, which was to be deemed 'Royal Property' as soon as the nuptials were complete and he was King.

As if to confirm this, all the church bells in the city rang out to celebrate the marriage of Sir Matt and the Princess – or, as we should now style them: His Supreme Royal Majesty King Mathew of all the

Kingdoms, and his wife, Her Royal Highness Queen Shazine.

The bell on the door tinkled as Monty Vanguard walked in. He looked relieved to see us – but concerned, too.

'Another hot chocolate, please, Bessie,' said Tiger, 'and better make that another round of buns.'

'I've just heard from the newly established Royal Attorney General's[44] office,' said Monty as he sat down. 'Anyone considered disloyal to the King will be subject to arrest and imprisonment.'

'How do they define "disloyal"?' I asked.

'However they want,' said Monty. 'Full Price and Lady Mawgon told the Attorney General that their loyalty was to Court Mystician Jennifer Strange.'

'I'm guessing that was the wrong answer,' said Tiger.

'Correct,' replied Monty. 'They're both now in jail.'

There had been other changes, too. All the clerks and analysts working to find a solution to the Troll menace had been assigned to other duties and Colin's job as 'Minister for Good Ideas & Kingdom Unification' had been given to someone 'less scaly'. The fencers, marksmen and worriers had all been stripped of any power and relevance, and the only people united

---

[44] She was previously a scruffy solicitor who was fired for sloppy property conveyancing.

against the New Order and currently at liberty were Boo, Tiger, Monty, myself and Colin – and the 'at liberty' part might change any second, as Sir Matt – I couldn't bring myself to refer to him as 'King' – had commanded we attend a meeting in an hour.

'Where is Colin, by the way?' I asked.

'In mourning. He said he needed to fly out of sight of land and tread air for an hour or two to gather his thoughts and contemplate life as the only remaining Dragon.'

We fell silent for a moment.

'Monty,' said Boo, 'we made a mistake. The Quarkbeast mass conjoinment will liberate far more juice than we thought.'

'How . . . much more?'

'2^{63} TeraShandars.'

Boo had to repeat it.

'That's . . . that's more wizidrical energy than the world has seen since magic even *began*,' said Monty in a low voice.

'By a large margin,' said Boo.

'He wanted to achieve immortality when we spoke,' I said. 'D'you actually think he could?'

Monty thought about it carefully.

'He'd have to dump ARAMAIC and RUNIX spell languages and restart work on SIMSALLABIM.'

'I've never heard of that,' said Tiger.

'It's a radically different spell-code,' said Monty,

'that's been worked on sporadically down the centuries. It's essentially a self-learning artificially intelligent spell language where you tell it what you want to achieve, and it runs itself backwards to a workable spell.'

'That makes *anything* possible,' said Tiger.

'That's exactly what it means,' said Boo. 'With SIMSALLABIM up and running, all Shandar has to do is want something – and it shall become so.'

We talked on and I mentioned D'Argento's revelation that Shandar had undertaken a 'self-soulectomy'. This interested Boo and Monty, as a soul can't be destroyed outside of a host, and the freshly removed Better Angels of his Nature had to have been sealed in a porcelain jar and then hidden.

'How would we find them?' asked Tiger.

'Zambini was the finest proponent of finding lost things,' said Monty. 'In laboratory conditions he once located a lost sock seventy-six miles away buried under six inches of concrete. Mind you,' he said, 'that was twenty years ago when there was more crackle about.'

'Even if we found his Better Angels,' I said, 'what could we do with them?'

'I don't know,' said Boo. 'As you might imagine, soulectomies are quite rare – I'll have to look into it.'

We lapsed into silence after that, still unsure of Shandar's ultimate plan. They, like me, didn't really go for Shandar's 'Everything Project'. It was too noble. There *must* be something else. While we munched unhappily on the buns, half-expecting Sir Matt's guards to arrest us, my mind turned to other matters. Namely: how wrong I had been about the Princess. I felt not only annoyed, confused that she hadn't consulted me – but also hurt. We'd shared stuff, dangerous stuff, stuff that bonds warriors in battle – and you don't bin all that for a massive twit with a lantern jaw and a deep voice – with or without the impressive singing career.

I gave Monty and Boo the Dibble Jars full of crackle, and while I took another sip from my hot chocolate they said they'd see what could be done with them. Things had looked really bad this morning when I left, but right now, with an idiot in charge, a tyrant about to become all-powerful, and Feldspar gone, things looked a great deal worse.

King Mathew Speaks

His Supreme Royal Highness King Mathew of all the Kingdoms, defender of the free and rightful ruler of all that anyone might survey, anywhere, didn't waste much time once he had assumed power. He at once dissolved all Conclaves, cancelled all outstanding plans and strategies that the Princess or I might have instigated, and at once convened a King's Court which I, as Court Mystician, was invited to attend – but I suspected really only to be fired.

'Thank you all for gathering,' said King Mathew as soon as we were assembled in the Queens Hotel ballroom, 'and my wife the Queen and I thank you for the kind notes of congratulations on our nuptials and the many pledges of allegiance and IOUs regarding presents which we have seen fit to embrace rather than publicly ridicule, as we first thought we might.'

No one said anything, so he continued.

'I've only got a few things to say, and I shall be brief. Firstly, I am to wield absolute power in all the Kingdoms, and anyone who has not signed the book of allegiance in the foyer will be considered an enemy of the Crown. But, to show my caring nature, they shall not be executed, but banished: thrown forcibly across the Button Trench in the direction of the Trolls after being painted with gravy. My Queen, your Queen, the only queen in what I am now calling the *United Kingdoms*, is currently resting in her suite upstairs, and will not be troubling her tiny female brain on anything more onerous than domestic affairs – and has passed all her powers to me. Any promises you made to her are now mine, all loyalty granted to her is with me, any promises the Queen made to anyone else will be looked at on a case-by-case basis. Any questions?'

Again no one said anything.

'It's now Saturday evening, and the deal with Shandar will go ahead as planned on Monday at dawn. We have until then to find the Quarkbeast, muzzle it and have it ready for the handover. Anyone who tries to stop us in this endeavour will find their life and property forfeit.'

'I have a question,' I said.

'Ah,' he said, 'Court Mystician and ex-knight of the realm. My wife has told me that handing out honours willy-nilly was a grave mistake that has now been retracted. You should really say "Your Majesty" when you speak to me, but I'll settle for "Sire". Now, what is the question?'

'The Mighty Shandar cares nothing for humans or Trolls,' I said. 'After you hand over the Quarkbeast, Shandar will be more powerful than any sorcerer has ever been. The only course open to you right now is *not* to do what he asks and try to figure out his plan – and a way of stopping him.'

King Mathew seemed unimpressed.

'Thank you, Court Mystician, for your valuable input, but you are *totally* wrong. This Mighty Shandar seems a reasonable man. We will give him what he wants, and if he breaks his word then we will be in the same state as if he hadn't got rid of the Trolls. All that it will cost us is a Quarkbeast, which is no biggie – I never liked the mangy little cur anyway.'

'You have no idea the evil that you are tackling, Sire,' I said. 'He will—'

'Are you loyal?' he asked suddenly.

'I am loyal to the wishes of the Princess Shazine,' I said.

'And her wish is that I am in charge, Miss Strange. Are you loyal to me?'

'I am loyal . . . to a just belief.'

'I'll take that as a no. You are to relinquish the Quarkbeast to my care. This is the way you are to serve the Crown. Your tenure as Court Mystician ends now, and the position will not be filled until there is some sense of loyalty from those in the magic profession.'

'You're making a huge mist—'

'That's all agreed, then. Miss Strange, you have until midnight tonight to surrender the little beast, and if you refuse I shall have you executed. Following on from that, all members of your entourage will be asked, in alphabetical order, to reveal the whereabouts of the Quarkbeast – and if they refuse, they too will be executed. Are we clear?'

'Yes, Your Majesty,' I said as tartly as I could, and left the conference.

Tiger and Boo were waiting for me in the dining room. The King, never one to shy away from publicity, had called in the local TV station to broadcast his every move and so, he hoped, cement his legacy as a great statesman who saved the Kingdoms from the Troll.

'Well,' said Tiger as I sat down between him and Boo, 'that could have gone better. Does that mean I'm not an earl any more?'

'I think it does.'

'Good,' he said. 'I never much cared for it.'

I looked at my watch. Midnight was still two hours away and Shandar's deadline the day after tomorrow at dawn.

'What are we going to do?' asked Tiger.

'I'm not giving the Quarkbeast to anyone,' I said, 'but I also like my head where it is. Round up everyone loyal to our cause and we'll meet in the Globe Late

Night Scone Joint – there's a room at the back. Only take care: the King's spies will be everywhere, although they're unlikely to be any good.'

I got up.

'Where are you going?' asked Boo.

'To see the Princess.'

'You'll probably need this,' she said, and passed me a glass globe about the size of a ping-pong ball.

'It's a 20:1 Quickener,' she said. 'Use it wisely.'

Boo, although a poor sorcerer herself owing to the loss of her index fingers, could still perform a few remote enchantments. Storing spells in globes has a long tradition as they only require you to break them open and the latent spell is activated – and then does instantly what it was intended to do.

I took the elevator to the hotel's top floor, which had been requisitioned so the Royal Couple wouldn't have to rub shoulders with ordinary people. I was going to have to speak to the Princess directly to get my head around her sudden turnaround.

The doors opened to reveal Princess Jocaminca, who was now head lady-in-waiting, responsible for helping the royal mind navigate its way around clothes, banquets, who to be friends with, that sort of thing. The best curtain-makers of Penzance had all been summoned, along with the local Farrow & Ball paint stockists and palace-designers so the Princess could make far-ranging and important decisions regarding the decor of the Royal Palace, wherever they decided it should be built, and of what.

'The King has commanded you do not speak to our Queen,' growled Princess Jocaminca.

'I just want her to confirm to me her mind,' I said. 'Ten minutes.'

She raised an eyebrow provocatively – princesses do that – and four of Sir Matt Grifflon's bodyguards started moving towards me, the wiry one with the wide-set eyes at the front. I wasn't here to chat so crushed the globe containing the Quickener in the palm of my gloved hand. At that precise instant the world – with Princess Jocaminca and the guards in it – suddenly slowed down as time ground to a near-halt, the noise captured at that precise moment now a low hum. The Quickener was fixed at 20:1, so although it appeared to me as though everything had slowed down it was only because I had sped up: the next twenty seconds of my time would take a second of anyone else's. It was the first weaponised use of magic, and the first to be banned. Not by the military leaders, obviously – they loved it. Armed with a Quickener even the most ham-fisted of swordsmen could kill ten others as they hurtled through time. No, they were banned by wizards themselves, who, unlike scientists and physicists in particular, often gave scant thought to whether if such a thing could be done, it should.

The Quickener had other uses, too, and not just to escape bears, for which it was originally intended. Move fast and you became a blur. It's not invisibility but about as close as you are likely to get. I dashed forward as soon as time ground almost to a standstill and ran down the corridor, knowing that the only hint I was there at all would have been a faint smear of colour as I moved past. I had to waste precious seconds weaving past people and then more time figuring out which was the Royal Suite, but when I found it, I quickly darted through the open door and locked it behind me. Inside was another princess-now-lady-in-waiting so I swiftly bundled her stiff and unmoving form into the cupboard, just as the Quickener ran out, and time returned to normal. The sound rose from a low hum, and outside, the seagulls that had been frozen on the wing continued their flight. I walked through to the bathroom, where the Queen was in a large onyx tub, filled with milk.

'Your Majesty,' I said in greeting, 'goodness - where did you get that much rabbit's milk?'

'It's actually long-life milk from cartons,' she said, 'bought from the Co-op. But in times of need, we all have to slum it a little. Who are you and what do you want?'

'It's Jennifer Strange.'

'So it is,' she said, suddenly looking nervous. 'My mind is made up, so you'd better leave. Guards!'

It looked like her, but it patently wasn't. Boo had been unable to detect any spelling around her, so whatever was making the Princess act like an idiot, it wasn't magic. There was only one possible explanation.

'I get it,' I said, suddenly realising. 'Where did Sir Matt find you?'

'It's not Sir Matt, it's King Mathew,' she replied in a huffy tone, 'and I think you are going to come to a very sticky end if you don't reveal where your Quarkbeast is.'

'It *is* Sir Matt Grifflon,' I said. 'He only gets to be King if he marries the Princess, and that's not you, nor ever will or can be. So again: how did he find you?'

'Very astute,' said the impostor, realising that I would not be swayed. 'I made myself known to him as soon as I heard my sister's body complete with royal interloper had made it all the way to Cornwall. I had to make a few sacrifices of my own, you know, so don't say I don't deserve this.'

She raised her right arm from the bath of milk. The real Princess had lost her right hand to Hollow Men a couple of weeks before and the impostor had severed her own hand too – if she hadn't, she could never have hoped to pass for the Princess. Judging by the level of healing, it looked as though she had used a rapid-healing balm, and that would have cost the same as a house. No one had been doing those spells

206

for years, and the cost of old stock rose higher each year.

'That's commitment to a cause,' I said, 'and you're going to be sorely pissed off when you find it was all for nothing.'

But the fake princess seemed to be made of sterner stuff, and wasn't going to be easily beaten.

'No one will believe you,' she said in an arrogant tone, 'and no one will believe the Princess even if she can escape and presents herself at court. I am the Queen, my husband is the King, we have the authority and the government and the army – and that's really all that matters. Give up the Quarkbeast, Miss Strange – it's the only play you have left.'

'This isn't over,' I said, as the shouts from the princess in the cupboard had alerted the guards, who were now banging on the bedchamber door.

'It is for you,' said the pretend Princess, 'but I'll throw you a bone. Give us the Quarkbeast and I will have the King reinstate you as Court Mystician. It will be mostly ceremonial, but even so – it's a job. So be a good little girl and do as we ask, okay?'

I said nothing, and without having thought of an exit plan, simply lifted up the sash window and stepped outside onto the roof, meaning to find the fire escape and go down that way. I didn't have to as Colin was waiting for me, seated on the roof parapet and reading a copy of *Mortal Engines*.

'I'm so sorry about your brother,' I said. 'He gave his life to me and the cause.'

'It's a worthy cause, Jen,' he said, wedging the book behind his ear. 'It's up to us to ensure his sacrifice – and that of others – was not in vain. Boo said you could do with an escape plan. Where to?'

'Just fly,' I said, feeling tired and lost and without ideas. 'Take me to Land's End to see the moon reflected in the sea. After that I need to contact William of Anorak – and then we'll hit the meeting at the Globe.'

208

The Meeting

It was just past ten when I entered the private room upstairs at the Globe, a late-night scone bar at the top of Queen Street, a place that served top-quality scones until the clotted cream ran out or a fight started, the one generally leading to the other. Colin said that he was too big and obvious to be upstairs at the Globe, and that he would be sure to raise suspicions – so he'd perch on the roof and, if anyone asked, he'd tell them he was doing a bat survey.

I was late to the meeting as William of Anorak had taken some time to find the information I needed, and I wanted to wait until he confirmed what I already felt I knew. I greeted everyone as I entered, Exhorbitus hidden in a large sports bag. Molly was there, dressed in the trenchcoat and fedora, as was Tiger, Once Magnificent Boo, Monty Vanguard and General Worrier.

'I know this is the wrong thing to do,' said the worrier, chewing his knuckles nervously. 'I'm going to be executed for sedition for sure – but if I'm *not* here, you'll think me a loser and coward and a drip and that would be worse, I think.'

Molly was there because the peace accord she'd made with the Princess was now null and void, and she didn't believe the Princess would marry Sir Matt either. I found out later she had driven herself here, then dashed in a side entrance under cover of a large blanket. Tiger was sitting with her, trying to find out which particular shade of cerulean blue the Trolls hated.

'How about this one?' said Tiger, showing Molly a Dulux colour swatch.

'Nope,' said the Troll.

'What about this?' he asked, showing her another with several subtly different shades upon it. 'Anything here you find even mildly offensive?'

'Nothing at all,' she said. 'In fact, I think I'd quite like the spare cave decked out in something like that.'

'How's it going?' I asked.

'Not very well,' he said. 'We've been through the whole Dulux catalogue, all of the Humbrol enamels, the Crown line, Revell, Tamiya, Little Greene and even Farrow & Ball, where we thought it might be something between "Inspid Blueberry" and "Choking Zebra".'

'Are those actually colours?'

'I don't think so. Tomorrow we're going to go through the Pantone colour range.'

'Keep at it. Hello, everyone. Guess who I found taking a bath of UHT milk in the Royal Bathtub?'

'*Identical sister?*' said Monty once I'd explained who the impostor was. 'How did Grifflon find her?'

'I think she found him,' I said. 'She strikes me as a particularly nasty piece of work. I just phoned William of Anorak, who did a quick search and found that her name's Betty Scrubb. Unlike her sister Laura, who was a Royal Dog Mess Removal Operative Third Class, Betty has been in and out of juvenile detention her entire life. Last time was for fraud, so a seasoned liar. The thing is, since the original Princess was body-swapped and the impostor had her hand removed and balm-healed, there's no foolproof test to tell who is and who isn't the real Princess, and while I could vouch for her as I did with the princesses, I'm not sure anyone is going to listen to what I have to say this time around.'

'It's not over yet,' said Tiger, punctuating the silence that followed.

'True,' I said. 'Thank you, Tiger. The situation is worse than it's ever been, but it's not hopeless. There are thirty-two hours until the Trolls cross the Button Trench, and we need to use that time productively. We need to find the true Princess, figure out a foolproof way of unmasking the impostor, de-king Sir Matt, get the Princess back on the throne, then defeat the Mighty Shandar and the Trolls. So, any ideas?'

'Is "de-king" a word?' asked the Troll.

'It is now.'

'We need to find when and where they were switched,' said Tiger, 'and see if that affords us any clues as to where she is now.'

I thought for a moment.

'We need . . . a group of people who will be so worried about making a mistake and ruining everything that they *won't* make any mistakes at all. We're going to weaponise fretting – but in a positive way.'

'Oh, blast,' said General Worrier, 'that's me and my team, isn't it? Well, okay, we'll give it our very best but don't yell at us all if we fail – we'll be too busy, anyway, sitting in a dark room and staring at the wall gently weeping to ourselves, crushed inside.'

'That's the spirit, General. Better get on to it. Find out where the Princess is for us.'

He sighed and gathered up his notebooks. With an army of terrible worriers desperate not to ruin everything, they were, oddly enough, highly motivated to do everything correctly. General Worrier opened the door to leave and Molly gave out a sharp cry. She held her head, the pain manifesting itself in a muscle spasm that resulted in a narrow cleft that ran vertically down her forehead.

'Close the door!' she yelled, and Tiger complied; the pain abruptly ceased.

'The doors must be open all the way to the street,' she said. 'I like my spaces small but also unbounded. You wouldn't like me if I came over all expansive.'

She then looked sheepish, mumbled an apology and the conversation switched again to what I'd seen at Shandar's Tower of Knowledge.

'Eternal life is probably the biggest bribe given to anyone, ever,' remarked Boo.

'It's not likely he'll deliver,' I said. 'He'll offer anything to get what he wants to fulfil his plans — whatever they are.'

'Speaking of which,' said Boo, 'Princess Jocaminca found a fantasy author before she became a fake queen's lady-in-waiting. He might be able to come up with something that's bigger and bolder than anything we can dream up.'

'What have we to lose?' I said in a desultory tone. 'Better bring him in.'

Tiger went out and came back a few minutes later with a middle-aged man dressed in chinos and a shirt. He looked around the room at everyone in turn, seeming astonished to be there.

'Goodness,' he said finally, 'is that a Troll?'

'Thank you,' said Molly in a huffy tone, 'for that piece of stereotyping. I would have preferred: "Oh, look there's a brave member of the resistance".'

'But you *are* a Troll,' said Tiger.

'Yes, that's true, but I'm more than *just* a Troll.'

'So,' said Boo to the author, 'what sort of stuff do you write? Science fiction?'

'More science *fantasy*,' said the author, who then

added, since we all looked a little blank, 'It's sort of "*impossible* worlds made real", rather than "*improbable* worlds made real".'

'I'm not sure I see the distinction,' said Boo, 'but then I'm not a big reader.'

'Me neither,' I said, 'but look, we need a fantasist to come up with a scenario that would fit the facts we know, but it's got to be bigger and bolder than we could dream up.'

'I'm not sure that makes much sense,' said the author, still confused, 'but I'll give it a whirl.'

'Wait a moment,' said Boo, 'we need to make sure you're up to the task. Tell us a weird idea you've come up with that's *totally* out there.'

'Well,' said the author, 'I made George Formby president-for-life of Great Britain.'

'Who's George Formby?' asked Tiger.

'What's Great Britain?' asked Boo.

'Okay,' he said, 'here's another: a book about Humpty Dumpty as a police procedural.'

'I think that's been done,' said the Troll. 'Everyone's always retelling nursery rhymes. I mean, it's not a massive stretch, is it?'

'How about a social order based wholly on the strength of your colour vision?'

'Better,' I said. 'is there a sequel?'

'Don't you start. I also wrote a thriller set in a world in which humans have always hibernated.'

'I like that idea,' said Tiger. 'What are you working on at the moment?'

'The last book in a series for children.'

'How does it turn out?'

He looked down.

'I'm only on page 215 so I'm not quite sure – but I think it all works out okay.'

'What were you looking at just now,' asked Tiger suspiciously, 'when you looked down?'

'Nothing.'

Everyone fell silent as we all contemplated the author, who started to fiddle with the keys in his pocket, and looked at the four walls nervously, as though they might be appearing to move or something. But since we had nothing to lose we asked him to sit down and then explained everything we knew about the Mighty Shandar, and when we had finished he looked at us long and hard.

'World domination?' he said.

'We can all think of *that*,' said Tiger. 'It's got to be much bigger and bolder than that.'

'How much bolder?' asked the author, an odd gleam in his eye.

'A *lot*,' said Boo.

'How about this, then,' he said. 'Shandar's not after world domination, he's after *galactic* domination. He doesn't want to be *a* leader, he wants to be *the* leader: God-Emperor of the Universe, with a thousand star systems quaking in terror at the mere mention of his name.'

'I would not have thought of that,' said Tiger.

'Me neither,' said Boo.

'There's a universe?' said Molly.

'Anything else?' I asked.

'He will need to launch his bid for galactic domination from here on Earth,' said the author, starting to get quite enthusiastic, 'and to travel the vast distances demanded by his megalomaniacal ambitions, he will need to be able to manipulate the very fabric of spacetime. To do that he will require not two raised to the power of sixty-three TeraShandars, but two raised to the power of eighty – or more. He'll get that by siphoning off the energy of the sun itself, and transform all that thermal energy into wizidrical power by the combined emotional outpouring of billions of terrified people crying out for him to spare them from annihilation.'

'Woah,' said Tiger, 'you think—'

'Hang on,' said the author, 'there's more. If all goes according to Shandar's plan, this time next month he will not be mighty or magnificent, but *Eternally Fabulous*, with power to control matter, energy, physical laws, light, distance – even time. Soon, entire star systems will quake in fear and plead for mercy as news of his awesome power spreads throughout the galaxy, bringing terror and destruction before it, while in his wake the Earth will be left a cold cinder drifting in space, devoid of all life.'

'Well,' I said, 'that's not—'

'Wait a moment,' said the author, '*still* more. We are on the very dawn of a new age of evil that will spread misery and fear to the very farthest corners of the galaxy. Defeating him isn't a global imperative, it's a *galactic* imperative. The freedom and wellbeing of the galaxy and everything in it rest squarely on your shoulders.'

There was a pause.

'Okay,' he said, 'I'm done.'

'Wow,' said Boo, punctuating the silence that followed, 'that *is* bigger and bolder than anything I could think of. Possible?'

'He's been planning it for over three centuries,' I said, 'so yes. Monty?'

'Harnessing the power of the sun would give him massive quantities of power – and given the number of suns in the galaxy, he can just harvest another as soon as his power wanes. But travelling to another star system? Really?'

'Eternal life to enjoy the bounteous fruits of his own megalomania would be pretty pointless if you couldn't move from sun to sun as they grew old and winked out,' observed Tiger. 'It's true: however bad he is right now, that will appear as nothing when he spreads his evil plans across the galaxy.'

'Was that helpful?' asked the author.

'It's certainly something to build on,' I said, suddenly realising that this whole deal was way bigger than the UnUnited Kingdoms or even the planet. 'If the rest of the world knows he can't be trusted, we might have powerful allies.'

'Glad to be of use,' said the author. 'Anything else you need me for?'

I told him there wasn't and asked him whether there was anything he wanted.

'I could chronicle your adventures,' he said in a hopeful sort of voice.

'A plate of chips was more what I had in mind,' I said. 'We've got a tab down at the bar.'

'Oh,' said the author, 'right.'

And he went out.

'That was all a bit far-fetched,' said Tiger.

'On the contrary,' I said, 'it explains the Tower of Knowledge and everything he is placing within it. Stores, furniture, art, books, DVDs of almost everything. It also explains the internal cross-bracing of the structure and the sealed windows. It's not his citadel, his fortress, his hideout: it's his eternal transport to the stars.'

'Criss-crossing the galaxy for eternity in a full-size replica of the Chrysler Building?' breathed Monty in wonderment. 'I can't condone it, but that is kind of classy.'

We all fell silent, contemplating the news.

'Now what?' said Tiger as we heard the cathedral clock striking eleven. 'We're meant to be surrendering the Quarkbeast at midnight.'

'Not going to happen. Boo, Monty, what do you make of this?'

I took the photograph out of my pocket, the one I had found in the glovebox of the Volkswagen, of me as a baby in the arms of Zambini with Mother Zenobia close by, the Quarkbeast at Zambini's feet. Everyone who hadn't seen it moved closer to get a better look.

'There's a child on the back seat,' said Tiger. 'You can see her hand and the top of her head.'

'This photo was revealed to me only yesterday,' I said. 'Zambini and Mother Zenobia never told me the truth as to who I am and why I was left at the orphanage.'

I turned the picture over and showed them where 'The Assetts' was written in pencil.

'He spelt "assets" wrongly,' said Molly.

'It doesn't matter. Zambini wanted me to see this, so I need to find out more. I'm thinking the Quarkbeast and I are pivotal in defeating Shandar. But how are we assets, and what do we do?'

'You need to ask Mother Zenobia,' said Boo.

'If she survived the Troll invasion,' added Tiger.

'Is she old?' asked Molly.

I nodded.

'Then she probably did,' said the Troll. 'Humans get

very stringy and inedible anywhere past fifty years old. There *are* recipes, but they generally revolve around extended boiling and an over-reliance on seasoning, so are rarely worth the trouble.'

We all stared at her.

'I've heard,' she added hastily.

'Good to know,' I said, looking at my watch. 'If I'm still alive in half an hour, I'll figure a way to get to what remains of the orphanage and ask her. Is there anything else to discuss?'

'Yes,' said Monty, 'the Trolls. Since they managed to overrun the UnUnited Kingdoms in a little under ten days with consummate ease – why did they never do it before?'

'Molly?' I said.

The Troll thought for a moment, trying to tap her Hive Memory for any clues.

'I think we *did* try it before,' she said, 'but it didn't work out because we didn't have the numbers.'

'You've got them now,' said Tiger, 'there are millions of you.'

'There aren't millions of *me*,' said Molly. 'I'm one of a kind.'

'I meant millions of Trolls,' said Tiger.

'Oh,' said Molly, 'right.'

Monty stared at the Troll and stroked his moustache carefully, then thought of something.

'I've an idea,' he said, 'but I'll need to research

previous Troll invasions to try and find a weakness. Molly, would you help me out?'

She said she would be delighted, so long as there was a moussaka in the offing and there was no outdoors or buttons or cerulean blue, and once this was all agreed, I took a deep breath.

'Okay, time to go and face the music. Tiger, would you fetch Kevin Zip and ask him to join us? We'll be in the ballroom.'

'Is there any point?' asked Tiger. 'If he's accurately predicting the near future, he'll be there when we arrive.'

I said goodbye to everyone and thanked them, told them to carry on the struggle without me if I didn't make it back, and departed with Tiger, because he said he wouldn't leave my side even if I yelled at him, and I wasn't going to do that.

The Quarkbeast, sensing something important was going down, followed us like a lamb.

Kevin sees it all

I wasn't going to be a coward and have any of Sir Matt's[45] goons searching for me, so I told the receptionist at the hotel I would be in the ballroom. The moonlight spilled into the dark room as I entered, the Quarkbeast and Tiger at my side. True to form, Kevin Zip was already there, waiting for us.

'Hello,' he said, 'I have an idea you need me here with you.'

'Do you know why?' I asked.

He smiled.

'It'll come to me.'

I turned to Tiger.

'Look,' I said, 'if I don't last the hour, you must give up the Quarkbeast. Just pop him behind the cold water tank in the loft and say it will take twenty-four hours to find him. With a bit of luck, the worriers will have found the real Princess by then, and we can have an adult in power again.'

'But—'

---

[45] I'm still not referring to Sir Matt Grifflon as 'King'.

'Don't argue with me on this, Tiger.'

He fell silent and I took off my coat, pulled on my leather gloves, drew out Exhorbitus and held the blade in front of me. It glowed a soft blue in the darkness, and faint sparkles moved across its highly polished surface.

'You accept with gratitude,' said Kevin to Tiger.

'What do I accept with gratitude?'

'You'll find out.'

'Tiger,' I said, 'I'm officially making you the Last Dragonslayer's apprentice, so Exhorbitus will be yours when I'm gone.'

Exhorbitus had a unique anti-theft device: if anyone but a Dragonslayer or their apprentice touched it, they were vaporised. As my apprentice, Tiger would be the only person able to touch it.

He looked at Kevin Zip, then me and said: 'I accept with gratitude.'

'And Tiger?' I said.

'Yes?'

'Thanks for everything.'

'Jen, there must be another . . .'

He didn't get to finish as five of Sir Matt's goons walked in. Leading them was the dangerous-looking wiry fighter with the wide-set eyes who didn't look as though he'd be easily swayed by reason or threats. The Quarkbeast was sitting behind me, head cocked on one side, watching the proceedings.

'Surrender the beast, Miss Strange,' said the wiry fighter. He had two cutlasses, their scabbards crisscrossed upon his chest. They were short weapons, but deadly when used in pairs at close quarters: like being attacked with a pair of very large scissors.

'You know what will happen if you . . .'

His voice had trailed off because Kevin Zip had spoken his *very same words at precisely the same time.*

'My . . . my argument is not with you, Zip.'

Kevin, once again, said the words at precisely the same time, even with the hesitation. Zip's maximum Prediction Event Horizon had been reducing since the HENRY took hold, which made his short-term future prediction astonishingly precise. In the brief pause that followed, I took up a defensive position and held Exhorbitus at readiness. I had sliced the top of the postbox earlier, so they knew what I and the sword could do.

'Step aside,' said the wiry man, 'or by order of the King your life is forfeit – *will you stop doing that?*'

He was talking to Kevin, who was still mirroring his speech – even the pauses and the 'will you stop doing that?'.

'I can see events unfolding,' said Kevin in a soft voice, 'but the future is not fixed, and you can change it.'

'Tricks,' said the wide-spaced-eye man, 'worthy only of a stage magician.'

Kevin said this with him too, also in unison. It was very clear to all present that this was *not* a trick, and there was an uneasy shuffling among the small group of men.

'The King also stated,' continued the wiry man to me, still trying very hard to ignore Kevin's word-mirroring, 'that your pretty young visage be untouched, so all would recognise your head when displayed on a pole. Now, where is the beast?'

I said nothing. This was Kevin's show.

'This is how it's going to turn out,' said Kevin, pointing a finger at the wiry man. 'You will make the first move towards Jennifer and be the first one dead. The next to die will be the left-handed guy on the right, followed by the two dressed in leather, who will both be cleaved in half with one swipe. The tall one at the back has a kindly face, so Jennifer will spare him – he will simply have his sword arm sliced off cleanly at the shoulder.'

'What about me?' said a young man probably no older than eighteen, who was at the back.

'When you see the first man die, you will wet yourself, drop your sword and run.'

They all exchanged nervous glances; it seemed a plausible scenario. The wiry warrior with the wide-set eyes took a deep breath.

'Perhaps that is so, but I have my orders, and I will carry them out. Others will follow when I am dead, and we *will* have the Beast, irrespective of blood spilt. Your call.'

I respected him for his words. Not only because he was taking us all seriously, but because he knew this might be the final minute of his life, and however misguided the order that brought him here, he was willing to carry it out. He had his ideology, and I had mine – and we would both defend it with our lives. He and I were true warriors both.

'You brought this fight to me,' I said. 'Leave now and you can save yourselves.'

'Our positions are clear,' said the wiry man. 'All that remains is the outcome.'

There was silence in the ballroom. No one stirred, and I felt a deep inner calm fall across me, for Kevin had already given me the moves I was to make. But then, I had a doubt – my assailants would *also* know my moves, and anyway, we were now past Zip's Prediction Horizon. What he had seen had not come to pass. I stared into the wide-set eyes of the warrior, and—

'Quark.'

The Quarkbeast had moved between us and Sir Matt's men and was staring at me with his large mauve eyes while wagging his tail in a doleful manner. I suddenly felt that he was telling me everything was okay, and that he'd take it from here.

'What?' I said, with a vague sense that this was

the Quarkbeast speaking through the Mysterious X, and that he wanted to give himself up to avoid bloodshed.

'You're sure?' I asked as the King's guards exchanged nervous glances.

'The Quarkbeast has told me he is surrendering to you,' I said, and the Quarkbeast wagged its tail vigorously. The junior member, the one who would have wet himself and run, looked at the leader, who nodded, and the lad stepped forward and nervously placed a collar on the Quarkbeast. But instead of allowing himself to be led out, the Beast walked to a corner of the ballroom and sat down, dragging his would-be keeper along the floor behind him. Quarkbeasts are as strong as they are stubborn.

'I think the Quarkbeast has decided that this is where he would like to be kept,' I said, inwardly applauding the Quarkbeast's guile and quick thinking, and thanking the Mysterious X for being the vector of communication, 'until he is handed over.'

'No,' said the wiry fighter, 'my orders are for him to be imprison—'

He was interrupted by one of the Quarkbeast's razor-sharp scales, which had flown off his back with an explosive report and embedded itself with a *thunk* in a painting of Isambard Kingdom Brunel, who although not actually Cornish, was thought engineery enough to be given honourable citizenship.

The wiry servant of Sir Matt stared at the Quarkbeast's carbide-tipped scale, which was stuck right in the centre of Brunel's forehead, then at me, then tipped his head in respect.

'This is a favourable outcome, Miss Strange. I shall report to the King that we have the Beast in custody.'

'He likes to chew anything metallic,' I said as we turned to leave, 'only not lead as it gets stuck between his teeth – and cobalt, which gives him the runs. He won't harm you, and he's fond of chess, so long as you play it without the knights. He doesn't like knights.'

'Who does?' said Tiger, and he and Kevin followed me out of the ballroom, the guards busying themselves with 'guarding' the Quarkbeast.

'Thank you, Kevin,' I said once we were out of earshot. 'I think you just saved those men's lives.'

'None of those men would have suffered so much as a cut,' he replied. 'I didn't foresee any of that stuff. Your shoelace is undone. With your first swipe you would have lost your footing and been killed by the wiry guy at the front. After that it would have been Tiger, then me.'

I looked down at my shoelace, which was indeed undone.

'You lied about what you could see?'

'The future is soft and pliable, Jen,' said Kevin with a smile, 'but we do what we can to guide ourselves towards positive outcomes. But I only bought us time. It was the Quarkbeast who saved our lives.' He smiled again. 'Well, that's me for now. If I hurry I've got time to catch *Back to the Future III* at the cinema.'

'There's a brilliant bit where the train time machine converts into a flying vehicle,' said Tiger, then: 'Oh, sorry, that was a bit of a spoiler.'

'It's okay,' said Kevin, patting him on the shoulder, 'when you can see the future, all you ever get are spoilers.'

We watched him walk away.

'Well,' said Tiger, 'what do we do now?'

'You do what you want,' I said. 'I've had about the longest day of my life. I will offer prayers for Feldspar and the crew of the *Bellerophon*, then I will be spark out asleep – hopefully for a good eight hours.'

The Worriers

I had a room on the second floor facing the sea, and slept through five storms, woke for the sixth, then was asleep for the next two. I had balanced a bottle on the doorknob to alert me in case anyone attempted to get in, but no one did.

And I dreamed.

I was back on the control deck of the Mighty Shandar's Tower of Knowledge. The Hollow string quartet were playing a piece by Pachelbel, and from the duct that would funnel the energy from the conjoining Quarkbeasts I could hear the distant murmur of the other Hollow Men and Women working far below, packing the treasures and necessities for Shandar's journey across an eternity of time and space. Shandar was sitting in a leather armchair and thumbing through a book of spells. Dreams were often a method of communication from sorcerers, so I assumed this was one of those, and waited to see what he had to say.

'Ah,' he said, lowering the book, 'Jennifer. The Quarkbeast is captured, my friends tell me. You shall be granted safe conduct to bring the little beast to me. It is important you are here to witness the conjoinment.'

'Delivering the Quarkbeast was never part of the deal.'

'The deal has changed.'

'We know of your plan,' I said. 'You would destroy the Earth and everything on it to pursue your self-serving megalomaniacal ambitions?'

He wagged a slender index finger at me.

'Total knowledge is a noble pursuit, and nobility always exacts a price. So what if I suck the life out of a few suns and lay waste to a star system or two? There are billions upon billions of stars out there, and I'm sure the universe can spare a dozen or so. No one will miss the Earth. You know what? I don't think anyone even *knows* about the Earth.'

'I know about the Earth,' I said. 'Agreed, it may have a few unresolved issues, but it is also full of beauty, and kindness, and love.'

'And hate,' he said, 'and cruelty, and hunger.'

'It's a work in progress,' I replied, 'and with optimism, diligence and wise guidance we may get to improve ourselves.'

'Wise guidance? From whom?'

'From people like the Princess.'

'Pah!' he said. 'Six months of absolute power and even your little well-meaning chum will start building bronze statues to herself and have her underlings avert their eyes in her presence. Humans are horribly flawed, and prone to morbid self-aggrandisement with even a sniff of power. You will miss nothing when you join me on this journey.'

'I shall not join you.'

'It is my wish,' he said evenly. 'You will not defy me.'

'I would sooner die.'

I stood up to yell, but in doing so I woke myself up, and I was back in my room, the day outside new and grey and drizzly with patches of sleet, sun, hail and snow. Someone was tapping on my door. It was Tiger.

'I heard some shouting,' he said as soon as I opened the door. 'Bad dream?'

'Nope – a mental leap to Shandar's Tower. He's going to ask me to deliver the Quarkbeast personally, and wants me to accompany him on his journey to the stars.'

'What is it with you and him?'

'I don't know. Were you sleeping outside my door?'

'I *always* sleep outside your door. I've got General Worrier here. He wants to talk to you about the Princess.'

The time was 6 a.m. General Worrier had his second-in-command, Major Worrier, with him, plus a half-dozen of his trusted *fretteratti*,[46] but they waited

---

[46] From the Italian slang for a group of people who constantly worry. Pronounced: 'fret-a-rar-tee'.

outside once they'd apologised profusely for getting in the way and hoped 'I was not inconvenienced', and told me how they 'could never forgive themselves if I was'.

'Because we were so terrified of disappointing you,' said the general, perching on the dressing table and looking at his notes, 'we set about organising ourselves into a tiered command structure so orders could be spread quickly and fast. With the thousand worriers divided into two cohorts commanded by five highly strung centurions each in charge of one hundred overwrought neurotics to recheck each others' work, we had enough worriers to make a huge number of inquiries, filter them for relevance, then pass all pertinent information on to a centralised committee to be flustered and fretted over minutely before being passed on to me.'

'It sounds super-geeky,' I said. 'I love it. Then what?'

'No one knows when the Princess was switched, but since the impostor couldn't have made it across the Button Trench due to the number of Trolls in attendance, she must either have flown here or arrived by boat.'

'Makes sense.'

'Right. So we sent our field agents off to knock on the doors of freight managers, shipping agents and immigration officials at the docks and Penzance International Airport, to see what we could find out.'

'Surely no one's keeping records in a time of war?'

'These are *bureaucropaths*,' said General Worrier. 'Bureaucrats who get all obsessive about procedure. Like us, they worry about everything. Whether the records are in triplicate, whether a form hasn't been filled in, whether there is a box which hasn't been ticked. Who arrived, are they here, and if they left, then when, and how. No, the records are one hundred per cent complete. Better still, they think Matt Grifflon is a total idiot, and are much bigger fans of you and the Princess. And this is what we came up with.'

He placed a photocopied passenger manifest on the table.

'She flew in yesterday morning, part of a refugee flight set up for people on the Eat List – they run mercy dashes from Bodmin, a place not yet overrun with Trolls. She came in under her own name: Betty Scrubb, aged sixteen. Nationality: Snoddian.'

He placed another photocopy on the table, this time of her identity card. The likeness to the Princess was uncanny.

'So what happened then?'

'Nothing. She got the bus into St Ives, and the trail goes cold.'

'I really hope there's more.'

General Worrier grinned broadly.

'And how. Checking the passenger manifests again, someone named Betty Scrubb flew out of Penzance

International Airport just before the nuptials yesterday afternoon. We had a word with the immigration officer and he said she appeared to be "in a bit of daze".'

'Drugged?'

'Most likely. But get this: her travelling partners were four of Sir Matt Grifflon's personal bodyguards. I ran their IDs and they must have been hand-picked to defend the Princess against rescue: all of them were convicted for extreme violence and murder, and each time pardoned by Sir Matt or his father, Lord Grifflon of Bedwyn.[47]'

'What was their onward destination?'

'The Isles of Scilly,' he said, 'about twenty miles west of here. As soon as the aircraft departed, "King" Mathew annexed the entire Isles of Scilly as a no-fly zone, and requisitioned all the castles there for his own use.'

He flicked over the pages of a notebook.

'After analysing all the potential castles for princess-imprisoning and grading them on suitability, isolation, lofty towers and dampness, we came up with this as the most likely.'

He showed me a postcard of Cromwell Castle on the island of Tresco, a tall, cylindrical stone tower with

---

[47] Granting 'dodgy pardons' for cash was the sole form of income for the diminutive duchy, along with jam-making, and exorbitant tolls on a 126-foot stretch of the Kennet and Avon canal.

one entrance, six storeys and a single window high up under the eaves of a pointed roof. It was perfect for imprisoning a princess, which was not surprising, as imprisoning princesses at the top of tall towers was a mini-industry in itself, and there were several purpose-made towers dotted around the country which could be had at a very reasonable weekly rate.

I opened the window and called up to Colin, who was sitting on the roof above my bedroom. He stepped off into a near-silent hover, and came down to see me.

'Hello,' he said, scratching himself, 'this bat survey stuff is actually quite fun. I've seen fifty-eight pipistrelles, twelve lesser horseshoe, seventeen long-eared and a Daubenton's. How did the meeting go last night?'

I told him about Shandar's plans.

'Dear oh dear,' he said, 'humans are *so* tedious with their overinflated mission statements and unbridled ambition. It would be better for all concerned to have more modest goals: like watching a sunset with friends, or making nourishing cabbage soup. They're much less harmful – and actually attainable. What can I do?'

I explained where we thought the Princess might be imprisoned.

'Ooooh,' he said excitedly, 'my first Princess-rescuing gig. If her guards try to stop me, can I vaporise them all with a scorching lungful of fire that leaves only a pile of carbonised bones, heat-distorted armour and the faint smell of a hog roast? I've always wanted to do that.'

'You . . . must use whatever force you feel is necessary to restore the true monarchy.'

'Good,' he said. 'I'll be off as soon as I've eaten seven cans of curried beans, nine cabbages, a dozen assorted fish-heads, four pints of soured cream and six dozen slightly-off eggs.'

I didn't need to ask why. A Dragon's fiery breath is basically methane,[48] which is generated in a separate stomach, then lit by a pilot light in the gullet before being expelled out of a nostril or the mouth. I shut the bedroom window and hugged General Worrier warmly.

'Thank you,' I whispered in his ear. 'You and your team have done the Crown, the Kingdoms and the planet a great service and it shall not be forgotten.'

'Not if she isn't rescued, we're all vanquished or we got it wrong,' he said. 'Then we'll all go from hero to zero faster than you can whistle the Catalina Magdalena Hoopensteiner song.'

---

[48] It is actually a lot more complicated than this, as the methane is mixed with pure oxygen and hydrogen, which is generated in a gland above the Dragon's throat. The resultant mix, sustained for long enough, will indeed melt armour – yet if controlled precisely and directed at a frying pan, can be used to make a very refreshing omelette.

'Not in my eyes.'

I looked at my watch. I had full confidence in Colin's princess-rescuing abilities, but I needed to find out why Zambini left me in the orphanage as a baby and what made Shandar so fearful of me. I had to visit Mother Zenobia, but the orphanage was back in Herefordshire and a drive would be too long and perilous, so I removed from around my neck the Cloud Leviathan's tooth that had been fashioned into a whistle, and blew on it. I'd not done this before, and knew only that Ralph would hear and help me if I asked. That's the thing about Australopithecines who are the result of an Evolutionary Master Reset[49] – they can be trusted on a favour if things really get out of hand.

The Cloud Leviathan's whistle made no noise, but I knew it had been effective as I heard dogs whine and bark outside. Ralph could be anywhere, but a Leviathan was swift.

Once everyone had gone I had a quick bath, dressed and came downstairs for breakfast. The new Queen was lording it over everyone in the ballroom, which was now a VIP breakfast area. I heard later that she'd had the Rice Krispies checked to ensure they were all the same size, and the porridge rejected nine times

[49] Cloud Leviathans, Australopithecines, Ralph and Evolutionary Master Resets are all fully explained in *The Eye of Zoltar*.

until the consistency was just right. The King was also present with most of his retinue, including those who would have killed me the night before if Kevin's strategic fibbing hadn't won the day.

The royals all had a separate, screened-off area in which to eat, but I also noticed the Quarkbeast had not yet moved from the spot he had adopted the night before. I winked at him as I walked past, and he winked back. He hadn't been captured at all by the King's men. The most they could hope to boast was that they knew where he was.

I sat down at a table with Boo, Monty Vanguard and Tiger. Colin had left soon after his methane-inducing feast, and although the Isles of Scilly would only be twenty minutes' flight time away, he had not yet sent word of progress. It would be safe to assume he would observe the tower first in order to confirm she was there, numbers in the garrison, the Btu[50] value of a human, that sort of thing. He knew the import-ance of the mission, and I trusted he would be cautious, yet victorious.

'Where are Full Price and Lady Mawgon impris-oned?' I asked.

---

[50] The British Thermal Unit. Simply put, just how much energy would it take to carbonise a human? It's only of relevance to fire-breathing Dragons. I don't know where he went to get the figure.

'In the Cornwall Department of Corrections in St Ives,' said Boo.

'They'll be free as soon as we get the Princess back,' said Tiger.

'How do we prove she's the Princess?' asked Boo.

'We'll cross that bridge when we come to it. What about the Trolls, Monty? William of Anorak told me the way to defeat Trolls might have been forgotten down the years and scrubbed from the archives by Shandar, eager to make their defeat impossible.'

'I've been doing a bit of reading,' replied Monty, 'and trying to work the problem backwards to figure out a solution. We know that fighting the Troll was a big deal during the Roman invasion of Britain, and Emperor Hadrian defeated the Troll by banishing them beyond the wall that bears his name. Later on, Emperor Antonine established a new wall sixty miles to the north. As far as we know that was the last time the Trolls invaded – each subsequent war was the result of humans attacking *them*.'

'The Roman Troll Wars are well documented,' said Boo. 'Battle re-enactors seem to do little else. Where are you going with this?'

'This: that defeating Trolls seems to revolve around having not *one* Troll wall, but *two*. The Modern Troll Walls were built three hundred years ago, and only ten miles apart, far closer than the Roman walls.'

'Is this significant?' I asked.

'I think so. But there are rumours of *another* Troll War, this time in the eighth century when they were defeated by King Offa, who, and I quote, "Builded a great wall of the purpose of which to Troll numbers greatly reduced".'

'What does that mean?'

'I'm not sure. Records are scarce or missing. But there is another dyke or wall behind Offa's Dyke known as Wat's dyke, and, well, here we have the double wall thing again.'

We remained silent. There didn't really seem much to go on, but Monty wasn't finished. He showed me a map of the UnUnited Kingdoms with all the ditches and walls built in antiquity marked on them. There were a lot in number: some running east and west, others running north–south – even a canal network built in part by the Romans that was fed by seawater.

'I think these defences were built to get rid of the Trolls,' said Monty. 'All of them have been found to contain buttons in great quantities. It also says that Offa's Troll War was "faced with many hundreds of thousands of the sinful beast, but we did by way of clever enclosure, two days from start of attack to the last Troll banished".'

'That's seriously quick in terms of defeating Trolls,' said Tiger. 'You would have thought mopping up the stragglers would have taken a month on its own.'

'Excuse me,' said one of the waiters politely, 'there's

an Australopithecine outside wanting to speak to a Miss Strange.'

'Ah,' I said, 'that will be my ride. Anything else, Monty?'

'I'll know more when you return.'

'Good. Tiger? You up for a trip to Mother Zenobia's?'

'Do I get to ride on a Cloud Leviathan?'

'You do.'

'Then yes,' he said, 'I'm *totally* up for this.'

Cloud Leviathan

The Australopithecine had a flattish face, a protruding lower jaw, deep-set eyes that were a bright blue and was covered all over in short coarse hair. He wore no clothes at all except a set of very worn Converse All-Stars and his only possessions were carried in a large handbag that always sat in the crook of his arm. Handbag and shoes aside, he looked like the sort of hominid that is often featured on the cover of *National Geographic*, along with weddings in Azerbaijan and men on rickety ladders collecting honey.

Ralph had originally been *Homo sapiens* like us but when he suffered a potentially fatal self-induced overdose of magic, Perkins had to subject him to a Genetic Master Reset – that is, he had taken him back to the time when he wasn't really quite human – a sort of hominid on the cusp, just between ape and man. It had saved Ralph's life, but left him 1.6 million years behind in human development. And while Ralph had trouble remembering where he left stuff or following even the simplest episode of

243

Bergerac, he knew a whole bunch about friendship and loyalty – and could ride a Cloud Leviathan like a master.

'Hello, Ralph,' I said, and he grunted in reply.

Swapping gifts is usual when you meet an Australopithecine. He gave me a Hot Wheels VW Baja – one I did not yet have in my collection – and in return I gave him a pretty marble, six marshmallows and a box of matches, while Tiger offered up a half-used scented candle and a pack of Zetor Tractor Top Trumps, and received, in return, a mousetrap and a used Q-tip. Ralph examined his gifts very carefully and, when satisfied, popped them into his handbag.

'How are you?' I asked.

'Good I am me better never,' he said cheerfully, his sense of word order not yet fully evolved. He had trouble with grammar and making plans more than a week in advance, and would often steal stuff that he liked, not really understanding the concept of ownership. But all things considered, he did pretty well on a third of a modern human's brain capacity. To be honest, he fared a lot better than many humans I knew with a *full* brain capacity.

'What do, Jen?' said Ralph, and I outlined as best as I could where I needed to go. A modern map was useless as his more primitive visual cortex could not interpret the writing, so I handed him a picture map I'd drawn that gave him landmarks to follow all the way to Hereford, then a picture of the River Wye and the castle at Clifford, a stone's throw from the orphanage.

The small hominid nodded, then started to look around, calling the Leviathan by name – it seems he had dubbed it 'Basil'.

'How can he lose a Leviathan?' asked Tiger as Ralph ran around the place, covering the ground urgently like a demented spaniel trying to find a lost stick.

'A Leviathan has chameleonic skin,' I explained, 'to merge into the background. They can't be counted, studied or even hunted because . . . well, you can't see them.'

The Cloud Leviathan was also known as an 'AltiHippo' or 'Skywhale', the latter giving the origin of the name of their native country, Wales. The creature was a coach-sized flying mammal that had so far escaped scientific scrutiny. Kept aloft by a diet of gravity-defying Angel's Feathers and propelled by four massive flipper-like paddles on the side of its body, it had a large blunt head with a horizontal mouth that could swallow a thousand starlings at one go, or strip a single tree of apples during a high-speed swoop. The tail was long and ended in a small triple fluke which was used for directional purposes, as well as fanning itself in hot weather, and arranging things in its nest.

'What's that?' asked Molly, who was driving past in her Mini, the window open a crack so she could talk, the car's suspension sagging under her weight.

'An Australopithecine friend of mine named Ralph.'

'A what?'

'I'll explain later—'

'That's it!' said Molly, pointing at the hominid. 'That colour. *Yukky yukky yukky*. I'm off.'

And she drove rapidly off down the promenade in the direction of Newlyn without a backward glance. I looked at Ralph, who had painted his body with blue warpaint, presumably the shade of cerulean that Trolls don't like. I made a mental note to ask him for the recipe.

'I think I've found the Leviathan,' said Tiger, pointing at a huge eye that had opened up in an area of shimmering emptiness, and was staring at him with a great deal of interest.

We called Ralph over. He climbed onto its back and he too promptly disappeared until a hand popped out from behind the chameleonic skin and helped us aboard. On the back of the creature was a very comfortable wooden wheelhouse built of recycled wooden pallets and lined with Welsh blankets.

We were off as soon as Ralph had donned a small pillbox hat and completed a largely unintelligible flight safety announcement – it seemed that his previous life as a human had been spent travelling a lot by air, and this had filtered through as the only way one should fly. On the one-hour journey we were served lunch and a beverage, then persuaded to buy duty-free chocolate, a model of a Leviathan that seemed to be Lego but disappointingly wasn't, and then a couple of scratch cards which Ralph had designed himself. Tiger won a 'good-quality stick suitable for burning' and I won a large brass button.

The journey took us up the north coast of Cornwall and Devon, then cut across the Severn estuary after we had circled twice so Ralph could act out the over-water flight safety briefing. We made landfall at Cardiff over the deserted airport, then carried on north before eventually descending on the far side of the Black Mountains to Clifford, the castle prominent on the river, and home to the Blessed Ladies of the Lobster for over six centuries.

'Go round a couple of times, would you?' I asked, and Ralph gently prodded the Leviathan, which began a wide orbit around the orphanage, which we could see was besieged on all sides by Trolls. The nuns were putting up a spirited defence, and were holding them at bay.

'Okay,' I said, 'take us down into the courtyard.'

The Leviathan swung around elegantly, paused to swallow two geese that had the misfortune to be flying past at that moment, then settled onto the grass. Ralph passed me an Angel's Feather tied to a house brick.[51]

'Release when ready.'

Tiger and I disembarked and the Leviathan lifted off behind us. A nun came out to greet us. It was our old PE instructor Sister Asumpta, who had roundly terrified us as children. She recognised us both instantly.

'Ah!' she said. 'Jenny and Tiger. Come just in time to take over the batting, have you? We're six players down and on a sticky wicket.'

Sister Asumpta always talked in cricket metaphors, taught cricket, thought that cricket was the best game ever, and always carried a cricket bat to stop the orphans – and anyone else – getting out of hand. Tiger and I bowed and curtseyed without even thinking. I explained that I needed to talk to Mother Zenobia as she could have information that would help us defeat Shandar and the Trolls.

'Very well,' she said. 'I think you'll find her in the rose garden. Tiger, you're with me – see if we can bowl a googly and knock the Troll for six.'

Tiger, who feared Mother Zenobia more than

---

[51] A single average-sized Angel's Feather has an uplift of two pounds, just under that of the average house brick. You can find out more about the uplifting power of Angel's Feathers in *The Eye of Zoltar*.

potential death at the hands of a Troll, needed no second bidding and went off with Sister Asumpta while I headed into the rose garden, a small nuns-only sanctuary on the sunny side of the house. As I walked through the orphanage the smell of gruel, cheap sausages, bleach and freshly clipped ear came back in a rush. I'd spent twelve years of my life here, and although never luxurious, the time had been on the whole happy and not without comedy, as the nuns generally had a good sense of humour. I passed through the main hall where during lessons we had learned skills relevant to our expected station in life as part of the UnUnited Kingdoms Orphan-Based Economy. We learned about retail, hospitality, mining, heavy manufacturing and fast-food operations. I'd been a diligent student. Even today I'd easily be able to flip burgers, drive a heavy goods vehicle or even sand-cast an eighteen-ton ship's anchor. I thought it was luck that had sent me off to Kazam, but now it looked more like a plan.

'Ah!' said Mother Zenobia as I walked into the rose garden. 'Jennifer Strange. How are you, my girl?'

'I am well, Mother.'

She invited me to sit.

'I thought it was you. You are wearing two socks on your left foot, the change in your pocket is three shillings and ninepence plus a brass button, three washers and a glass bead – either green or blue.'

'Blue,' I said. 'That was quite remarkable.'

'Pah!' said Zenobia, but it *was* remarkable. Zenobia was over one hundred and twenty-six years old, and had been blind for so long that the skin had grown across her empty eye sockets. Her powers of hearing had developed into something indistinguishable from a super-power.

'The Trolls have come,' she said.

'Shandar helped them,' I told her, 'to divert the Kingdoms from upsetting his own plans.'

'Sneaky of him. You are part of the resistance down in Penzance, I hear?'

I told her that we had achieved very little, but suspected that Shandar had spelled a memory fog to occlude the knowledge of how to beat the Troll.

'I know little of Trolls,' said Zenobia. 'Tell me everything.'

So I explained about Shandar, how he wanted me to accompany him on his journey to the stars, his plan for galactic domination, the harvesting of the Quarkbeasts and even the power of the sun to further his ambitions – and how he was telling me it was all about the pursuit of knowledge, nothing more. As I spoke she nodded her head wisely, and when I had finished she went quiet for almost a minute. But when she spoke, it wasn't about Shandar.

'You did not come all this way to tell me that. You

found the photograph in the VW's glovebox, didn't you?'

Mother Zenobia was always astute.

'I did.'

'It was only a matter of time. You were not abandoned, you were not orphaned. We could have told you more, but we did not. We lied to you. But it was necessary. Are you angry?'

I thought for a moment.

'Yes,' I replied, truthfully enough.

Mother Zenobia took a deep breath.

'Twenty years ago Zambini came to me with evidence that Shandar was planning something of unprecedented evil. I agreed with his findings and we discussed countermeasures. Zambini and I could be the only ones who knew of our plan – even a whiff of our scheme against Shandar would have seen us both killed – and you, too.'

'Zambini was vanished,' I said. 'You think Shandar suspected something?'

She gave me a small and almost imperceptible smile.

'It's equally likely Zambini self-vanished so he couldn't reveal anything. He had . . . weaknesses that could be exploited. Me, I'm of sterner stuff. Luckily, your trajectory was already determined – when you saved the Dragons it would have been obvious to Shandar what you were, and just how difficult it would be for him to destroy you.'

'So who am I?' I asked.

Mother Zenobia took my hand in hers.

'To defeat the Mighty Shandar we needed to use something that he could never destroy, something that all tyrants come to fear and which eventually defeats them.'

'You know that superheroes aren't real, right?'

'I'm talking about their *weaknesses*. Whether it is incompetence, greed, stupidity, arrogance or, in Shandar's case, common decency.'

She let these words soak in for a moment.

'Shandar can't kill you, Jennifer, because, in part, *you are him.*'

I rubbed my temples, and stared at the ground, where I could see a small grasshopper rubbing its hind legs together. I closed my eyes and said in a quiet voice:

'I'm the Better Angels of his Nature, aren't I?'

'They are only a part of you,' said Zenobia. 'Zambini knew that Shandar dare not destroy a part of himself, so after four years of searching he found the Jar – and placed them in you.'

'Am I . . . real?' I asked.

'One hundred percent human. Zambini sourced you as a baby so I don't know who your parents were, but they were good people, who trusted Zambini when he said that the vessel for Shandar's rejected

Better Angels had to be someone with a Human Moral Worth Index that was off the scale – and you fitted the bill. Your parents understood that, shouldered the sorrow of your loss and gave you up, knowing that there was vital work for you to do in the Grand Scheme of Things.'

I was silent for a moment, trying to take this in. But I wasn't thinking about the parts of Shandar that were me, I was thinking about my parents, and that, given the finality of Zambini's farewell, I had missed any chance to find out who they were, and who I was.

'So why would Shandar want me on his journey to the stars?'

'Shandar knows that while utter ruthlessness is a useful skill for taking power,' said Mother Zenobia, 'it's overrated when it comes to *keeping* power. To maintain a sustainable dictatorship, he needs to harness those skills he foolishly cast out: tact, diplomacy, magnanimity, mercy. They can all be powerful weapons, especially when a thousand star systems are looking to marshal their forces against him. He knows you have them, and that without you and he seamlessly working together, his empire will barely last ten thousand years – it's amazing how quickly subjects tire of their tyrants once the mass murder begins. Tea?'

'What? Oh, yes, yes, I'd love a cup.'

A novice nun had been hovering at the entrance to the garden, and at a signal from Mother Zenobia trotted in with two cups of tea and a couple of Chelsea buns. I nibbled on one, and wrapped the other in a napkin for Ralph and Tiger. I sat and thought for a while, sipping my tea. Now my purpose was clear, everything suddenly seemed to shift into greater focus. My function in the Grand Scheme of Things was to defeat the most powerful sorcerer the planet had ever seen.

'So,' I said, 'I can get close to him, but how do I destroy him?'

'Ah,' said Zenobia, putting down her tea, 'our plan was not without a few wrinkles. We have engineered only an *opportunity* but without clear instructions. Your power and strength lie in your Moral Worth, courage and sense of intuitive action. Sometimes it's better not to think too much about something, and assistance, when times look bleak, can often come from unexpected quarters.'

'Zambini said something similar. What does that mean?'

She didn't answer, simply smiled, reached out for my hand again, and squeezed it.

'It is up to you now,' she said with a weak smile. 'Goodbye, Jennifer, I hope it all works out. You were our star orphan, my girl, there was none better.'

She took a deep breath.

'My work is now done. Will you stay with me until I am gone?'

'I would be honoured, ma'am.'

So I held her hand until her breathing stopped. I sat silent for a minute or two until her novice returned, then kissed her gently on the forehead and returned to the courtyard.

'What have you learned?' I asked, meeting up with Tiger ten minutes later.

'That Trolls don't like cricket bats,' he said, 'and nuns *really* frighten them, especially violent ones with a steely-eyed sense of purpose.'

'That's not a surprise to me.'

'Me neither. Sister Asumpta's platoon succeeded in corralling them into the walled garden. They caught eighteen of them that way, but most escaped almost immediately.'

'Why didn't the others free their comrades?' I asked.

'They're not sure.'

I untied the Angel's Feather from the house brick and let it go, whereupon it started to rise into the air, along with the faint sound of a chorus and a shaft of light. As good as his word, Ralph came down to pick us up and, five minutes later, we were heading southwest, back towards Cornwall and Penzance.

'What about you?' asked Tiger.

'I learned that when you have less than twenty years to defeat a plan over three hundred years in the making, it's okay to cut a few ethical corners.'

'Meaning?'

I explained what Zenobia had told me as we winged across the Severn estuary. He stared at me incredulously for a moment once I had finished.

'How do you feel about all that?' he asked at length.

'Calm,' I told him. 'Now my purpose in the Grand Scheme of Things has been revealed, everything is quite clear: I am to defeat Shandar. All other concerns are secondary. *Nothing else matters.*'

We were silent for a minute or two until we made landfall and then followed the North Devon coastline. Tiger asked me what our next plan of action would be.

'I guess we wait for events to unfold and act accordingly.'

'*That's* your plan?'

'You have a better one?'

'No.'

'Hang on,' I said as an idea popped into my head, 'Let's take a detour and see how Colin's getting along.'

I drew a rough map of the Isles of Scilly on a sheet of paper and showed it to Ralph.

'Ook,' he said as we sped low across Dartmoor, annoying a group of Trolls doing their mid-morning religious veneration.

Or perhaps they were stretching to alleviate indigestion. I don't know.

Colin and the Princess

Aside from the odd detour so the Leviathan could feed on a flock of seabirds, we made good time, and were soon winging our way across the sea between Cornwall and the Scillies, the white foam of the cresting waves almost close enough to touch, the smell of salt spray in our nostrils. Ralph was flying low because he didn't want us to be seen, and although the Leviathan's four paddles made à thumping noise as they rhythmically beat the air, they would hopefully be mistaken for the sound of the sea. We approached the island of Tresco from the north-east, crossed the rocky shore and then glided softly up the hill to alight at an abandoned castle, where we found Colin and one of Sir Matt Grifflon's men, bound up with rope. I recognised the latter as one of the minstrels, last seen at the Co-op. There was a walkie-talkie on the grass next to him.

'Hello!' said Colin cheerily. 'I was wondering when you'd arrive.'

The jar containing the Mysterious X was sitting on a low wall, the loose collection of charged particles that made up the nebulous entity firing like fireflies. Colin must have brought X with him in case he needed to communicate some ideas across the ether.

It was no coincidence I had turned up.

'Hello, Colin,' I said, 'that's Ralph. He's an Australopithecine.'

'Is he, by gum? Hello, Ralph. I like your handbag. I'm a Dragon.'

'Ook,' said Ralph politely, although clearly unimpressed. When you can ride a Leviathan, Dragons don't have quite so much 'wow' factor.

'So,' I said, getting straight down to business, 'do the Princess's kidnappers know you're here?'

'If they do they're pretending they don't,' he said. 'I was going to charge in and carbonise them all in a terrifying frenzy of barely concealed rage, reclaim the Princess and then fly away triumphantly across the sea like the badass Dragon I always wanted to be.'

'What happened?'

'My pilot light went out,' he said, opening his mouth wide so we could see. The small flame at the back of his gullet was indeed extinguished.

'So I overpowered Chuckles here, who was on guard duty, and tied him up. Actually, he tied himself up. They call in for an update every fifteen minutes. Do you have a lighter or a box of matches?'

Unfortunately, evolution had not so far supplied the Dragon with a natural method of reignition in the event of a pilot light outage, so they relied on either a man-made spark, a mouth full of flint, or a smouldering lightning-struck tree. Annoyingly, none of us had matches or a lighter, not even Ralph, who emptied his large handbag on the grass to check.

'Crumbs,' said Tiger, surveying the contents of the handbag, 'you've come tooled up, Ralph.'

He had indeed. Among the collection of gold doubloons, romantic novels, a half-finished sampler, a CD of Rick Astley's greatest hits and six fidget spinners was a large flintlock pistol complete with powder flask and six lead balls. Like most people, I wasn't fond of projectile weapons, and even knights and other warriors regarded them as 'the weapon of a snivelling coward', preferring instead to use a sword, rapier or dagger. If you were going to kill someone, the saying goes, 'only the worst cowards do it anonymously from a distance'.

'Can you load one of those?' I asked Tiger, and he nodded.

'Then do so – and make it a double charge.'

'High Ground, check in.'

The words had come from the two-way radio lying in the grass, and Colin picked it up. He placed it next to the captive guard's ear, and then a razor-sharp claw on his opposite temple.

'I lost my brother yesterday to this little caper,' said Colin in a low growl, 'so I'm feeling a little prickly right now. You're going to reply that everything's okay up here. Do you understand what I will do to you if you try to trick us?'

The minstrel nodded and Colin pressed the transmit button.

'All clear up here.'

'Well done,' said Colin, 'you have earned yourself another fifteen minutes of life.'

'Miss Strange?' said the captive in a plaintive sort of voice. 'Please tell your friend not to kill me.'

'He's a Dragon,' I said. 'They kind of make their own rules. Do you want a piece of advice?'

'That I should do what he says?'

'You learn quickly.'

We crawled to the edge of the derelict building on the hilltop, hid behind a stone arched doorway and peered down the slope opposite. Cromwell's tower was right on the edge of the sound between Bryher and Tresco, and looked about the most perfectly positioned tower for imprisoning a princess, and not by chance. Kidnapping royalty, as previously stated, was a growth industry in the UnUnited Kingdoms, not helped by the plethora of insurance companies which had sprung up to cover the cost of a safe return. In fact, some thought that the insurance companies might even have encouraged it, as pretty much every important person — and a few pets — were currently covered against ransoming.

'How many?' I asked as we peered at the tower.

'Five,' said Colin, 'all heavily armed. If I can't get my pilot light relit, I don't really rate our chances. My leathery hide will stop most small-arms fire, but not for ever. What's Tiger like in a fight?'

'What he lacks in stature he makes up for in ferocity – and he's good at throwing knives.'

'Could he kill someone?'

'I'm not sure,' I said, 'and I can't say whether I could either.'

It was a good point. Owing to the relentless depiction of death on TV, in theatre and the movies, killing someone often appears an easy choice and a satisfactory and acceptable way of dealing with conflict. I had serious doubts about this, and whether I could actually do so myself, if I had to.

'A negotiator would be handy right now,' said Tiger. Kidnapping princesses had generated a new profession: ransom negotiators and re-snatch squads would either work for the insurance company or even be employed by royal families in order to save losing their no-claims bonus.

'I'm not sure we have the time to find one,' said Colin. 'If we don't get the Princess back on the throne, Sir Matt will be giving the Quarkbeast to Shandar and negotiating with the Trolls.'

'You're right,' I said, 'this calls for more of an "on the hoof" plan. Tell me: how did you manage to talk to the Mysterious X when you wanted it to get in touch with me just now?'

'I imagined myself back in the lobby of Zambini Towers and then imagined myself yelling the words.'

'Think you can again?'

'Sure.'

A half-hour later I was approaching the tower on foot from along the access road. As I walked, I could see one of the guards step out of the front door to meet me.

'Far enough,' he said when I was about fifty yards distant. He was a nasty-looking character, the sort of person I would use to make sure a kidnapped princess stayed kidnapped. He had leathery skin, wore military armour, and had recently been knighted as a chevron was hastily sewn to his shoulder. A knight was the King's own guard and loyal to death – there would be little point in trying to talk him around.

'I've come for the Princess,' I said, 'and I will not leave without her.'

'Then you will not leave at all,' he said. 'The choice is yours.'

'We *will* retake the Princess,' I retorted. 'She *will* return to the throne, and she *will* show mercy to you and your garrison so long as you step away. Refuse, and your next thought will be as carbon. What say you?'

'I say that's bold talk coming from a little girl,' said

the knight, and drew a revolver from a holster by his side, cocked the hammer and fired. I heard the shot zip past my ear, nicking my earlobe. Either it was the wind or I was lucky; if he fired at me ninety-nine more times, I think he would have got me square between the eyes every time. He was surprised himself, and pulled back on the hammer once more to place a fresh round behind the hammer.

But at that moment there seemed to be a commotion at the very top of the tower. The knight did not move, well aware that a distraction is a popular ploy. He perhaps should have. As he fired the second shot I brought out Exhorbitus and held it in front of me, and felt the bullet ricochet off the burnished blade and fly over my left shoulder. He fired again and Exhorbitus moved again, instantly changing my pre-thought to action, and the third slug was deflected from my abdomen and pinged off the roadway behind me. It was the last shot he fired. Above him, a lit oil lamp came sailing out of the highest window, just a random thought planted in the Princess's head by the Mysterious X. Colin, waiting unseen on the back of the invisible Leviathan not sixty feet above the knight's head, caught the lamp in mid-air and in one seamless move ignited the gaseous breath from his methane-producing stomach, pointed himself vertically downwards and let fly with an oily burst of fire.

I'm not sure of the precise ratio of methane to hydrogen to oxygen in Dragon breath, but what I do know is that Colin's first attempt at carbonising went spectacularly well. In less than ten seconds the knight was transformed into a perfect charcoal facsimile of himself with every pore and eyelash preserved as a fragile carbon matrix that had once been complex life. As we watched, the blackened gun with the hand still attached fell to the ground, followed by the plates of armour in his coat. Within a few moments he had crumbled into a charcoal-coloured heap on the ground, only his lower legs remaining to show where he had once stood.

'Woah,' said Colin, who had alighted by my side. 'That was necessary and just, right?'

'He was trying to kill me,' I said. 'You did the right thing. Come on.'

We split left and right as a heavy machine gun opened up from a second-floor window, the bullet strikes chasing us along the ground as we ran for cover. But Ralph and the Leviathan's work was not yet done, and seemingly from nowhere a large hole was punched into the tower, the bulk of the Leviathan suddenly visible as its chameleonic skin rippled with the shock. The front of the tower fell out, the machine gun was silenced, and I scrambled over the rubble to enter the building. I sliced left and right as I entered the ground-floor room, removing the arm and a hand of two potential assailants. There was the crack of a weapon from upstairs and I rushed up the narrow staircase while Colin flew in a tight orbit around the outside, acting as top cover for the operation.

I reached the second storey, saw nothing remiss so moved to the top floor, where I found the last guard holding the Princess tightly from behind, a dagger at her throat. Tiger had got there ahead of me, and was pointing the old flintlock in their direction.

'Drop the dagger and you live,' said Tiger.

'You will kill me anyway,' said the guard, 'I have nothing to lose.'

'You have in your hands the true and just ruler of the Kingdoms,' said Tiger in an impressively calm voice. 'We need to vanquish the Trolls and the Mighty Shandar, but Sir Matt Grifflon has only his ambitions to think of. Before today, you were merely an unthinking drone of an arrogant despot. After today you will be the one that saw sense, the one who made all the difference. You need to do the right thing.'

The guard stared at Tiger, then at me, then dropped the dagger. The Princess wriggled out of his grasp, but did not run to join us – she jumped upon the fallen blade and held it to the guard's throat.

'You little fool,' said the Princess, who I could see had not been having the best of days, 'this is what happens to—'

'Wait!' yelled Tiger, who still had his weapon held

high. 'We don't kill unarmed prisoners, ma'am, that's not who we are.'

'A liar and a brigand and guilty of the highest treason,' the Princess shouted back. 'Who is to stop me?'

'I will,' said Tiger in a calm voice. 'Harm the prisoner and I will shoot you stone dead, Your Majesty.'

'Jennifer?' asked the Princess, who seemed to have reverted to her previous obnoxious self after all the stress. 'Will you let him do that?'

'I most assuredly will,' I replied. 'A queen who defies the law and murders one who has surrendered and offers no resistance is a queen who does not have the moral authority to rule. Do as Tiger says, Your Majesty.'

She looked at us both, and her face crumpled. The dagger fell to the ground for a second time, and we rushed forward to retrieve it.

'I'm sorry,' said the Princess, and collapsed in a heap.

'Thank you,' said the guard, moving to a corner of the room, breathing heavily, a slight nick on his throat where the dagger had drawn a little blood.

'It's okay,' I said to the Princess, 'it's not been a good day for any of us.'

'I thought you wouldn't come,' said the Princess. 'I thought all was lost.'

'Then you don't know me as well as you thought you did. Come on, we have a throne to reclaim.'

I whistled to Ralph, who brought the Leviathan into

a hover outside the window. We moved the Princess out of the window and across to the Skywhale, and in another minute we were all heading in formation back across the sea towards the mainland.

None of us said a word. Tiger had his face covered and my heart wouldn't stop racing. No matter what anyone says, rescuing princesses from towers is never plain sailing.

The One True Monarch

We made landfall at St Ives, and flew low across the Button Trench, where thousands more Trolls seemed to have gathered ahead of the order to invade. Shandar had said he'd remove the Trolls if we gave up the Quarkbeast, but he'd likely renege on the deal. Either way, we'd be fighting the Trolls – unless Shandar was serious about extracting the power of the sun to kickstart his galactic dominating aspirations – in which case battling the Trolls became somewhat pointless. Like rearranging the chairs on the deck of the *Titanic*.

The Leviathan dropped us off outside the Queens Hotel, and after I had hugged Ralph, thanked him for his help and he'd given me a gallon of blue warpaint that he bought cheap off a 'fella he knew', Tiger, myself and the Princess marched towards the main entrance, where, predictably enough, there was the same crowd that I had almost battled when they came for the Quarkbeast. The wiry one with the wide-set eyes was at the front but to the Princess's credit, she didn't break step as she walked towards them, and when they made no sign of moving, she stopped and spoke in a measured yet menacing tone:

'I am your Queen. Step aside and you will be pardoned; block my way and you shall be beheaded. Choose well, choose fast, choose wisely.'

The wiry one at the front seemed to go through nineteen mixed emotions in the space of about four seconds. He knew, after all, that she was indeed his Queen. They all did. So he said, hedging his bets completely:

'I agree . . . that you look very like our Queen. I will escort you to Their Highnesses so the truth of this matter be known.'

His colleagues, clearly relieved at an outcome that batted the decision to higher authority, all nodded their heads vigorously, and with a clanking of armour we were taken to the ballroom, which had been rapidly converted into a throne room, with the two most luxurious chairs in Penzance hastily painted gold with a spray can. Seated upon them were Sir Matt Grifflon and Betty Scrubb, dressed in royal finery and surrounded by a retinue of princesses, dignitaries, legal experts, guards and a whole heap of hangers-on, all eagerly working out how to set up a new constitution whereby Sir Matt could wield absolute power with just the thinnest veneer of democracy. A large copy of *The Rulebook of Rules about Ruling for Rulers* was laid out on a table, and a lot of people seemed to be discussing it. Or ways to get *around* the more democratic bits, anyway.

The room descended into hush as we marched in. Sir Matt, however, did not at first see who I was with.

'Arrest that girl,' he said when he saw me, 'and the younger sidekick. Have them put to death.'

'With or without due process?' asked one of his aides.

'Oh, *definitely* withou—'

His voice halted abruptly as he saw the Princess. Next to him on the dais, Betty Scrubb, usurper to the throne, simply stared daggers at us both, then calmed herself. Sir Matt Grifflon, slippery little eel that he was, might have been expecting something like this.

'Goodness,' he said, 'a royal lookalike. Most useful in case of a kidnap threat. She shall be employed. Have the others beheaded.'

'Wait a moment,' said the Princess. 'I am the rightful Queen of these nations. You kidnapped me, put this impostor on the throne and claimed my authority and lands illegally as your own. This is treason, plain and simple. I am willing to settle for your banishment, if you admit the plot right now, relinquish all rights and apologise in an appropriate manner.'

Sir Matt stared at her.

'So you're the Queen, are you?'

'You know I am.'

He smiled and settled back into the throne.

'Prove it.'

'I will vouch for her,' I said. 'The so-called Queen up there is none other than Laura Scrubb's identical sister Betty, a commoner and a thief. I call on the princesses present who knew Princess Shazine to ask her any questions you wish. This princess will be able to answer them, the usurper queen on that throne will not.'

'I will not submit to parlour tricks which are below my dignity,' said Betty Scrubb, 'and you shall not put the burden of proof on me. You heard the King. If you are the Princess, then prove it, here and now. If not, get out.'

I looked at the Princess, who stared back at me. That was the problem about bodyswaps. There was no real way of telling who you really were. Add an identical twin sister to the mix – especially one who had gone to extreme lengths to perfectly match the Princess's lost hand – and well, that was a bigger problem. Worse, it was indeed up to us to furnish the proof – and it would have to be beyond convincing. It would have to be airtight.

'I appeal to the princesses,' said the Princess, 'all who knew me before. Who is most like the real Princess Shazine Snodd: myself or the person currently on the throne?'

The princesses all looked at one another in shock. Most were unused to being called upon to actually do anything substantial, relevant or responsible.

'It's not our decision,' said Princess Jocaminca. 'This is a succession issue and is between you and the reigning monarch.'

The other princesses either nodded, sighed or twiddled their fingers. Jocaminca was no one's favourite, but if there were a nominal head princess, she was it.

'I think we're done here,' said the King.

'Um . . .?'

One of the princesses had her hand up. It was Princess Tabathini, the second-tier princess who had only been invited to make up the numbers.

'Yes?' said the King.

'May I make a suggestion?'

'Does it involve potentially finding a way to prove or disprove this charlatan's plans?'

'It does.'

'Then no, we don't want to hear your suggestion.'

The tall and slightly gawky-looking princess stood up.

'I'd like to hear what Princess Tabathini has to say.'

She said it in a quiet, timid-sounding voice.

'I'm getting a little fed up with this,' said the King. 'Don't make me decree that we de-princess some of the princesses. There are . . . how many are there, my dear?'

'Twenty-six,' said the Queen.

'Exactly. *Far* too many, especially when one considers there aren't nearly enough princes to go around. Perhaps a downgrading to "ordinary person" might be a good idea. It might even' – he chortled a bit here – 'increase your marriage options, something I feel you girls worry a lot about, hmmm?'

In retrospect, I think that comment was probably his downfall. A de-princessing doesn't just affect one princess, it affects them all. The whole point about being a princess is unearned privilege for life: and someone cancelling that right was an insult to the institution as a whole. The mood in the room suddenly changed. Say what you like about princesses, they can stick together when it's needed.

'According to the *Rulebook of Rules about Ruling for Rulers*,' said Princess Tabathini, suddenly sounding more confident, 'in Section 54, subsection G, paragraph 5, line 9 it states: "if a visiting princess wishes to speak at court, she is allowed to do so".'

'It won't make any difference,' grumbled the King, 'but we'll hear it anyway. Just have thoughts of living in a bungalow with no servants and waitressing at SmileyBurger in the forefront of your mind.'

Princess Tabathini took a deep breath.

'Being a princess,' she said, 'is not simply about external beauty, deportment, grace, accessories, tiaras, footmen, castles and so forth, it's what's *inside*. An impostor could look like the real thing, take on all the trappings and even appropriate a castle and staff, but they could never truly be royalty, for the haughty dismissiveness and deep sense of entitlement to an empty life of conspicuous wealth and luxury – the very soul of a princess – can never be learned.'

The other princesses met this with a ripple of applause, and one or two even sniffed into their handkerchiefs.

'We need a test that only a true princess could pass,' continued Tabathini, 'and this is it: the *real* Princess Shazine Snodd won the Pan-UnUnited Kingdoms Pout-Off three years running.'

There was a murmur from the crowd. It was true. Princess Shazine had stood head and shoulders above the most spoiled and indulged girls in the Kingdoms, and her level of obnoxious indifference to anyone but herself was envied far and wide. Tiger leaned towards me and whispered:

'I thought she was going to suggest mattresses and a pea.'

'So did I,' I whispered back.

'If you *are* the rightful heir to the Kingdom of Snodd,' said Princess Tabathini, staring at the Princess, 'you'd better show us that winning pout.'

The Princess looked at them all in turn, and they stared back at her. It was, in actual fact, a terrific test. Princessy pouts are rare and terrifying things, and exist solely as a way of *instantly* bending others to your will. They can take years to perfect, are often handed down mother to daughter, and the finest even have names.

'Hmm,' said the Princess thoughtfully, 'so you want to see "*El Carisma*",[52] do you?'

'If you can,' said Princess Jocaminca. I don't think she'd ever really forgiven the Princess for taking over when we arrived.

'Yes,' said the Queen, betting the farm on this, 'give it your best shot – servant girl.'

The Princess looked at me, a sudden sense of doubt etched on her features. If she couldn't prove that she was a princess, then everything we had fought for was gone. She leaned towards me and lowered her voice.

'Get ready to make a run for it if I can't pull this off,' she said. 'Trouble is, I've never tried "*El Carisma*" with this face and I'm not sure it has the muscle tone for it.'

'An obnoxious pout that withers all it falls upon comes from within,' I whispered in her ear reassuringly. 'A sense of royal bearing, an utter contempt for and indifference to anything but your own precious

---

[52] Spanish for 'The Charisma'. Unlike 'La Calienta' (hot) or 'Las Llamas' (The Llamas), which are all well known, 'El Carisma' has only been mastered by three known princesses. No one knows why they are all named in Spanish.

ego. You were that princess once – you can be her again.'

She nodded, took a deep breath, turned to the princesses and the King and the Queen and gave them the full *El Carisma*.

The room fell instantly silent.

I was beside her so only got a profile, but even then I felt it – a sense of chilling social inferiority, as though I'd wandered into a drawing room full of duchesses with my underwear on my head. The assembled princesses felt it too and they instinctively bowed their heads in obedience. Somewhere a dog barked, several courtiers ran off to hide and Princess Tabathini started sobbing quietly to herself. Three waiting staff at the back of the lobby who were accidentally looking in our direction both hurriedly left the room backwards, bowing as they went, and even the usurper Queen went pale and started trembling uncontrollably.

Jocaminca was the first to react in the empty silence that followed, and knelt in front of the Princess.

'Forgive me, Your Majesty,' she said, 'I did not know what I was doing.'

'I think you probably did,' said the Princess, 'but no matter. You are forgiven.'

The rest of the princesses started to kneel, and it moved like a wave around the room. Even Sir Matt's retinue kneeled before her, and that included the wiry one with the wide-set eyes, and the shabby curate with the ill-fitting hat.

'This is despicable,' said Sir Matt, rising from the throne. 'Guards, arrest that impostor and have her executed on the steps outside, then hung in one of those metal cagey things as a lesson to—'

'Hush,' said the Princess. 'Your days of ordering people around are over. Minister for Justice?'

The man with the oversized wig obsequiously moved forward, bowing so much that he was soon on his knees. By the time he reached her it had devolved into a fawning grovel.

'Yes, Your Majesty? Would you like me to have these two charlatans executed? We could conduct a trial if you want, but I think the verdict is pretty much foregone.'

'No. You are to find a hovel somewhere, of two bedrooms, with two acres of stony ground and a pig. It shall be given to Mr and Mrs Grifflon here, to enjoy their married life together. There shall be no executions today.'

'Wait,' said Sir Matt, 'all that marriage stuff was just to get the Crown. I didn't actually *want* to marry a commoner with poor diction, a string of convictions and a dangerous personality disorder – it is annulled.'

'Cheek,' said Betty. 'Thanks to you I've cut my own hand off for nothing.'

'Was the marriage legal?' the Princess asked the shabby curate.

'It was, my Queen.'

'I'm a knight,' muttered Sir Matt. 'It's not permitted for me to be treated in this way.'

'Not any more,' said the Princess. 'You are stripped of all honours, lands, titles and privileges. Your recording backlist and all rights thereto are to be given to orphanages, and your sword, armour, impressive mane of blond hair are all forfeit – but you may keep the moustache and the clothes on your back, aside from your cloak, which will be made into rags to polish the floor.'

'I will have my revenge on you for this,' screamed Betty Scrubb.

'You will not,' said the Princess, 'for precisely the reason you failed in your coup. Yes, you are dishonest and scheming, but you're really *very* bad at it. Get used to your hovel and your new husband, and if you know what's good for you, serve your nation wisely. And you, Mathew Grifflon, ponder upon the great kindness I have shown in not having your head struck from your shoulders. Serve your marriage well and obey your wife. If I hear a whisper of sedition, I may review my kindness. Do you understand?'

Mr Matt Grifflon looked empty, defeated and, for the first time, almost apologetic.

'I do, my Queen.'

'Good. Take them away.'

And they were, by the very people who they thought would protect them. I retrieved the ring of state from Betty Scrubb's finger and handed it to the Princess, who placed it on her own.

'Where is Princess Tabathini?'

'Here, ma'am.'

'For your quick thinking, I make you head lady-in-waiting. All other princess rights are unchanged, the threat of demotion forever removed. Your vacuous levels of self-absorption are now a right enshrined forever in law. Jennifer, you are once more a knight, and Tiger, you are again Earl Prawns, adviser to the Crown.'

'Your Majesty,' said the Minister for Justice, 'your throne awaits you.'

'You can hand them back,' said the Princess. 'There shall be no thrones, no crowns, no baubles, no grovelling, no averting of eyes. I shall not be crowned until this nation is safe, for until then I will not have deserved it. Although we have seen off the usurpers, there is still tyranny afoot in my Kingdom. That we shall defeat the Trolls and the Mighty Shandar is not certain, but by the memory of my mother and father and all those who gave their lives to defend these islands, we will not stop trying while there is a last gasp in our bodies.'

There were three loud 'Huzzahs!' at this.

'Good,' she said. 'We reconvene in an hour to discuss Shandar and the Trolls. Now,' she added, oddly reverting to the part of her that would always be Laura Scrubb, 'I've got to spend some time in the khazi. They gave me curry for dinner last night and I think it's going to be bad.'

Molly Reveals Herself

The Princess and I visited the Button Trench around teatime. Sorting out the chaos of the two recent changes in administration took a frustratingly long time, especially given that time was something currently in short supply. It was now Sunday afternoon, and the Troll invasion was slated for dawn the following morning. The Quarkbeast had been returned to us by Grifflon's men, but we still had no intention of giving him up.

We'd released Full Price and Lady Mawgon, who re-established the intelligence network and regained contact with our observers and resistance groups. Many had dutifully remained at their posts in case our fortunes changed, and, although patchy, the picture of the Troll invasion was generally consistent: they were now everywhere, and it did not look as though their appetite for human flesh would be appeased any time soon.

We stared at the Trolls on the other side of the trench, and they stared back at us in the sort of way we might stare into a fridge if feeling a little snacky.

They had vanquished the human with little difficulty; a further small addition of land in the extreme south-west tip would not make a significant difference, the ten thousand or so souls the equivalent of just one more larder in a house not noted for its lack of larders. It was said that more people turned vegetarian during the Troll invasion that at any time in the Kingdom's history. Being a carnivore suddenly looked a little iffy when you or your children were on someone else's menu.

The Princess and I stared across the trench. We had asked to speak to whichever Troll was nominally in charge, and one was now lumbering up to talk to us. It looked a lot like the Troll Wife we had seen a few days ago. She recognised us both, but on reflection that might just have been the Hive Memory.

'Yes?' said the Troll.

'This is the Supreme Ruler of the United Kingdoms,' I said, indicating the Princess, 'and she wishes to speak to the Emperor.'

'Oh yes?' said the Troll Wife. 'And for what *possible* reason would he want to talk to you? It's sort of like the starter wanting to have a chat with a guest, just before a banquet.'

'It's about the Mighty Shandar,' said the Princess. 'He will break any deal he has brokered. Our species will be better served by working together to defeat a common enemy before we find a peace of our own.

I want to forge a new history between your people and mine so that we can live in harmony, rather than aggression.'

'I'm sorry,' said the Troll absently, as her attention had wandered, 'did you say something?'

The Princess patiently repeated herself, but the Troll was no less dismissive.

'You're breaking my heart. But I'll let you into a secret: the Mighty Shandar will build bridges over the Button Trench no matter what you do tomorrow at dawn, and we *will* invade. So standing there bargaining with us is a little pointless – although out of courtesy we may ask if you would prefer to be steamed or boiled. Personally I'm against such concessions, but the 13.33 per cent bleeding-heart liberal Troll faction will have their say.'

We came away from the Button Trench without having made any headway, but at least some understanding of what we were to expect.

'It looks like you were right about Shandar,' said the Princess as we drove back into town. 'Helping us rid the land of the Trolls was never part of his plan.'

'Mind you,' said Tiger, who was also present, 'defeating the Trolls may not be relevant at all if the Mighty Shandar decides to leave the Earth as a frozen wasteland devoid of life, floating in a forgotten corner of the Milky Way. Shouldn't we take the fight straight to Shandar?'

'The Troll is currently the most immediate threat to our liberty,' said the Princess. 'We'll fight them first then deal with Shandar.'

I liked her optimism, but wasn't sure just how we could fight either right now.

We pulled up outside the Queens Hotel. The marksmen, eager not to sit on their hands doing nothing during a time of jeopardy, had been busy repainting the yellow lines outside the hotel, conveniently adding a 'Monarchs Only' parking slot.

Monty was waiting for us as we pulled up, and seemed to be looking positive about something, which might at least portend good news, even if it wasn't *actual* good news.

'Did that shade of cerulean blue that I gave you work?' I asked, since I'd passed Ralph's warpaint on as a possible weapon of war. A gallon of paint against several million Trolls didn't seem like much, but it was something.

'It did,' he said, 'but there's something else I want to show you. It's over at the Leisure Centre on Claire Street. Can you drive me up there?

'What we do know,' continued Monty, as we drove back up the hill, 'is that brute force alone doesn't work against the Troll's ferocity. So the worriers and I were looking once again at the problem and three things struck us as mutually incompatible: first was the sheer number of the Trolls.'

'It goes against all scholarly extrapolation of likely numbers, and every reconnaissance mission ever undertaken over Trollvania,' said the Princess.

'Right,' said Monty. 'Every Troll War was fought on the same assumption: that there weren't very many and they must be easy to defeat. But every time humans opened the massive gates in the Troll Wall to give them a bit of a pasting, there were always far more than expected.'

'Someone not doing their homework, it sounds like,' I said, pulling up outside the Leisure Centre, which was now being used to train anyone who was willing to fight. Pointed sticks, kitchen implements, fists, feet, sarcasm, Trollphobic jeers – we were getting desperate.

Monty led us through to the main sports hall, which had been divided by large curtain partitions. There were desks set up with chairs, filing cabinets, phones and photocopiers, and the walls were liberally covered with pictures, diagrams, maps and charts. There were also about a dozen of General Worrier's top worriers – including Major Worrier, who saluted smartly, bit his lip and then, the stress getting the better of him, had to be led away and sat down with a glass of water and a cool flannel on the back of his neck.

But in the centre of the curtained-off space was Molly in her Mini Traveller, doing some knitting.

'Hello!' she said through the window. 'Glad to see

you back, Jennifer. Sorry about Feldspar. He seemed a decent sort.'

'Thank you,' I said, 'he was.'

'So,' said Monty, showing me an old map of the UnUnited Kingdoms, 'my second point is the extensive use of multiple barriers required to defeat them in the past.'

He pointed at the various features on the map.

'As I mentioned before, we've got Offa's Dyke cutting off the whole of Wales, Wat's Dyke behind it, the others that criss-cross the land, the two ancient Roman walls at the borders of Trollvania, and now the two modern Troll Walls.'

We nodded, but didn't see where he was going with this.

'You had three points?' said the Princess.

'Ah yes: the Hive Memory. We know thoughts and memories are not universally shared, only among specific groups of individuals. And then there's the shared tattoos. We thought it was a wise Data Integrity policy, but now we're not so sure.'

'You've lost me,' I said.

'And me,' said the Princess.

'And *me*,' said Molly, 'and I'm a Troll so I don't have an excuse.'

'Okay, then,' said Monty, 'I'll demonstrate. Molly, do you trust me?'

'Yes.'

'*Really* trust me?'

Molly looked at the Princess, who nodded.

'Yes.'

'Good. I need you out of the car.'

Molly looked at us all in turn, then nervously at the sports hall, which even though only half its total size still seemed only *just* the size she might feel comfortable with. She opened the door and then, with an odd sinuous movement that reminded me of a circus contortionist climbing in and out of a small barrel, she squirmed elegantly from the car and was soon standing next to us.

'What do you want me to do?' she asked.

'I need you to be yourself,' said Monty, then, in a louder voice: '*Now.*'

The curtain partition must have been rigged with quick-release hangings or something, for it fell to the floor, instantly doubling the floor space in the sports hall. The effect upon Molly was instantaneous: the crease we had seen running down her forehead the previous evening at the Globe reopened, and as we watched she tensed in anticipation, then dropped to her knees as her head seemed to stretch sideways.

She cried out in pain and we all took a step backwards.

'She's grown another set of eyes,' whispered Tiger in astonishment, as Molly's head continued to stretch. Her extra eyes weren't the only things that were growing. Her legs were dividing down the centre, as were her arms, along with her body, which was separating down the middle, taking the new limbs and head with it, until, less than ten seconds later, there wasn't one Molly standing in front of us – *but two.*

Molly looked at the other Molly and then gave her a sisterly hug.

'Molly?' I said.

'Yes?' replied both the Mollys in unison, seemingly oblivious - or at least unsurprised - to what had just happened.

'I think I get it now,' said Tiger, who was fairly quick on the uptake.

'Lucky you,' said the Princess, 'because I don't.'

'The Troll,' said Monty in a quiet voice, 'is a variable-population-density life form. They do not live as a fixed number, but as a ratio. *Their numbers expand and contract to fit the space available.*'

He waited a moment to let this sink in.

'The two Troll Walls are there to keep the Trolls in a fixed space geographically,' he explained, 'just as the Romans used the walls, and King Offa a set of dykes. The way to defeat a Troll isn't with weaponry, or force, or entrapment – it's by *enclosing* them.'

I looked at Molly.

'Did you know this?'

'Look,' said the Troll, 'I'm not huge on the whole

counting gig – as far as I'm concerned, there's only one of me. One here, and one over there. One times one is?'

'One,' said Tiger.

'There you go,' said Molly, 'as clear as the nose on your face.'

Monty explained that there were roughly ten thousand or so Trolls living in between the Troll Walls, but as soon as the gates opened they could expand to over three million as they spread out to meet their preset density ratio, which was based on food supply, terrain and area. It sort of made evolutionary sense, too, for in this way a creature could never exceed the limits imposed upon them by their environment.

'That's why they hate us so much,' said the Princess, 'for humans can do what they cannot: expand unchecked beyond the levels at which their environment can support them.'

'There's a moral in there somewhere,' said Tiger.

'So hang on,' I said. 'Molly told us that 6.66 per cent of Trolls were vegetarians. That's ridiculously precise unless . . . she is the only one. In which case—'

'There are only *fifteen* individual Trolls,' said the Princess, who was a little quicker at maths than the rest of us. 'But we can check. Molly, can you name all your fellow Trolls?'

'Sure. There's Keith, Uuuurg, Estelle, Dave, Ugrax,

Gluuurg and Charlotte, who is my mum. There's also Gretal, Grnxtly, Polly, Ug, Dexter, Simon and Daphne.'

'Yup,' said the Princess, 'fifteen. Molly, as a percentage of all the Trolls named Molly that are anywhere, how many are in this room now?'

'One hundred per cent,' said the first Molly, while the second stared at the diagrams on the wall and then turned to us and added: 'I bounded myself in the Mini so that I should not suffer any indignities from any Troll anywhere in the Kingdoms.'

And she sighed deeply. Monty ordered the room divided in half again, but this time not by a curtain, but by a long string embroidered with buttons. Since it was an imposed boundary, it had the same effect as the curtain, and within a couple of seconds Molly had recombined herself back into a single Troll. It wasn't so painful, and she looked much relieved.

'I feel better as unit one' she said. 'If you want me I'll be in the Mini.'

We all thanked her and within a few moments she was happily back inside the small car. The Princess, Monty and I all exchanged looks. We knew then the method by which we could defeat them.

'I know,' said Monty, 'but with only a single night to prepare, there's only a slim chance of victory.'

'I'll alert the necessary parties,' said Tiger, going to find a phone, 'and warn Lady Mawgon to stand by to receive orders – and also to alert Mabel that everyone will be pulling an all-nighter, and to get the sandwich and coffee-makers on stand by.'

'I'm still not sure I fully understand what's going on,' said Molly, munching on a cucumber sandwich.

Humans v. Trolls

The Princess and I were ready and waiting as the sky lightened into a rich pre-dawn the following morning. Mist had formed in small pockets around the Button Trench, and the Trolls, up at first light, had shaken the sleepiness from their heads and were now waiting, motionless, and hungry.

General Worrier was with us, worrying as usual. His fret-based command system, whereby all possibilities of failure had been erased by the very real and unacceptable spectre of failure itself, was probably the most efficient command and control system that I had ever seen. He and his team had done all that was humanly possible. A failure now would not be theirs, but the result of an unsound overall plan or poor communication of orders.

Aside from the general, the Princess and myself, there was also Tiger, who wouldn't leave my side, a small contingent of royal guards to protect the monarch if things turned sticky, and a semaphore communications officer. It was their job to signal to another communications officer waiting at a phone box a hundred yards down the street, who would relay commands to the control centre back at the hotel, and from there to the resistance cells up and down the country.

In truth, the Princess shouldn't have been there, but had refused all entreaties to be taken to a safe place because 'she would never command others to face dangers that she was not willing to face herself'.

In due course it would cement not only her popularity, but the moral leadership required to rule a newly United Kingdom. She leaned closer to me and touched my hand.

'Is this going to work?' she asked.

'We'll know in half an hour,' I said, 'or at least you will – I'm on the First Eat List.'

We stared at the massed army of the Trolls facing us. If things went well, we at least had a sporting chance – and with a bit of luck, without a sword needing to be drawn, or a shot fired.

Actually, not a bit of luck – a *lot* of luck.

It had been a long night, but the fencers and marksmen, along with the team of terrible worriers, had been of inestimable value – far more than a traditional army. Killing a Troll would not diminish their numbers at all, for a new one would be generated to sustain the density ratio, and all that would be gained would be tired muscles and a blunted sword. No, we needed to build *barriers*. We needed not soldiers but fencers – and not just any old fencers, but masters of their art. Ones who could build in the dark, build stealthily, across rivers and streams, hills and forests, and who could instruct others in the craft over the phone if necessary, and call upon others to build the single greatest network of button barriers that was ever created – *and do it all in a single night.*

I looked towards the east, where already the sun was beginning to burnish the trees on a distant hillside, edging them with deep orange. Shandar's bridges across the Button Trench had already begun to build themselves. They were of tree roots, growing and entwining together so to eventually give a firm base upon which the Trolls might walk. The Trolls reacted by picking up their clubs and ensuring their salt and pepper grinders were loaded and in their holsters, ready to be utilised in case of emergency seasoning requirements.

The reason that we had left it so late to launch our counterattack was simple: we had no idea how much of our grand plan had been carried out and we needed to leave it as long as possible to ensure that it had. The marksmen and women were not quite so well organised as the fencers, but on the plus side anyone with a brush could in effect be a marksperson, so long as the paint had been mixed to the precise hue.

'General Worrier,' said the Princess, 'give the order.'

He nodded to the man holding the semaphore flag,

who signalled to the woman in the telephone box, who gave the order to Lady Mawgon, who relayed the order to the Regional Commander of the Devon Resistance Group, who signalled his deputy to order that the flare be fired. We could not see it from here, but the flare that arced up out of Bridgwater was significant, for teams of marksmen had been busily painting a continuous unbroken cerulean blue line between the estuary at Bridgwater on the northern coast and the inlet near Axmouth to the south. It mostly followed roads, as it was easier, but there it was: a thin blue line, which would, so long as it was unbroken, bind the Trolls within Devon to a fixed geographical area.

As we found out later, the team standing by to finish the line responded with a flare back to their regional command centre as soon as they had, and the 'order completed' signal was relayed back to us. The message took about thirty seconds in each direction.

'The Thin Blue Line has been completed, ma'am,' said the communications officer. 'Thirty-eight miles of unbroken paint.'

'Good,' said the Princess but without much enthusiasm, as annoyingly the Trolls were undiminished in number. It didn't seem to have worked, and the bridges across the Button Trench were now half complete. The Trolls were limbering up, drawing weapons, sharpening spoons and readying themselves for breakfast.

'Well,' said the Princess, 'it was a good idea. Maybe what works in sports halls doesn't extend to entire peninsulas.'

'So it's Plan B,' I said, drawing Exhorbitus out of its scabbard. 'Fight like hell. I suggest you retreat, ma'am.'

At that very instant the first rays of the new day bathed the scene in an amber glow.

'Ma'am, your retreat path is waiting,' said Tiger, pointing towards where the open door of my VW was waiting for us, engine ticking over. Colin would be waiting at the hotel, ready to whisk her off to the Isles of Scilly, where there would be no Trolls.

'Not yet,' she said. 'General: order every barrier closed.'

The general transmitted the new order, but this went not just to one regional headquarters, but all of them: to the 173-mile fence that had been constructed along the old Offa's path by an army of over ten thousand, who built the barrier from whatever was to hand, at night, by the light of torches and lanterns. It was decorated with buttons, and the last gap was completed, as we found out later, just as the sun rose. The fencers, their work complete, their hands and fingers bleeding, collapsed exhausted on the grassy flanks of the huge earthwork that would, for the second time in history, stand as a bulwark against the Troll.

Offa's Dyke wasn't the only one. Nine other barriers had also been constructed or painted, each restricting the open area in which the Troll could expand. From north to south and from east to west, following canals, and rivers, and estuaries, and roads. Sometimes walls, sometimes a blue line, sometimes a dyke built from earth, and at other times a beautifully pleached hedge – all decorated with buttons or painted cerulean blue. We learned later that over a hundred thousand people had worked on their construction, and from all walks of life: princes shoulder to shoulder with peasants, geeks alongside lingerie models, game-show hosts beside epidemiologists. All were committed to the destruction of the common foe, the cause of freedom, and to have vengeance for those who had been killed and eaten.

The sun's face was only just clear of the distant horizon when the root-bridges touched the opposite side of the Button Trench, and the Trolls, savouring their moment of triumph, tied bibs around their necks and gave out silly grumpy chortles. They were taking their time, and they wanted us to know it.

'It's a beautiful morning, isn't it?' said the Princess.

And it was. A perfect late summer's day, the distant clouds tinged with orange. It would be warm today, with a light breeze, and puffy white clouds would play across the sky. It was a shame I wouldn't get to see it. I would take out a few, even many, but their numbers would eventually be too much for me, and I would be overcome. There was no running, no hiding – this was where it ended. The Mighty Shandar could just walk in and take the Quarkbeast – there would be no one left to defend it.

'This is all my fault,' said General Worrier, sobbing quietly. 'I'm so sorry.'

'No,' said the Princess, 'the plan and execution were sound, we just didn't have enough time. I promote you to field marshal.'

'I *really* think you should retreat, ma'am,' said Tiger.

'No,' said the Princess, looking up at me, 'shoulder to shoulder, side by side. See you on the other . . .'

She had stopped talking as the Trolls had changed behaviour. Instead of waiting to invade, they were instinctively seeking out an identical partner and reabsorbing into one another, like spilled mercury. They did it without noise or complaint, just stoically accepting their new density ratio as their biology dictated. In less than half a minute their numbers had decreased by about a half.

'That's a relief,' said Field Marshal Worrier.

It was indeed. We didn't know it at the time, but the planned final gap of the Thin Blue Line that cut off Devon had not been the last one: farther down the line and unknown to the rest of the team was *another* group of painters, and it was this group that completed the line and precipitated the Trolls' sudden reduction in numbers. Many of the surviving Trolls turned to go in order to seek partners to conjoin, while others stood there, looking foolish and unsure what to do next.

But their defeat was not yet complete. We knew we couldn't get rid of them entirely since even the area the size of a sports hall could accommodate at least two – hence the second phase of our plan, when Field Marshal Worrier gave the order that the Troll Gates were to be closed. We knew the gates had been heavily guarded, but with the Troll numbers depleted by their enforced geographic bounding, their numbers might be small enough to be defeated by twelve hundred 'gate pushers' picked for their strength, bravery and willingness to be painted head to toe in cerulean blue. The field marshal gave the order, and we waited.

'I don't know about you,' said the Troll Wife, who was one of only perhaps thirty left at the Button Trench bridges, 'but I fancy a working breakfast.'

And they started once more to walk across the bridge. I drew out Exhorbitus and readied to do battle. But I didn't need to, for every single Troll stopped, merged with a partner if it had one and, if not, wandered off to find one. It would take another six days for them to merge back into a minimum of fourteen,[53] and two weeks for that small group to reach the Troll Wall, their progress assisted by the button barriers being raised and lowered as they walked.

The invasion was over. We had won.

But we didn't celebrate or jump up and down, we just felt . . . *relieved*. Generally speaking, those who celebrate at the end of a conflict are the ones who were not directly involved. For those of us in the front line, for all those who built fences, dug trenches and painted blue lines while at risk of being eaten, all we wanted was to get home and back to normality – and to try and forget that our mother, brother, sister or children ended up in a large cauldron to be eaten with badger sauce, or boiled down into a sticky mass, frozen and then sold on a stick at a Troll carnival.

'Bravo,' came a voice accompanied by a slow hand-clap, 'that was really *very* impressive.'

It was the Mighty Shandar, who had been watching while seated on a deckchair. I hadn't noticed him until now. With five thousand Trolls about to treat you as little more than a live buffet, I think I could be excused that.

I didn't say anything; I knew what he'd come for.

---

[53] Molly, the fifteenth, was with us. She never did go home.

'Are you ready to go?' he asked, looking at me. 'I have a date with destiny and she doesn't like being kept waiting.'

'While I still have air in my lungs, Shandar,' I said, 'you will never have the Quarkbeast and I shall never be party to your heinous plans.'

'Never say never, Jennifer. See there: the little fellow understands what he is, and what he was always meant to do.'

'Quark,' said the Quarkbeast as he trotted up. He looked up at me with his large mauve eyes. I felt him very clearly speaking in my head. Through the Mysterious X, I imagine.

'It's okay, Jennifer,' he seemed to say, 'sometimes death brings about opportunity. Don't be afraid.'

I turned to Shandar.

'You like deals. Here's mine: if I come with you to be your strategic moral compass, will you spare the planet?'

He stared at me for a moment. Shandar was not called 'The Mighty' for nothing, and his power, against mine, was vast. There are occasions when you have to be realistic, and get the best deal you can in a bad situation. It was the first time I had put something on the table, the first time I had even conceded that he might have a winning hand. But then I think he *knew* I would – that the Better Angels that were once his were powerful indeed, the sort that would trade themselves for others. If he'd kept them, he might have been a good man.

'Are those your terms?' he asked.

'They are,' I said.

'It's a big ask,' he said. 'I need the power of an entire sun before I can warp spacetime significantly enough to travel the distances I need – but no matter. We'll drop off at Proxima Centauri[54] and harness the power of that star instead. It'll take us thirty-seven years to get there, but with time eternal, I'm not troubled. We've got a lot of books and all the music we could want. I think I packed some jigsaws, too. With the Hollow Men and Women to wait on us, it'll be fun. So yes, I agree to your terms – with one proviso.'

'And what's that?'

'When you turn eighteen, you marry me. Not a big party. Just you and me and D'Argento and the empty suits. We'll be a husband-and-wife galactic domination team. I'll order the killings and the torture, and you can handle the mercy, diplomacy and soft furnishings. You'll save billions of lives, Jennifer. What do you say?'

'Is that a deal-breaker?'

---

[54] It's the nearest star to ours, about 4.2 light-years away. If Shandar was planning on getting there in thirty-seven years, he was going to have to circumvent some pretty big physical laws.

'It is. Marriage to me – or Planet Earth dies. What's it to be?'

I tensed inwardly, but showed no outward emotion. 'Deal.'

'Then that's all agreed,' he said with a grin. 'It's going to be quite a journey, and one that I don't think you'll regret.'

'I'll need to say my goodbyes,' I said, 'and I'd like to bring my Volkswagen. Where I go, it goes.'

'Agreed. I'll have them leave a space – and I'll get the Hollow Women to stock up with some spares. What engine does it have?'

'The twelve hundred – and with six-volt electrics.'

'You never had it upgraded?'

'It has a cast pedestal[55] so I couldn't without swapping out the engine.'

He made a note.

'Okay, then. Don't forget the Quarkbeast, now – oh, and nothing magical is allowed on board the tower. No amulets, Dibble Storage Jars, no tricks – nothing.'

'It'll be just me and the Beast and the car.'

'See you later, then.'

And he vanished, but this time without the dramatic pillar of fire.

---

[55] This is a geeky in-joke reference to early Volkswagens. You can safely ignore it.

I looked at the Princess and Tiger, who were staring back at me.

'What?' I said. 'It's a no-brainer, and a good deal in the circumstances.'

'It's not a good deal for you,' said the Princess. 'I mean . . . *marrying* him?'

I thought for a moment and took a deep breath.

'Y'know what? Although Zambini and Mother Zenobia moulded me to defeat him, perhaps I don't get to thwart Shandar's plans after all, but simply to *relocate* them – and a long way away. Besides,' I added, 'I save billions of lives on Earth, and countless more on planets I've never heard of during eons that are yet to begin. I may even get to save alien species that haven't yet evolved. That's a weird one to get your head around, but it's the best and biggest and finest gig anyone will ever get, no matter which way you look at it.'

I sighed. When Zambini and Zenobia had only a few decades to counter a threat three centuries in the making, they did what they could, not what they wanted.

I stared for a moment at the now-redundant Button Trench.

'It served its purpose well,' said Tiger, following my gaze, 'and no one should forget that Wizard Moobin gave his life to build it.'

'All sacrifices have been noted,' said the Princess.

'All those who gave themselves to defeat the Trolls will be honoured.'

We all lapsed into silence for a while.

'Let's go and have some breakfast,' I said finally. 'I think we've earned it.'

We say goodbye

The conversation over breakfast was mixed in tone. The defeat of the Trolls was good news, but the Princess and her group of advisers were concerned that until Shandar was gone, caution should be the watchword. I was resigned to my future by now, but I think the Princess was annoyed and nervous in my stead, as was Tiger. After breakfast Lady Mawgon sought me out and took my hand, squeezed it and then gave me the brooch she always wore. It was of jet, with a dark sapphire in the centre the size of a pigeon's egg.

'Take this as a gift,' she said, 'to remind you of happier days at Zambini Towers. I regret not having been more pleasant to you, Jennifer, but it was my way. The Great Zambini was right: you are a very special person. The brooch is valuable. You are to carry it with you always.'

I mumbled my thanks and Lady Mawgon gave me a crusty hug that smelled of old wardrobes.

'You will have the good grace not to mention to anyone I was kind to you?' she asked. 'These things can get around, and coming over as dismissive and aloof has really worked well for me down the years.'

I gave her a hug back.

'Your secret's safe with me.'

She smiled – the first I'd ever seen cross her grim visage – then moved quickly away. A lot of people wanted to speak to me, and their concern, although heartfelt and justified, made me feel as though I were more like a condemned convict up for a spell in the clink, rather than someone who was about to embark on a journey of unprecedented discovery until the end of time. But, weirdly, now I knew I was a countermeasure and my life had led up to this, accepting it as my destiny wasn't really such a huge deal. This was Zambini and Mother Zenobia's plan all along, and given that we'd avoided the destruction of the planet it was, in almost any way you looked at it, a dazzling success. Leaving everybody I'd ever known and loved, and the unanswered question about my parents, was just something I had to do.

Others had given far more.

'Look,' I said to the Princess after breakfast, 'I'm not going to draw this out. It's been a real pleasure knowing you, and I couldn't think of anyone better to take the new, unified and pro-Europe Kingdoms into the modern world.'

The Princess didn't reply. She just hugged me tightly. I'd been a friend and confidante and adviser to her, sure, but in the month we'd known one another, she'd become something closer to family. A sister, perhaps.

'I'll try and send a comet or something back with news,' I said, knowing that this really wasn't likely. She looked at me, her eyes brimming with tears.

'I was an obnoxious waste of space good only for popping out royal heirs and choosing curtains until you chanced along,' she said. 'You made me what I am. Everything I will become I owe to you – and I'm really not sure I can do it on my own.'

I smiled.

'Sure you can. You're going to be a great ruler, and I can't recommend Tiger highly enough if you ever need some straight-talking advice. Oh, and you know what? I may not have just chanced along. There was a plan here. If ever the Great Zambini returns, you can thank him for that – and once again from me.'

We hugged again and I turned away. I didn't look back, either, just trotted out to the front of the hotel where I had parked my car. The Quarkbeast was already waiting for me, as was Tiger. His eyes were full of tears and he hugged me round the waist.

'I have to go,' I said.

'I know that,' said Tiger, 'and have no argument with it: You're totally doing the right thing. It's just that . . . I'm going to *really* miss you.'

'And I you. Mind you,' I added, 'I always thought I'd die young, not miss out on dying altogether. Funny how things turn out, eh?'

'Funny how things turn out, yes. I never thought I'd be an earl and a key part of a transition government before my twelfth birthday. You know what?' he said.

'What?'

'I wish I'd had you as my big sister.'

'It would never have worked out,' I said with a smile. 'I'd be forever on your back to do your homework and wash behind your ears and chewing you out for messing with my stuff.'

He smiled back at me.

'Even so.'

I opened the door of the Volkswagen and the Quarkbeast jumped inside. I climbed in, shut the door and wound down the window.

'Look after the remaining sorcerers,' I said. 'Zambini Towers will need rebuilding, and Lady Mawgon, Boo, Monty and Full Price will require a lot of help to restore the mystical arts into a useful and well-regulated power only for good. We can't risk another Shandar.'

I paused.

'So long, Tiger. It's been good.'

'So long, Jenny. I won't forget you.'

He waved at me and I drove off. I didn't look in

the rear-view mirror, and blinked away my tears. Even without my own family, I'd still had one. Sure, Zenobia and the other nuns had been harsh, but there was love there. At Zambini Towers it had always been hard work, but they looked out for me, even Lady Mawgon.

I stopped to say goodbye to Once Magnificent Boo, who was waiting on the corner.

'Good luck,' she said. 'If I'd been into the whole "having a daughter" thing, I'd have hoped she'd be just like you.'

'I'd love to have had you as a mum, Boo.'

She squeezed my arm.

'Thank you, Jennifer. That means a lot to me. Give the centre of the galaxy my love.'

'I will.'

I put the car in gear, meaning to be off, but Boo leaned closer.

'It must be wonderful,' she said in a brooding tone, staring at me with her dark eyes. 'With eternal life must come unlimited power. Do you understand?'

'Not really, no.'

'You will.'

She then handed the Quarkbeast a transfer gearbox[56] from a MkII Land Rover for him to chew on the

---

[56] A 'transfer gearbox' is the secondary gearbox that engages four-wheel drive and lowers the gearing ratio.

journey, winked one of her dark eyes, clasped my shoulder with a rare sign of affection and stepped back.

I drove on, but soon realised I wouldn't need to figure out the route to the Tower of Knowledge. Word had got about through the worrier network that I was leaving with Shandar, having secured the sun's continuing ability to pour bounteous warmth and light onto the planets, and all the fencers, marksmen and other support personnel were lining the route, eager to see me on my way. As I drove through the shattered remains of the Kingdoms, I realised just how much damage had been done in such a short time by the Trolls. It was all rebuildable, but at least now with the Kingdoms united and under wiser and more considered leadership, they could come back better.

After a couple of hours, I came within sight of Shandar's mighty tower. I took the motorway exit where it was signposted 'Shandar Plunder Traffic Only' and drove along the newly built access road. There were still trucks moving in and out, but the Hollow Men, far from regarding me with suspicion, simply inclined their empty hats in my direction as I passed.

I drove down a ramp to the first sub-basement and was directed to a large, roped off area in which to park. I turned off the engine and climbed out, the Quarkbeast at my heels.

'Ah, Jenny!' said a voice behind me. 'Welcome to your new home.'

The Mighty Shandar

Shandar seemed more relaxed now I had agreed to his terms and the question marks over my compliance had at last been lifted. He shook my hand warmly.

'So glad you could make it, my dear,' he said as a team of Hollow Men heaved the blast doors closed behind us. 'Don't think me suspicious, but you were once a formidable opponent so I want to make trebly sure there are no tricks up your sleeve or well-laid plans in your mind. Is there anything you'd like to tell me about now? For I will insist on searching you – mind, body and luggage.'

Just me being here *was* the plan, but I suppose he was right to be suspicious.

'I have a Pollyanna Stone,' I said, digging it out of my pocket. 'I used it to conjure up who I thought were my parents in times of stress.'

'Family are overrated,' said Shandar. 'When you need them they're not there, and when you don't want them they're on your back wanting part of Cumbria or a castle or a pet Leviathan or something.'

The Mighty Shandar's family were now assumed casualties of his Soulectomy. Wagging tongues said they were turned to stone and used as garden ornaments.

'You are to surrender the stone and anything else with an enchantment attached,' he said. 'It's a wise precaution, I think you will agree. Where is Exhorbitus?'

'I gave it to Tiger.'

I didn't tell him, I just left it in his bedroom with a note.

'Just as well you did,' said Shandar, 'for I would have had to destroy it. There will be no magic in Shandar's Tower aside from mine.'

I handed over the Pollyanna Stone and Shandar crunched it to powder between thumb and forefinger, the residual wizidrical energy fizzing out as orange sparks.

He put out his hand to touch my head, fingertips glowing a bluish colour.

'Do you mind?'

'Knock yourself out.'

He placed his fingertips on my temple. I had thought it would feel creepy, but because I was made of the better parts of him, it felt weirdly as though I were touching my own head, only with thick gloves. I could also feel his mind inside mine, teasing and looking, searching and ferreting, as though drawers were being pulled out and the contents dumped on the floor in a search for well-laid plans or magical contraband, similar to the early-morning raids the nuns used to pull on us back at the orphanage. As Shandar delved I had little flashbacks of the past couple of weeks as he teased the information from my head, but I feared nothing. There was no plan; I had agreed to his deal, and was quite willing to keep my side of it.

'Nothing sinister there,' he said, 'but I can feel the goodness that was once mine – it comes across as old fashioned and stale, like listening to the tiresome and idealistic rants of a naive youth. I can also sense you despise me. A couple of hundred years will bring you around to my way of thinking. I'm really quite endearing when you get to know the better of the worst parts of me.'

'I'll have to take your word for it.'

He ran his hands over my small amount of luggage, and then the Volkswagen.

'Any spells hidden anywhere? A sorcerer miniaturised and hiding in the glovebox? A Dibble Jar full of crackle waiting to do me some mischief?'

'Nothing,' I said.

'I still need to be cautious,' he said. 'There are always a few naysayers who want to rain on your parade when you contemplate galactic domination.'

He gently laid his fingertips on the Beetle's bonnet, and there was a low humming noise. Shandar paused, like a tuner listening to a piano. He moved down the rear panel, then reached right under the car in the area of the engine and pulled out a small Bovril jar that had been tightly stoppered with red wax.

'What's this?' he asked.

'You've just been inside my head,' I told him. 'I don't know – and you know I don't know.'

He sniffed it delicately, then covered it with both his hands.

'Well, well,' he said, 'a timed thermowizidrical explosive device, due to go off in twenty-six minutes and eight seconds. Written in ARAMAIC V3.4, to give a low wizidrical signature. It looks like one of Monty's. I will concede he's a good spell-writer. If he'd been able to do magic as well, he may even have been relevant. It's a little crude, though. A *bomb*? I thought they would have been more imaginative.'

'Powerful enough to start a chain reaction?' I asked.

'No – it would just have taken a sizeable chunk out of the tower and enough to topple it. Your friends just tried to kill you,' he continued with a smirk. 'Funny how people turn on their chums when they get desperate, isn't it?'

'I would only be collateral damage in the assassination of a tyrant,' I replied. 'They would have happily accepted the same fate, even if engineered by me. And I would have,' I added, fixing him with my best steely gaze.

'You pompously self-righteous people are all the same,' he said, 'horribly—'

'Pompous and self-righteous?' I suggested.

'I was going to say "disgustingly smug". And I'm not a tyrant. In fact, I'm probably the least tyrannical person you know.'

He didn't go on to explain why he thought this, or even why he thought I should believe it. He then crushed the explosive device in his hands, and the stored wizidrical energy flooded into his body.

'Happy now?' I asked.

'No,' he said, continuing his search in and around my Beetle, 'for if *I* wanted to assassinate someone, I would place two weapons – one hard to find, and the other almost impossible.'

He was right, and eventually found the second, which had been suspended inside a glass jar filled with water – always a good way to cloak wizidrical energy. It was well concealed, too – Shandar had to actually reach *through* the metal to retrieve it.

'*Much* more impressive,' he said, showing me the jar, which was glowing a soft shade of emerald green in his hands.

'Now *this* might have kicked off a chain reaction,' he said, almost admiringly. 'D'you know, I almost respect your wizardy chums. There was only a 4% chance I wouldn't find it, but at least they *tried*.'

He absorbed the power from this one, too.

'We're clear,' he said finally. 'One of the Hollow maids will show you to your quarters.'

'When do we leave?' I asked.

'Leave? My dear girl, we've already left. We're currently 20,000 feet above the Earth, travelling at roughly fifty times the speed of horse. We'll pick up more speed once the Quarkbeast conjoinment occurs, but we won't be leaving the solar system straight away – as chance would have it, Jupiter and Saturn are in conjunction, so we can drop off for a look-see on the way out. After that, I'll ramp up the speed and we'll head off across interstellar space to Proxima Centauri, allowing me to refuel myself, then jump into a more richly inhabited part of the galaxy – somewhere that will give me greater scope for the crushing of worthless peons who dare to oppose my might.'

I stared at him.

'Or,' he added quickly, 'to a place where you can advise me how best to temper my worst excesses to maximise the size and reach of the Shandarian Empire. Now say goodbye to the Beast and I shall elevate myself to immortality.'

The Quarkbeast had been sitting there, quite happily, and wagged its tail as I knelt down to say goodbye. I'd never hugged it before as its sharpened scales didn't lend themselves easily to cuddling unless there is a large tin of plasters and a bottle of iodine to hand, but as I approached his spines folded flat into his back and he closed his mouth tight so his fangs wouldn't show. I placed my hand on his back and he purred at me.

'Sure you're okay with this?'

He wagged his tail and licked my face, which felt raspy and smelled of rusty hammers.

'You've been a good friend,' I said. 'Thank you.'

'Goodbye, Jennifer. The best view of Jupiter is from the orbit of Ganymede.'

'What did you say?' asked Shandar.

'I didn't say anything.'

I hugged the Quarkbeast tightly. I'd had to trust Maltcassion the moment before I slayed him, and the Quarkbeast had told me that death brings about opportunity. I'd also learned that death is sometimes not the worst thing that can happen: it can be a gateway, whereby old things pass away and new and better things arrive in their place.

I relaxed my grip on the Quarkbeast, and he wagged his tail again, gave me a wink, laid his paw on my hand and then trotted off towards the central stairway and the Quarkbeast Deck.

'Quark,' he said as an afterthought once in the stairwell. 'Quark-Quark-Quark.'

'Why do you shed tears for something that isn't real?' asked Shandar, staring at me.

'You couldn't possibly understand,' I replied.

He smiled.

'But you will teach me. Now: I'm going to give you free rein to move around the tower, but if I suspect you're getting up to any monkey business, I will have you bricked up in your quarters. The one thing I've learned about Jennifer Strange is that she's very resourceful, but since you have no plans or magical gadgets to help you out, I have little to fear from you. But the threat of bricking you up in your quarters remains. Understand?'

'I understand.'

'Good. The Hollow maid will show you to your rooms.'

And so saying, Shandar vanished.

The Hollow maid was dressed the same as the other Hollow Women, but with the addition of a white apron with pockets. She, like the rest of the Hollow people, was just empty clothes hanging in the air.

'Lead on,' I said, and she walked me towards the elevators.

'Mind the step,' she said in a weirdly empty voice.

'You can talk?' I asked.

'The Glorious Leader has great plans for make good benevolent domination of galaxy,' she said mechanically. 'We are earmarked for Mandrake Sentience Emulation Protocol upgrades. His Mightiness believes eons better spent more comfortably with servants who have personality. Is this good?'

'Yes. You'll enjoy the protocols.'

'I do not feel real today. Will I, in time?'

I thought about the Quarkbeast and the Transient Moose, both of whom had a personality, despite being little more than a spell.

'Whether biologically or wizidrically based, it makes no difference. Once you care for others, and understand kindness, empathy and the value of friendship and selflessness, you've got what it takes to be human. Nothing else matters.'

'Your word I will take for this.'

'Do you have a name?'

'I would like you to name me. I think you will be good at that.'

'Blousie.'

'I like that,' said Blousie, 'it is a good name. Do you want to hear a joke? I tell jokes well. It is about a family of balloons during a thunderstorm. I think you will laugh.'

'Maybe later. For now just show me to my quarters.'

Jupiter and Beyond

My quarters were modelled on Zambini Towers with all the shabbiness included — water stains, peeling wallpaper and rickety furniture, I think to make me feel more at home. I had an entire floor to myself — the fifty-third storey — comprising sixteen rooms including library, gym, sitting room, reading room, den, workshop, two laboratories and six more empty rooms 'to expand into'. I also had a walk-in observation chamber that was built on the outside of the tower, with a large semicircular viewing port the size of my car. There was a comfy armchair in the centre from where to sit and watch the heavens, something that even in my sullen and dejected mood rarely failed to entertain.

We'd been travelling for two weeks now, and the Quarkbeast conjoinment had taken place on the second day. I stayed in my quarters when it happened, as there was no pleasure in witnessing the Mighty Shandar elevate himself to the status of an immortal: ridiculously overblown acts of self-aggrandisement he could do on his own. The song of the Quarkbeast had echoed through the building when they recombined to liberate the 2^{63} TeraShandars of pure wizidrical energy, and even with my pillow held tight to my ears, it still got inside me, and I wept, not for my Quarkbeast, but for all of them, and what this meant for Shandar, and his ambitions, and his unbridled, misused power. The Eye of Zoltar had done exactly what it was supposed to do: absorbed and then focused the raw wizidrical energy directly into Shandar's body. Every cell of his being now coursed with energy, elevating him to a level of unheard-of power.

It didn't stop him being a massive twat, though. I'd avoided him for a week afterwards. But even in the seventy-seven storeys of the tower this was tricky as he would often teleport in to where I happened to be, as if by accident, and want to talk about how terrific he was and how fantastic were his plans.

I'd be hard pressed to find a fortnight I enjoyed less.

I was in the observation room staring out of the port, still in my pyjamas even though it was past ten. I hate to admit it, but I was thinking about myself. I was feeling self-pity, and that was worrying, because I'd always viewed it as a wasteful, destructive emotion. I had been surrendered by my parents to be brought up as a countermeasure, my personality inextricably bound to a rejected group of emotions.

My lot, my destiny, my purpose, was to simply dilute the more violent impulses of a megalomaniacal idiot.

How successful I would be in controlling Shandar's worst excesses was yet to be seen, but was also something of an ethical dilemma: do you give tacit support to a tyrant to ensure he murders *less* than he would have? And could you ever justify that position?

So here I was, stuck on a replica New York skyscraper with a sorcerer of almost infinite powers heading off to who-knows-where. Shandar had to be stopped, *yet I had nothing in the plans chest*. What could someone who had zero magic do against someone who had enough power to achieve immortality, travel to the stars and even rewrite the laws of physics?

There was a knock at the door.

'Good morning, Miss Strange,' said Blousie, who was now my official maid. She'd been matching herself to my personality over the past few weeks to make our social engagement easier, and oddly, she was turning out to be like Tiger – mildly sarcastic with an odd sense of humour.

'Hello,' I replied. 'What news?'

'His Supreme Mightiness would like to have a chat,' she said. 'He's on the control deck.'

'What does he want to talk about?' I asked.

'His favourite subject, I imagine,' said Blousie, 'himself.'

Shandar fancied himself as a living god, but I

disagreed. There were six basic qualities to being a deity: omniscience, omnipresence, empathy, humility, guidance and forgiveness. The only one he had on the list was the second – and only a bit of that. Which gave him about a ten per cent pass rate. Not even an 'E minus' – I'd got a higher grade for baking back at the orphanage. But I think he was after another god-like attribute, which wasn't on the list at all: the unswerving adulation of a large group of zealously committed followers.

'Will you go?' asked Blousie. 'I'm meant to convey your message back to Miss D'Argento.'

'Tell her I'll be ten minutes.'

I always told them that but often took half an hour – or didn't turn up at all. I went back to the observation port, where Jupiter was looming large and dominant. When the planet first hove into view, Shandar had summoned me to the control deck and asked me to describe what I felt about the gas giant, as the rejected Better Angels of his Nature had included his sense of natural beauty and aesthetics. A successful Tyrant, he argued, must be able to destroy beautiful things without hesitation if it furthers their cause. I described Jupiter as best as I could, but no words could do it justice. From here we could easily see the colourful gaseous clouds that swathed the planet and the Great Red Spot, a perpetually raging storm the size of Earth. We couldn't actually see the clouds moving, but occasionally an aurora would crackle around the poles, shimmer for a while and then die down. It was spectacularly beautiful.

The Earth and Moon had shrunk rapidly in size as we'd pulled away, until they were distant, then small, then dots, then almost impossible to differentiate from anything else on the velvety backdrop of stars. There were eight days of apparent emptiness – Mars was on the other side of the sun, and couldn't be seen – then Jupiter began to loom larger and larger until it dominated our view. But there was no enjoyment to be had in any of it. My friends, although safe, were now far behind, and our task, to vanquish Shandar, had failed. He would travel to the stars, he would do all that he set out to do. His centuries of planning and preparation had been time extremely well spent.

I watched as the largest of Jupiter's moons moved into the periphery of my vision: Ganymede. It looked a little like our moon, grey and pocked with craters, but with a grooved surface and polar caps. Why, precisely, the Quarkbeast had suggested that the view from Ganymede was something to behold, I wasn't sure. But then I had a thought. Maybe the message wasn't in the message. Maybe the message was *the fact that I had received a message at all.*

I had a quick shower, dressed and made my way to the control deck, the nerve centre of Shandar's ambitions. The steel-clad spire with serried ranks of triangular windows had been replaced by a large transparent dome which gave a better view than from my observation deck, and the lack of any reflections on the polished crystal gave a seamless ringside seat to view the cosmos. The sun was a quarter of the size I had been used to, but still too bright to look at with the naked eye. As we watched, it set behind the planet and the thin corona around Jupiter's edge became a lively myriad of colours. The lights on the control deck dimmed and as our eyes became accustomed to the dark, the billions of stars in the Milky Way became clearly visible.

'It's quite something, isn't it?' said D'Argento, who had been trying very hard to make friends. She'd told me all about her time with Shandar since the age of sixteen, one of the dynastic family agents who had looked after the sorcerer for centuries. I had not been interested.

'The sun seen through the plumes of the marzoleum plant back home used to wobble and shimmer quite beautifully,' I said, 'and the views I saw in the Cambrian Empire were something really quite special.'

'Meaning?'

'Meaning you don't need to come four hundred million miles to find something of beauty.'

Shandar teleported in next to me. Too close, in fact, and I took a step back so he wasn't in my personal space.

'The stars are our destiny,' he said, sounding terribly grand. He did this a lot now, and reminded me a little of Grifflon's ornamental hermit – full of faux wisdom.

'They're *your* destiny,' I said, 'not mine.'

'I spared six billion souls on your account, Jenny,' he said. 'I delayed my plans thirty-seven years to accommodate your feelings, so a little bit of gratitude might be in order. Brunch?'

I looked at the dinner table. It was the only place to eat in the tower, and he insisted that D'Argento and I always dined with him. It was Shandar who chose the topics of conversation, and for the most part dominated it. Things he had done, spells he had cast, the beasts he had created. He spoke of the Dragonpact from his viewpoint, as it seemed it was less about 'freeing mankind from the loathsome worm' but ridding himself of a dangerous adversary – and how it would have worked perfectly, if not for my tiresome meddling. He talked about his future plans, too, in more detail. They were quite ruthless, and as he talked I often felt my concentration lapse, then wander to happier times. Hide and seek in the orchard back at the orphanage, in a place free of the Sisterhood's attention; my early times at Zambini Towers under Zambini's wise counsel; the search for the Eye of Zoltar. Tiger, the Princess, Perkins. Boo, Mawgon, Wizard Moobin. All fine people.

'I want you to both have a look at these ideas for

my Emperor of Everything costume,' said Shandar once we were seated, pointing to a pile of notebooks on a sideboard. 'It's either long robes in crimson or something more like leathery armour – both have their advantages.'

'What if there's no one there?' I asked.

'No one where?' asked Shandar.

'Out there,' I said, pointing towards the heavens. 'What if all the advanced intelligence in the galaxy was living on a pale blue dot orbiting a medium-sized sun on an outer spiral arm of a none-too-unusual galaxy? What if the best you get to rule over is something jelly-like that has only just dragged itself out of a shallow sea?'

'It's a good point,' said Shandar, 'and one which I have considered. If life has not yet emerged, then I will create my own, and populate worlds with creatures made in my image. I will truly then be a god. Not one that assumes or has assumed their power – but a *real* one. A Creator. A Controller. A Grand Architect. The One Who Is All Things To All Creatures.'

'You can't create things just so you can control them,' I said. 'That's not being a god – that's just being a massive bully led by a galactic-class ego – a child building sandcastles on the beach so he can knock them down.'

I saw Shandar clench and unclench his fists.

'You test me daily, Miss Strange.'

'You said you wanted to learn about your Better Angels: this is called humility.'

'I disagree with your approach,' he replied. 'You are to bring my Better Natures forward as a conductor brings up the bassoons – only when required, and in moderation.'

There was silence for a few moments.

'You must have some of this kedgeree,' said D'Argento nervously, 'it's really very good.'

'I have some toast,' I said, nibbling on a corner. Shandar's power and ambitions weren't the only thing worrying me right now. My goading of him had another purpose: to remind myself how much I despised him. He had decided during his self-spelled immortality to de-age himself back to about thirty-five and to make himself more handsome. To Shandar, there was no point becoming a god if you were walking around in a body not fit for purpose. In this I had little interest except that, worryingly, and despite everything, I found myself thinking that he was not unpleasing to the eye. Worse, on another occasion I thought one of his jokes hardly rubbish at all. There could only be one explanation for this: he was *beguiling* me with his new-found power. If this were to run to its logical conclusion, my resolve would be removed entirely and with it any chance to potentially save the lives of the trillions of sentient lives which currently had no idea at all of their possible annihilation.

It would be preventive tyranny at its very finest. So long as I could act.

'How are your quarters?' Shandar asked.

'A gilded cage is still a cage,' I replied.

'Your humour is very surly at present,' said Shandar, helping himself to more kedgeree. 'Something wrong?'

'Where do you want me to start? I am here because I was coerced. You have kidnapped me and expect me to do your bidding.'

'You came of your own free will,' said Shandar. 'You could have refused my deal and died with your species and planet. That option was always open to you.'

'It was no option and you know it.'

'There you go with that ingratitude of yours again,' said Shandar. 'I am about to elevate you to the status of a god. What can you possibly have against me?'

'The Better Angels of our nature are there to prompt us to a better place,' I said, 'and to offer virtuous judgement to guide us all to honourable conduct. You want to manipulate mercy only to feed your personal ambitions. Besides, I am mortal, and to be honest, what is stopping me from taking a one-way trip out of the airlock? You need the better side of yourself to achieve lasting domination; you said so yourself – evil alone is not enough; a stick is valueless without the carrot, criticism worthless unless tempered by praise.'

He stared thoughtfully at me for a moment.

'Agreed,' he said finally. 'You are too valuable during this early re-educational phase to be lost.'

He pointed a finger at me. I experienced a brief shudder and suddenly felt stronger and lighter and more buoyant. I moved my hands and they seemed to work with greater precision and speed.

'There,' he said, 'I have given you immortality and invulnerability.' He paused to let this sink in. 'You are now like me, a superhuman whose destiny is to lead. You may not see it straight away, but you'll come round to it. And you will admire and respect your master for what I am doing, given time.'

'I'm immortal?'

'You're welcome. You will age naturally until you are twenty-two and perfect in every way, then stay that way for ever. Our wedding party will be delayed until our first planetary conquest: no point in making a star go nova[57] without any witnesses, eh?'

'You should really say thank you,' said D'Argento. 'This is an honour not yet even bestowed upon me, and I am the Mighty Shandar's most loyal subject.'

'Everything comes to those who wait, my dear,' said Shandar, laying his hand affectionately on D'Argento's.

---

[57] 'Going nova': an exploding star. Shandar's idea of a firework display. I don't suppose he cared whether that sun was home to a friendly system of planets.

She moved slightly as he did, and for a fleeting moment I thought I could sense disgust on her face – but then it was gone and she pressed her other hand on his and smiled sweetly.

I'd never thought of what it would be like to be immortal – one doesn't, really, but I could muse on it now. It seemed only a mere flash since I left the orphanage. If that's what the passage of time felt like, the inevitable end of the universe would doubtless come cantering up with annoying rapidity. I thought again of how the view from the orbit of Ganymede was something to behold.

'What did you say?' said Shandar, his tone sharper than normal. He'd heard it when the Quarkbeast communicated it to me the first time, and the suspicion I'd had earlier about the message suddenly made more sense. I had a daring thought. But if I was right, I didn't want to raise his suspicions.

'I was just thinking,' I said, 'why don't we drop into orbit around Ganymede? We could use the time to acclimatise in a place closer to home – and study Jupiter, or at the very least collect some data to analyse at our leisure.'

He looked at me, eyes narrowed.

'Are you up to something, Jennifer?'

'I just think a moment of reflection before departing our home solar system would be time well spent, that's all.'

'I disagree. My decision is made, I need no time for reflection.'

'Since Jennifer is your empathy consultant,' said D'Argento in a rare moment of support, 'I think it might be a good idea.'

Shandar stared at D'Argento, then back at me.

'Very well,' he said finally. 'Ganymede, eh? It will be a good opportunity to see how well I can manoeuvre the tower at close quarters. A useful skill I should hone now, before we head over to Proxima Centauri. Besides, you are still not fully understanding the brilliance of my mission. Perhaps you need a couple of weeks so we can straighten it out in your head. Who knows? By the end of that fortnight you could have completely changed your mind about me.'

He smiled as he said it. My suspicions about a beguiling were correct.

'That might indeed help,' I said. 'Would you pass the Waldorf salad?[58] I seem to have developed something of an appetite.'

'That's good,' said Shandar. 'I do so hate girls who pick at their food.'

So we ate, and chatted, and Shandar, now more relaxed, was saying that if he couldn't get enough

---

[58] Named after the Waldorf-Astoria Hotel, this salad is made of apple, celery, walnuts and grapes on a bed of lettuce, liberally drizzled with mayonnaise.

power from sucking the energy out of Proxima Centauri, we'd pop on over to Barnard's Star and harvest that one too. He made it sound like nipping down to the corner store for another packet of crisps. But while he was talking, it suddenly made a lot more sense that Monty had left those crude and easily discovered thermowizidrical devices in my car. They were never going to detonate; they were always going to be found. They were simply diversions in case Shandar was suspicious about the lack of an attack. If he found those, he would look no further. *And it worked. He didn't.* The real plan was much subtler – and given Monty, Boo and Mawgon knew Shandar would search my mind for any clues, anything they cooked up I couldn't know anything about. They would have to trust me to figure out what they were up to.

And I'm quite good at figuring stuff out.

But they knew that, too.

'What are you smiling about?' asked Shandar.

'Because I'm lucky.'

'To be here with me now on this adventure?'

'No, I'm thinking that even out here, I have friends. The sort that have your back and give you the tools to do the job you need to do. They understand you, they trust you, they take care of you, and they never give up, no matter how bad things appear.'

'That's a heart-warming little story,' said Shandar,

plopping his napkin on his plate as a Hollow waiter moved his chair so he could stand up, 'but I have work to do. The tower is the size of six cathedrals, so manoeuvring it into Ganymede's orbit will be a little like trying to reverse an ocean liner into the Panama Canal at top speed blindfolded – not for the faint hearted, and requiring skill, dexterity and a sound understanding of mass, gravity and converging veloc-ities. Why not watch? You might learn something.'

'I'll watch from here while I finish my breakfast.'

Shandar nodded, then walked to the elegant wooden pulpit in the middle of the room, which looked as though it had been swiped from a cathedral some-where. He raised his hands and I felt the tower move as he warped the space beneath us to shift the mass of the skyscraper towards the Jovian moon. I looked up to see D'Argento staring at me in an odd manner.

'Something on your mind, Jenny?' she asked.

'Can I ask you a question?'

'I will answer as honestly as I can,' she replied.

'What do you get out of this?'

'I get an opportunity,' replied D'Argento thought-fully, 'to be in the right place at the right time, to assist a truly great person in their moment of triumph.'

'Are you sure about that?'

She looked me straight in the eye.

'I've never been so sure of anything in my life.'

'I think I'll have some of the kedgeree after all,' I

said, and walked to the sideboard, where a Hollow waiter handed me a plate. I took a good spoonful – it smelled delicious – then walked off to a seat by the fire.

While Shandar and D'Argento were distracted – he placing the Chrysler Building into orbit around Ganymede, she flicking through the designs of suitable Evil Emperor costumes – I placed my hands on the brooch that Lady Mawgon had given me. When she had, she'd made up some stuff about how she wished she'd been more pleasant – probably also a diversion – but then crucially had given me the order that 'I was to carry it with me always'. Not unusual, you might think, but it became more relevant when added to other events: when Once Magnificent Boo said goodbye she had added that 'with eternal life must come limitless power'; and, crucially, the Quarkbeast communicated with me when I first came into the tower, even though he can only do that one way: *through Mysterious X.* I think it meant two things. Firstly, that the Mysterious X had snuck on board hidden among the atoms in Mawgon's brooch, and secondly, that there was nothing particular about Ganymede that was important. The real message was this: *We have your back – and whatever you do, don't let him leave the solar system.* There was something else, too. Zambini's second message, the one I got through Molly: *Help will come from an unexpected quarter.*

If all this was true, the time of action was right now.

I got up from the table, and with Shandar amusing himself by manoeuvring the tower, I walked down the stairwell from the control deck, out of sight of him, D'Argento and any of the Hollow staff. Colin had told me how he had spoken to the Mysterious X, so I closed my eyes and imagined myself back in the lobby of Zambini Towers, standing at reception, the old oak growing to the ceiling, the delightful shabbiness. I then imagined myself shouting as loudly as possible the following words: 'If you can hear this, answer by sending a single charged particle through one of the light receptors on my retina, because when you speak to me, Shandar hears. Everything you've put in my head so far he's picked up.'

In an instant there was a small white flash in the periphery of my vision. The Mysterious X was listening. I imagined myself shouting again, but this time, it was my plan. It was simple and audacious, was in two parts, and required the Mysterious X to tap into my life-force to harvest the energy he needed. I had to hope he could, because I now contained a lot of power: I knew from both Perkins and Wizard Moobin's early passing that if a sorcerer runs out of wizidrical energy there is always somewhere else to go: your own life-force. Because essentially, all magic *was* life-force, the power of human emotion – love, anger, sadness, jealousy, grief. Perkins could tap into a lot of power because he was young, Moobin less so because his time on Earth was already up. I had more in reserve than either of them. I had life immortal, and I could trade that for potentially limitless amounts of wizidrical energy.

Annoyingly, so could Shandar. But unlike me, he wouldn't actually want to. He needed his immortality to live for ever: I only needed mine to defeat him. Which kind of gave me the edge – so long as the Mysterious X could spell strongly enough and the unexpected help was both real, and actually helpful.

There were two flashes in my eye to show X understood my plan, and my heart began to beat faster as I felt the Nebulous Entity go to work weaving and spelling inside me. I felt stronger, more powerful, more confident. A buzz started at my shoulder and then worked its way down my arm until I could feel my fingertips start to tingle. I pointed at the nearest Hollow Man and he turned to brown paper in an instant and fluttered to the floor. I smiled to myself, and walked back upstairs to the control deck.

'What do you think?' asked the Mighty Shandar. The Chrysler Building was now moving slowly around Ganymede, sixty miles out. The view was spectacular, but that wasn't foremost on my mind right now.

'Impressive,' I said.

'Indeed,' replied Shandar, staring at me with a look of surprise on his face, 'and so are you. How did you smuggle a sorcerer on board?'

'I don't know what you mean.'

'I can feel you radiating wizidrical energy like a hot stove,' he said. 'Who gave you that power?'

'It doesn't matter,' I replied. 'The stars are not your destiny and you will not spread your tyranny into the galaxy. This all ends right now.'

He seemed unimpressed by my threat.

'Better Angels are an overrated commodity,' he murmured. 'I shall take them back and bestow them upon someone more willing to embrace my will.'

He pointed a finger towards me and I instinctively put out the flat of my open palm to stop him. I felt pressure on my hand, holding back his power, and then in an instant he had overcome me and I was hanging upside down about eight feet up, my arms tightly behind my back, a soft sphere of sparkling blue light around me. I was trapped.

'Well, well,' said Shandar, moving towards me. 'Looks like we may have to bring our once cosy relationship to a premature close. That's a shame, Jennifer, dear, because once I had properly assimilated your heart and mind to me and my cause, you would have been a dazzlingly good ambassador and a delightfully compliant wife. It wasn't just my Better Angels I needed to use – *it was yours*. A righteous person utterly corrupted would have been an awesome diplomatic weapon, but it is of no matter – I will simply retrieve what is mine, take what is yours and abandon you on Ganymede. A Jennifer Strange but with all the very best bits taken out. You will live life eternal in isolation as an embittered angry wretch, a twisted knot of hate, anger and jealously.'

His pretence of charm had all but vanished. I was a threat, this was business, and in business he was ruthless. He pointed a finger at me and I felt my insides begin to move and shift, along with a curious draining feeling as he began to draw out the Better Angels – his, and mine. I started to feel not anger and fear but petty jealousies in that D'Argento was better looking than me, had better clothes and more money, and I wanted that stuff too, and would steal it from her when I got the chance. I stopped breathing and felt myself collapse inwards as my vision began to fade. I think I saw Shandar laughing, and then, quite abruptly, the pain stopped, and all jealousies vanished as the Better Angels snapped back inside me, the blue sphere vanished and I fell out of the air to land, fortuitously, on an armchair, but in an untidy heap. By the time I had got up, Shandar had dropped to his knees and his mouth was wide open, face contorted in pain. Behind him, Miss D'Argento was holding the Eye of Zoltar in a pair of blacksmith's tongs and pressed hard on the small of his back. The Eye, suitably reversed, was doing what it did best: absorbing and then focusing wizidrical energy. Only this time it was taking it *out* of Shandar, and the energy was streaming in a narrow beam out of the window and to the surface of Ganymede.

'I've waited so long for this moment,' said D'Argento, lips pressed together in a single line. I looked at her, then at Shandar, whose arms were now stretching out in length to more easily dislodge the jewel from D'Argento's hold.

'I don't understand,' I said.

D'Argento looked at me and smiled. But it wasn't the smile of Shandar's agent, it was the smile of someone closer. A friend perhaps, or even a family member.

'You asked what I was to get out of this,' she said. 'I told you "an opportunity to assist a truly great person in their moment of triumph".'

'So?'

She smiled.

'I wasn't talking about Shandar. Now: that plan of yours, whatever it is – I know you have one – make it happen.'

The sorcerer's arms were plucking uselessly at the jewel, trying to dislodge it from the tongs held tightly by D'Argento. He was still on his knees, head down, greatly weakened by the effort and the power that was flowing out of him. I stepped forward, but then hesitated as Shandar's creepily long arms plucked the Eye of Zoltar from D'Argento's grasp.

'That *really* hurt,' he said, panting with the exertion. He was still kneeling on the floor, sweating profusely. His arms cracked and squeaked as they returned to their normal size, and the Eye vanished from his grasp – teleported, I presumed, to a safe place.

'Winning the bout is not winning the fight,' he gasped, trying to stand but falling back to his knees, 'but I am the Mighty and most magnificent Shandar, more powerful and fabulous than you can possibly imagine. You took some of my power, but not enough to make a difference – harvesting your sun will easily replace the shortfall. You cannot defeat me.'

In this, I think, he was correct. While X could channel a huge amount of power through my life-force, X or I would never have the skills to defeat him on a wizard's field of battle. I was the rowboat, and he the battlecruiser. But I knew what I had to do. I knelt down in front of him and wrapped my arms tightly around him.

'I don't need to defeat you,' I whispered in his ear, 'all I need to do is what you asked: help you understand the lost opportunity to have done something truly useful with your life.'

The Mysterious X then spelled the first part of my plan: to give Shandar back the Better Angels of his Nature. All of them, every last little bit. And in that moment of self-realisation, the true understanding of his heinous crimes and the depth of his malevolent intent, his face crumpled.

'Oh my good God,' he said in a quiet voice. 'What have I become?'

He started to sob, as the many burdens of his inflicted sorrows flooded his mind, as if all the people he had crushed and defeated and murdered were crowded inside his head, questioning him, condemning him, and finding him wanting.

But I knew this would not last for long. The evil that was Shandar was greater than the man, and would reject the Better Angels as he had before. No, I needed him weakened by the burden of his guilt so I could make my last and only play, the second part of my instructions to the Mysterious X: *a thermowiz-idrical detonation large enough to achieve criticality.* Shandar, myself, D'Argento and the tower and the Hollow Men and all the spells herein, utterly annihilated in an uncontrolled explosion of epic proportions. I held on to him and yelled: 'Now, X, now!'

I closed my eyes tightly, ready to welcome the nothingness that would announce my success.

'Was something meant to happen?' said D'Argento, and I opened my eyes. I looked down at Shandar, whose evil personality was beginning to re-form as he once more expelled the Better Angels. Worse, even in his weakened state, he was still more powerful than me.

'You little fool,' he said in a weak voice. 'You do not have the emotional energy needed to focus your powers to initiate a criticality. You are weak, as you have always been. But never fear, I shall give you the end that you so desire – only it will be on your own: sad, unremembered and unmourned, abandoned on Ganymede to watch as I suck the sun dry of its power.'

He paused, weakened by the speech. But already I could feel his power returning; it would not be long. He would succeed. He was all-powerful.

I felt a hand on my shoulder, and D'Argento's voice close to my ear. It was soft, and warm, and caring.

'Our parents live in a village outside Leominster,' she began, 'in a small house with a wisteria on the gable. There is a swing in the garden under an apple tree and the paddock leads down to a brook. In the springtime, the blossom drifts around the house like snow, and in the summer the hedgerows are alive with the creamy scent of meadowsweet. Our father John looks after the house and our mother Lynda is head nurse at the local hospital. She is good at her job, and much admired. Zambini came to them and explained what was needed, what we, and they, had to do. You at Kazam and me embedded with Shandar. They followed our progress, and love us, miss us, and will be proud. But they knew that we had a function to play in the Great Scheme of Things, they understood that, and put aside their sorrows, and love us just the same.'

I felt my eyes fill with tears. I thought of the photograph I'd found in the glovebox, and the unseen child in the back of the VW Beetle. I also remembered the misspelling of the writing on the back. Only it *wasn't* a misspelling.

'Assett is our surname, isn't it?' I said.

'Yes,' she replied. 'I am Belinda, and you are Catrina. You are my little sister by four years.'

'Catrina Assett,' I said whispering my birth name for the first time.

Belinda hugged me tightly, as a big sister might do.

'Thank you,' I whispered, and she told me I needed to act while there was still time.

Because I could, now.

Magic is an invisible energy field that flows about us, powered by the force of human emotion: anger, sadness, greed, hope, love – and *joy*. The joy of knowing who you are, who your sister is, and that she, and your parents, love you.

'You lose,' I said, holding Shandar even tighter, 'as you were always going to.'

'Wait, what?' he said, struggling to get out of my grasp. I think in that brief moment he felt real terror, and the anger and ignominy of defeat.

I didn't. I imagined myself back in the lobby of Zambini Towers, but I was not alone. Moobin was there, and Zambini, and Feldspar, and the Quarkbeast, and Perkins, and Captain Lutumba and her crew and all the others who had not made it this far. And they were all smiling, because I had done what I had set out to do. The right thing, for them, for everyone.

I felt Shandar struggle ever more violently to get out of my embrace, but Belinda added her arms to mine to hold him close, to ensure that the wizidrical detonation went critical.

'No, wait,' he said, 'you can't—'

'Now,' I said, but I wasn't speaking to Shandar, I was speaking to the Mysterious X.

And there was light.

And there was heat.

And then . . . there was *opportunity*.

. . .

Epilogue

'How can you be sure what happened to Jennifer right at the end?' asked Tiger as he finished reading my typewritten notes. 'Especially as no one really knows whether the Mysterious X was real, or just a few orphaned good ideas in need of a hypothesis.'

'I can't,' I replied, 'but we are all agreed that Shandar and his tower were utterly destroyed. Astronomers have noted a disturbance in the orbit of Ganymede, as though a large chunk was blown out of it – and two comets were ejected from the conflagration, fast and dense enough to easily overcome Jupiter's gravitational pull and accelerate off out of the solar system.'

We were speaking at a small café in the main square in Hereford. Most of the damage inflicted by the Troll invasion had been repaired by now, but even so, two years on, there were still blackened façades and boarded-up buildings. The plinth next to the old Black and White house now carried a bronze of Jennifer and was surrounded, as usual, by fresh floral tributes. Her effigy was simple, rather than heroic. Lifesize, with

Jennifer leaning on Exhorbitus, the Quarkbeast by her side.

'She triumphed, that much is clear,' I said. 'The galaxy is safe.'

'I sincerely hope so,' said Tiger, 'but again: how can you be *so* sure any of this happened as you say it did?'

I didn't know at first, either. The ideas just popped into my head, the same way they did when I was asked to think up something 'big and bold' for Jennifer upstairs at the Globe, the only time I met her. I needed to know more, and on a hunch I drove to Leominster, and after a lot of exploring found what I was looking for: a small cottage with an apple tree in the garden and a wisteria on the gable, the paddock leading down to the stream. There was only one way I could have known that: the ideas had not been mine. John and Lynda Assett were polite and cordial, proud of their daughters, but didn't want their identities revealed. Humility runs in their family.

'It just rings true,' I said, 'don't you agree?'

'I do,' said Tiger, 'every word.'

I wasn't guided to write *everything*, though – only the part in the Chrysler Building. The rest I pieced together from a multitude of sources over two years, and speaking to the participants had often been a humbling experience. Jennifer had inspired those around her to a sense of higher account – no one embellished anything, or made her more heroic and selfless than she was. There was really no need. I'd asked Once Magnificent Boo what she had thought the Mysterious X actually was, and she told me that maybe something, *somewhere*, keeps a careful eye on potential usurpers, and works in mysterious ways to defeat them. I *think* I understood what she was talking about.

'Did you hear Lady Mawgon became court mystician?' asked Tiger.

'A wise choice,' I said, 'and Colin is leading a delegation to ensure the newly formed United Kingdoms are more closely aligned with Europe.'

'He's a good negotiator,' said Tiger, 'even if he does have a silly sense of humour. The coronation was quite something, wasn't it?'

Tiger was being ironic. There was no huge coronation, just a five-minute ceremony. The Queen's low-key approach to her new-found status was well received in the islands, along with her decision to transfer power to a representative democracy within twenty years.

'It might be the first and only time an all-powerful leader divested themselves of limitless power,' said Tiger. 'A pointer for tyrants and dictators everywhere.'

There was a pause. Tiger had been invaluable in giving me the basics of the story as he had known Jennifer the best, and had established himself as the go-to person for any Jennifer Strange consultations.

Without Tiger's say-so *The Last Dragonslayer Chronicles* would not be simply unpublishable, they'd be dead in the water. Tiger had invoked Jennifer's spirit in his decision:

Get it right or don't do it at all.

'I say go for it,' he said, handing me back my outline notes – four books, each dealing with a different part of her story. 'I can't see how else this should be told.'

'Thank you,' I said, placing the sheaf of papers in my bag. 'What's with the Quarkbeast?'

I had noticed the small creature when I arrived, sitting on Tiger's foot and eating the copper windings from a starter motor. It was about the size of a guinea-pig and had markings like those of a silver birch.

'I don't know,' he said. 'Perhaps there is trouble brewing up ahead. Legend says the Quarkbeast appears to those in need of assistance, but I think I've got some time. It won't be fully grown until I am almost ninety.'

'About the same time the twin comets from the Wizidrical Criticality return,' I mused, as astronomers had already tracked their journey, and seen hundreds of smaller comets break from the two and streak off in all directions. They would be visiting new worlds, outside ours, as if on a journey of discovery. The smaller comets would never return, but the larger two would. Officially, they were known to science as B769-D; unofficially as 'The Two Sisters'.

I finished my coffee and stood up.

'There's just one more thing I need to run by you.'

'Is it about the Queen's skin rashes?' asked Tiger. 'I think you should leave that bit in, no matter what she says.'

'I have — no, it's just that I wanted to tell the story from Jennifer's viewpoint. What do you think?'

'I don't know the first thing about writing,' said Tiger with a shrug. 'It's whatever makes the best story, I guess.'

I screwed the top on my pen and closed my notebook. All I had to do now was to sit down and write it.

'It's decided, then,' I said, with some relief. 'I'll tell her story using a first-person narrative.'

So I did.

THE LAST DRAGONSLAYER

Book one of The Last Dragonslayer series

In the good old days, magic was powerful, unregulated by government, and even the largest spell could be woven without filling in magic release form B1-7g.

Then the magic started fading away.

Fifteen-year-old Jennifer Strange runs Kazam, an employment agency for soothsayers and sorcerers. But work is drying up. Drain cleaner is cheaper than a spell, and even magic carpets are reduced to pizza delivery.

So it's a surprise when the visions start. Not only do they predict the death of the Last Dragon at the hands of a dragonslayer, they also point to Jennifer, and say something is coming. Big Magic . . .

'Jasper Fforde has one of those effervescent imaginations' – *Independent*

The Song of the Quarkbeast

Book two of The Last Dragonslayer series

A long time ago Magic faded away, leaving behind only
yo-yos, the extremely useful compass-pointing-to-North
enchantment and the spell that keeps
bicycles from falling over.

Things are about to change. Magical power is on the
rise and King Snodd IV of Hereford has realised that he
who controls Magic controls almost anything. Only one
person stands between Snodd and his plans for
unimaginable power and riches.

Meet Jennifer Strange, sixteen-year-old acting manager
of Kazam, the employment agency for sorcerers and
soothsayers. She may only have one functioning Wizard
and her faithful assistant 'Tiger' Prawns to help her.
But one thing is certain: she will not relinquish the
noble powers of Magic to big business and
commerce without a fight.

'True literary comic genius' – *Sunday Express*

The Eye of Zoltar

Book three of The Last Dragonslayer series

The Mighty Shandar, the most powerful wizard the world has ever seen, returns to the Ununited Kingdoms. Clearly, he didn't solve the Dragon Problem, and must return his fee: eighteen dray-weights of gold.

But the Mighty Shandar doesn't do refunds, and vows to eliminate the dragons – unless sixteen-year-old Jennifer Strange and her sidekicks from the Kazam house of enchantment can bring him the legendary jewel, The Eye of Zoltar.

The only thing that stands in their way is a perilous journey with a 50% Fatality Index – through the Cambrian Empire to the Leviathan Graveyard, at the top of the deadly Cadair Idris mountain. And it's a quest that sees Jennifer fighting not just for her life, but for everything she knows and loves . . .

'Seriously funny . . . packed with magic and invention . . . watch out, Terry Pratchett!' – *Sunday Express*

Discover more from

JASPER FFORDE

Sign up to the newsletter for exclusive content:
www.hodder.co.uk/landing-page/
jasper-fforde-newsletter-sign-up/

Keep up to date at:
www.jasperfforde.com

And follow on social:
🅕 jasperffordewriter
jasperffordebooks

🐦 jasperfforde
HodderBooks

📷 jasperfforde
hodderbooks